A SEASON IN FITZROVIA

A SEASON IN FITZROVIA

K. A. Lalani

The Book Guild Ltd

First published in Great Britain in 2023 by
The Book Guild Ltd
Unit E2 Airfield Business Park,
Harrison Road, Market Harborough,
Leicestershire. LE16 7UL
Tel: 0116 2792299
www.bookguild.co.uk
Email: info@bookguild.co.uk
Twitter: @bookguild

Typeset in Aldine401 BT

Printed and bound in the UK by TJ Books Limited, Padstow, Cornwall

ISBN 978 1915853 400

British Library Cataloguing in Publication Data.
A catalogue record for this book is available from the British Library.

In memory of Kenneth John Page

CHARACTERS

Paul Crowley: A talented young artist starting his "fresher" year at the Slade. He has the ambition to become the "star" of his generation.

Lynette Crowley: His sister. At home she was in his shadow. Now will be her chance to shine.

*St John Crowley: Their elder cousin. A decadent art critic/patron.

Mercedes Campion: Her interests include art and literary mentorship.
   She uses her villa on the French Riviera as a bolt-hole.

Jayne Campion: Her youngest sister. Paul's celebrated portrait of her makes her a star, but will their romance survive?

Jack Trevelyan: A beautiful young man with a mercurial artistic talent.
   He is deemed to be a great rival to Paul, but can their friendship survive?

Alicia Savernake: A beautiful model, whose romance with artist Jack helps to heal the loss of her beloved brother during the war.

Laura Savernake: Her younger sister, also harbours ambitions for modelling
   but an ill-fated liaison is almost her undoing.

Nicola Fearns: She wins her place at the Slade by a bursary and feels out of her depth, but Paul Crowley and her cousin Martin are her champions.

Matthew Fullerton: A one-time tennis star, he swaps the court for a career in journalism and having severed ties at home begins a romance with Nicola, but is he destined to remain on the periphery of his talented artistic friends?

Laurence Naismith: A novelist in his mid-forties, struggling to regain his pre-war eminence. A friend of St John Crowley.
                              ★ [pronounced Sinjohn]

Alexander "*Rollo*" Savernake: Father of Alicia and Laura, he still grieves for Miles, the son he lost in the Great War.

Daphne Milford Savernake: His wife. A stunning beauty in her youth, she had many suitors and was famously painted by Nathaniel Gilbrandsen.

Gervaise Trevelyan: His wealth and the estate in Cornwall made him good husband material to Margot Phillips. They developed an understanding, but he knew he never fired her passion.

Margot Trevelyan: Once the muse of the fiery Gilbrandsen, she agreed to marry Gervaise on her patrician father's say-so.

Hugo Trevelyan: Her eldest son. He survived the war while his two closest friends didn't and he sees his parents grow further apart.

Caroline Trevelyan: His wife.

Adam Trevelyan: the middle son, he finds his niche in the Civil Service.

Nathaniel Gilbrandsen: the mercurial artist, he exiled in Spain, when he lost Margot to Gervaise. Dynamic, talented, a law unto himself.

Martin Fearns: the elder cousin of Nicola. Invalided out at Festurbet, he becomes the inspiration for her art.

Sybil Horton: A stunning beauty. Orphaned in her teens with her brother, Ralph, she is "adopted" by the Savernakes and the Trevelyans, and falls for the boyish Miles. The great love of her life.

Lieutenant Hayden Ballard: A Canadian soldier badly wounded at Vimy Ridge, he gives Sybil a cause to fight for and their romance helps to heal her losing Miles.

Edgar Trentham: Partner in Trentham & Westmacott. He won't risk the reputation of his publishing house to save the career of Naismith at any cost.

Austin Westmacott: As his father steps back, he learns more of the business with Edgar as his "mentor" but he sees adding Naismith is coup for him.

PRELUDE

Alexander Savernake's expression darkened visibly from the moment he walked into the entrance hall of the family home and heard the unmistakable voice that he had hoped never to hear under his roof again. His eldest daughter, Alicia, was standing on the landing of the double staircase, above which stood the portrait of his wife, Daphne Milford Savernake. The man stood next to her was St John Crowley, who Alexander knew had coveted Daphne for himself, so he had never forgiven him for having got her to the altar ahead of him. The fact that he knew she had never entertained any idea of marrying St John or had ever given him the tiniest hint of encouragement in that regard notwithstanding, they had barely tolerated each other in the years since and Alexander was seething at his intrusion.

'Alicia, you didn't alert me to the fact we had guests.'

She turned at the sound of his voice and he looked at her quizzically, thinking how much she resembled her mother; that it could easily have been Daphne standing there, were it not for the fact that she was staying at the Campion villa in the south of France and that he had received a telegram that morning informing him that she was extending her stay, which had not helped with the sourness of his mood. He knew, however, that Crowley would be aware that Daphne was away, as she had mentioned prior to leaving that Laurence Naismith, the man standing beside Crowley on his landing, had been furious that *her* invitation meant his request to stay at the Campion villa had been denied.

Alicia Savernake looked desperate and he guessed she must have felt ambushed by the two men who had arrived while he was with his estate manager. She looked uneasily at him as St John Crowley half turned, offering Alexander his best saccharine smile of insincerity, before sauntering downstairs as Alexander reluctantly went to greet him.

He shook hands with both men and kissed Alicia gently on the cheek to reassure her and turned back to Crowley, taking a deep breath to marshal his anger and hope he kept his resentment sufficiently concealed.

'Crowley, what brings you down to Hampshire?'

'We are on our way for luncheon at Ashburn Park, as guests of Charles Trentham. Thought we would divert here as it is on route and say hello, but your delightful daughter informs us Daphne is away...'

'Indeed. A fact of which I thought you would be aware. How is the book going, Naismith?'

Laurence Naismith smiled wanly. He hadn't wanted to make the diversion as he knew Daphne Savernake was in France. Truth be told he had been reluctant to accept the invitation to stay with Trentham. He was more an acquaintance of St John's and now *he* felt embarrassed.

'It's progressing, thank you...'

'Splendid. Well, I can see you have enjoyed a long look at my wife's portrait, *again*, and we mustn't detain you further from continuing your journey to... Dorset, is it?'

'Perhaps we will see you and Daphne in London soon, once she has returned from her painting sojourn.'

'We will see what can be arranged.' He kept his tone neutral and patting St John gently on the back he led them to the door.

When he returned from bidding them farewell, he stood for a moment, gazing up at the portrait of his wife, painted when she was around the age Alicia was now and he had started courting her.

'Alicia, couldn't you have waylaid them?'

She shook her head. 'Not without going against everything you and Mama ever taught us about good manners. No!… Besides I don't want to put Lynette offside, by being rude to her cousin…'

Alexander smiled weakly. 'I understand. It's just that St John always manages to irritate me without even trying. I don't think he has ever really accepted that your mother chose me.'

Alicia raised an eyebrow at her father. It was a claim she had heard numerous times before, but didn't entirely believe.

'Doesn't the fact that St John Crowley appears to have remained a confirmed bachelor indicate that he's no competition now?'

Alexander smiled as he led her into the morning room and reached for his newspaper. He suspected his daughter had a different understanding of the definition of the term "*confirmed bachelor*" to what men of his generation understood it to mean, but he was not inclined to divulge further.

'Maybe… He is still overly fond of her and he doesn't appear to care how inappropriate it appears. Besides which I have always thought Naismith an odd fish… You would be wise to stay away from him.'

Alicia nodded. 'I agree with you about him. Did you see him squirm when you enquired about his book? I hear he has been forced to accept a role writing a society column in one of the national papers.'

Alexander opened his newspaper and smiled. 'Really. The

mighty have fallen! He has always viewed himself as a literary giant… Poor Naismith!'

Alicia had heard the rumour about Naismith having fallen on harsher financial ground via Lynette Crowley and she didn't know the extent to which it was true, however it had put a gleeful smile on her father's face and she was grateful for that.

★ ★ ★

In the rear seat of St John Crowley's chauffeur-driven car, Naismith lit a cheroot and sat back, sighing heavily.

'Shouldn't we be getting a move on, St John, if we are going to make lunch at Ashburn? I have to say that was *so* embarrassing! I would never have agreed to making this detour if I had known I was going to be confronted by Savernake… Did you notice the smug tone in which he enquired about my book?'

St John rolled his eyes, but decided not to comment. He laughed lightly instead as he had only accepted Charles Trentham's invitation to lunch as an excuse to come down to Chelcombe Lacey. Of course he had known Daphne wouldn't be at home, as his companion had been whining ever since he had his invitation to stay at Mercy's villa declined. Although, as he usually expected his stay to be offered *gratis*, St John suspected that was sufficient motive for Mercy Campion to decline.

'There's no hurry, Larry. I wanted to familiarise myself with the portrait and I know how my presence here always riles Rollo…' He smiled again, reminded of how much Alexander also despised the nickname that he had earned at Oxford which had been derived from his middle name.

Laurence Naismith exhaled heavily as St John gave the signal to his chauffeur to drive on, the cloud of blue-grey smoke momentarily obscuring the smug smile on St John Crowley's face.

Jayne Campion lay supine on the chaise-longue, enjoying her post-clitoral bliss. Her left shoulder was still bare as Paul Crowley had instructed she should wear her black silk kimono robe thus and she was trying her best to appear enigmatic, though their lovemaking had been so awesome it made enigmatic difficult to achieve. She had to admire how he swiftly refocused his attention to his art. He was beautiful. That was the only way she could describe him. Handsome didn't quite cut it for Paul, though she knew he hated the compliment. As he said, it made him sound frivolous and that wasn't how he wanted to be viewed by the artistic community.

He looked at her, his brows pleated as she shifted slightly.

'Try to stay still while I finish this section.'

'If you knew just how difficult sitting still for as long as it takes you to get me right is, you might show more understanding.'

Paul Crowley nodded. He knew by the lightness of her tone that she was teasing him as she increasingly inclined to do. His expression remained a study in concentration, until he let it relax into a smile.

'I could always find someone else to sit for me. There will be plenty of willing volunteers in life classes at the Slade…'

'Ah, but will they be as stunningly beautiful as your current girlfriend, unless you prefer to paint older women?'

He smiled at the provocative tone in her voice and chose not to take the bait, but he smiled.

'I'm nearly done. I know my timing could have been better, but I wanted to capture that look…'

'I hope it will all be worth it when the portrait's finished…'

She paused to stub out her cigarette as Paul put his brush down, adding, '… To think I declined the south of France to stay here so you could fit some more sittings…'

'I am nearly done. I thought Mercy was there, hosting Alicia's mother?'

Jayne nodded. 'She is but I was asked along. See, I found your company more alluring even in an unseasonably mild August.'

Paul opened his arms expansively and said, 'Don't I look like I appreciate the gesture?'

'Whenever I watch you working, you look too engrossed to enjoy anything.

I need a cigarette.'

'OK! Now you can relax. Light me one as well.'

Jayne nodded, reaching for his cigarette case and catching the rueful look he sent her way.

'So which other artists have you sat for?'

Jayne smiled uneasily. 'Only a few…'

She lit two cigarettes, putting one between his lips. Half turning from him, he saw her sense of unease and said, 'Was one of them Jack?'

Jayne nodded.

'So why be shy? Evasive, even.'

'I wasn't sure you would like it. You are supposed to be rivals, aren't you?'

Paul sighed heavily. In his view, the rivalry attributed to him and Jack Trevelyan was over-blown, but he knew he didn't want it to become an issue between him and Jayne as he realised she had become too important to him for that.

'Artistically speaking, yes, but I hope we can remain friends. The art will always come above everything. I am sure it will be the same for Jack.'

'We haven't… you know…' Jayne blushed and he found her candour endearing.

He smiled.

'Thanks, but you don't owe me that explanation.'

Given that she and Jack were briefly together before he took up with Alicia, he understood that must have *hurt*. He removed his smock, and then his shirt. His torso gleamed in the light from silken shades as he joined her in bed. Jayne felt her arms around his neck, as he kissed her, their lips meshed as one. Was it possible Paul Crowley could become the man to heal her after years of grief? Could she achieve the happiness with him that she had been denied because of the war? Which Jack Trevelyan hadn't managed to bring her? It was still too early to tell, but she knew that he was coming closer to helping her feel whole again, more than any other casual beau that she'd had in years, and that was a positive start.

1

Chelcombe Lacey, Churchyard – Hampshire

Alexander Savernake bent to lay the flowers on his son's grave and straightening, he accepted Alicia's arm through his, as her sister, Laura Savernake, laid a third bouquet. He still felt raw inside on occasions like this. Hollowed out like the husk of an old tree, so he supposed he should have been more understanding of Daphne's decision to stay away.

Despite that, he needed her here. The girls needed *her*. The war had been over for nearly four years and yet it cast a long shadow on his remaining offspring and their friends, who by virtue of good fortune and a certain date on the calendar had escaped the action and the danger of becoming another member of the lost generation.

Laura sobbed slightly as she stepped back, before stifling a third strangled sob and looking to her father for any sign of censure, but he gave her a reassuring smile instead. He wasn't usually inclined to submit to his emotions in public, but this anniversary always got to him. Even so, both she and her sister knew what he usually expected of them.

The unexpected visit from St John Crowley had put him in

a foul mood for the rest of the previous day and this had come on top of their mother's decision to remain on the Riviera. Laura knew her parents had always been close. She and Alicia had benefited from the tight family unit, as had Miles growing up, but his decision to volunteer for action had been a severe bone of contention between them as their mother had urged him to discourage their son from going and then she had railed at him for not trying hard enough when his efforts had failed. Subsequently, she never coped with this anniversary. Miles' birthday and Christmas were also difficult, but she managed them in her way, so it hadn't surprised Laura that their mother sought a reprieve. However, her father's smile of reassurance when she feared she would submit to her grief had been welcome.

Laura half turned at the sound of footsteps crunching in the recent early fallen leaves and she smiled as Jack Trevelyan joined them, taking Alicia's hand in his. He lifted his bouquet and half smiled as Alexander nodded for him to add it to the others they had placed there.

'I didn't want to intrude until you had laid your floral tributes. This is from us all, especially Hugo.'

Alexander smiled at his daughters and then at Jack, squeezing his shoulders. There was no intrusion as far as he was concerned as he recalled the many occasions on which Miles had been warmly welcomed into the Trevelyan household.

'You are always welcome, Jack.'

Alicia moved slightly as Alexander moved forward again, and ran his hand along the top of Miles' gravestone and whispered something that he didn't intend the others to hear.

Laura linked her arm through his and Alicia turned to Jack.

'You will join us for tea?'

Jack hesitated and Alexander said, 'Please do.'

Alicia held back, letting her father lead the way back to the house, urging her sister to keep pace, while she whispered into

Jack's ear. She didn't yet know where the relationship with him was going to take her, but she was prepared to bide her time. She was following him to London when he started the freshman term at the Slade. She had received some very positive feedback from agencies that she had approached for assignments as a fashion model and she had strongly urged Jack to retain the studio he was renting here on the estate.

As they made their way into the house she told him about St John Crowley's visit and how furious her father had been, and Jack smiled.

Knowing Paul and Lynette's cousin as he did, his empathy was entirely with her father.

The Campion Villa – Cap St Vincent, France

Daphne Savernake sat in companionable silence with her friend and hostess Mercedes Campion on the terrace of the villa which looked down on the sparkling blue of the Mediterranean, as the sun began its slow descent below the horizon. She had temporarily abandoned her canvas and oils for a sketch pad and pastels as she captured Mercy's legendary beauty, which she shared with her younger sibling Jayne.

Daphne and Mercy – as she was usually known by those who knew her best – had been debutantes together, so they had danced with the same men at countless soirées and balls during The Season and while Daphne had no doubts about saying yes on the third time of asking by Alexander, just so that she was sure he was serious, Mercy had been more selective, marrying later to an older man. There were rumours that she might once have accepted a proposal of marriage from Laurence Naismith, if he had ever plucked up the courage, but she had always quashed them as idle nonsense.

Daphne felt out of sorts. The latest telegram from home

had been terse and to the point and she felt hurt by Alexander's lack of understanding. She wasn't taking any responsibility for St John Crowley's surprise visit, even though she accepted her husband's assertion that Crowley had been causing mischief by descending on Chelcombe Place when he would have known that she was away.

Mercy turned to her and said, 'So you are glad you took my advice and didn't rush home to soothe Alexander's furrowed brows and calm his ire?'

'Yes. Because he can cope. I know St John knows how to rile him, but that isn't the major reason for him being offside with me. I always struggle when it gets close to the anniversary of Miles' death and it usually results in a quarrel, so I decided to spare him and the girls the residual tension this year. Alexander never understood why I was so against Miles rushing off to fight and I guess he will never reconcile himself to his grief and the possibility that had we tried harder to dissuade him, events might have turned out differently...'

Mercy looked at her as Daphne's voice grew weaker and then trailed off and she offered her hand, as Daphne continued.

'I know it sounds irrational and I am not the only mother who feels that way, but giving Alexander and the girls the freedom to grieve their way and for me to do it on my terms, seemed like the best idea and if he cannot see that yet... I am sure he will in due course...'

Mercy smiled. She was pleased to hear Daphne asserting herself and although she couldn't instinctively know how Daphne felt, she had been one of Miles' godparents, so she felt the loss in her own way.

'I guess my invitation must have put Naismith's plans awry?'

Mercy nodded, smiling broadly.

'Yes and it will do him good not to look upon my villa as his personal fiefdom. One that he expects to be at his disposal whenever it suits him and usually *gratis*. So I had no hesitation in declining him in your favour.

'He can find another artistic friend to descend on and see how generous they are to his whims. Much like his friend St John, Laurence Naismith thinks that his scintillating wit and good company – his reputation as a raconteur and novelist of some note – notwithstanding make for him being an irresistible house-guest. He may find another of his friends not as accommodating as I have been over the years.'

Daphne smiled and laying down her sketch pad she stretched luxuriously as Mercy turned to her. 'Finished the sketch?'

Daphne nodded. 'For the time being.'

'Good, because it's well past my cocktail hour…'

Daphne laughed as Mercy rose and disappeared inside the villa.

The air was cooler now the sun had set; the sky blazed orange, but soon it would be dark.

This break was exactly what she had needed and she was determined to make the most of what remained.

2

Fullerton Chase – Dorset

Matthew Fullerton lit another cigarette and sitting back in his deckchair, he sighed heavily. Lifting his face against the late summer sun, he felt the bitter aftertaste of another family quarrel over his future career prospects and the conflict between how he saw his future and *their* expectations. His parents and siblings had always been very supportive of his ambitions in the sport of tennis and he had come to the conclusion recently that they possessed a greater belief in his potential than he had, hence the fierce opposition to him abandoning plans of continuing competing in major tournaments and turning his attention towards a career in journalism. He had known for a while that he lacked the necessary killer instinct required to be a winner in the sport. The kind of ruthless determination to win that the likes of New Zealand-born Anthony Wilding and the American Bill Tillden possessed which had seen them win multiple titles, before and since the war.

He was also aware that his father, Denys Fullerton, disapproved of the louche lifestyle that he aspired to lead in London and that this prejudice fuelled the opposition to the change in career. He didn't doubt his father still believed he could win the men's singles title at Wimbledon or perhaps the US Open one day, but *he* didn't share that faith and it was time for him to retire gracefully from tennis before the sport retired him, with numerous early-round knockouts and the bitter disappointment that came with them.

As he took the last drag on his cigarette, he saw his eldest sibling, Giles, appear at the conservatory door and he grimaced. Giles hadn't helped matters by forcing his way into what should have been a private discussion and injecting his opinion, until their father had demanded he leave them. It was an unfortunate fact as far as Matthew was concerned that as the eldest son, he would inherit Fullerton Chase, with all the responsibilities that came with it. An honour he would be happy to see conferred upon Giles. He could see a circumstance when the time came for him to inherit, where he would do just that, aside from the fact that Giles would see it as a charitable act and resent the gesture which he didn't really deserve, but one which would afford *him* his freedom.

'So your future is no closer to being resolved, Matt?'

Matthew could hear the smug gleefulness in his brother's voice, although a swift glance in Giles' direction showed he had managed to keep his expression neutral.

'If you have come out here just to goad me, Giles, don't bother. I am not in the least interested in jousting with you today.'

'So you really have lost your competitive edge then?'

Matthew looked at Giles and smiled.

'That was what I had been trying to say to Father and you before he demanded you left... It's a pity you don't have the basic skills to make it in the sport as you definitely have the killer instinct.'

Giles blushed crimson and took a deep breath to moderate his rage.

'Is that meant to be some kind of jibe?'

Matthew stood, stubbed the butt of his cigarette beneath his shoe and strode towards Giles, gently shouldering him aside.

'Take it any way you wish.'

'Do you think Rosalind will stay interested for long if you are in London all week and only deign to come down for the occasional weekend?'

Giles was still trying to stay the right side of neutral, but Matthew wasn't fooled when it came to Rosalind. His brother had always coveted the idea of having her for himself. Matthew understood his frustration because Rosalind's mother had always envisaged a liaison with the eldest Fullerton and in that ambition she had an ally in *their* mother.

Matthew shrugged as Giles looked at him, the taunt lurking in his eyes striving to break free.

'Well, if she isn't, that will open the door for you. Then you will have to convince Mrs Marriott that marrying the second Fullerton son might be an adequate alternative to her long-held plans...'

Giles bristled angrily.

'You can't expect to keep the girl wondering forever. So if your interest is waning you had better put your best neutral face on, as Rosalind has been invited to play tennis tomorrow afternoon, followed by tea and you know Mother will do her best to nudge the two of you towards a formal announcement...'

While Matthew knew Giles was doing his best to provoke him, there was a lot of truth in what he said and *he* didn't want to hurt Rosalind, but she, like his father, saw his future pursuing a career in tennis and theirs together mapped out as a couple.

'To what end, Giles?'

'A formal announcement of your engagement!'

'You're not joking, are you?'

Giles shook his head, grinning gleefully.

'So you had better be ready to pledge your future to

Rosalind or else withdraw with honour and incur Mother's disappointment as deeply as you have Father's wrath…'

Matthew swore under his breath. He hadn't been expecting this revelation but he knew enough where his mother's instincts lay to be certain that it wasn't Giles's attempt at subterfuge. It would suit Giles to see his relationship with Rosalind scuppered however it happened and although he liked Rosalind Marriott well enough, the feelings on his part had never hitherto been so strong to compel him to formally ask for her hand, despite his mother's constant urging. He knew Rosalind wanted the life in Dorset that they could still have, that she didn't share his allure for the city life in London, that he now envisaged for himself. To what extent would she make sacrifices for them to remain together and move towards marriage?

Was it even fair of him to ask that of her?

Rosalind had been more than patient with him over the years and Giles was right to point out that he couldn't keep her waiting and wondering forever. His heart had to be in it as strongly as hers had always been. He also had to be convinced in his mind that marrying Rosalind was *still* the right move for him. He had made one major life altering decision this evening, with all the residual disappointment it had unleashed given the expectations of others regarding *his* future. It appeared that now he would have to look to making another which had the potential to cause an even greater hurt.

Despite his goading, he could see why Giles was struck with envy about Rosalind as she did fit most men's dreams of a potential wife, and as different as she was from the likes of Lynette Crowley or Jayne Campion, who he had only met a few times, or the elder of the Savernake girls, who it appeared was moving towards a relationship with Jack Trevelyan. He found their artistic lifestyle in London increasingly exciting and vibrant, pulling him away from the rural life in Dorset which seemed stifling by comparison. Yet this was the life that he had been born into, the one that Rosalind Marriott craved as his wife.

Despite her youth at nineteen she had experienced the hurt of losing an older brother in the last weeks of the war. A sibling that she had idolised. He had heard a similar story from Jack about Alicia's brother, Miles Savernake. Another story of family tragedy wrought by the devastation of war among so many. The stories behind the countless names that had been carved into the stone of monuments to the fallen.

He was just one of the lucky generation who had escaped action in the trenches by a hair's breadth. So if he had a legacy worth anything, it was to live the life the fallen never got the chance to live. To fulfil the promise that fate had denied them and to become the best version of himself, wherever that journey took him.

Giles looked at his brother, his brows suddenly pleated with concern.

'Matthew, are you all right?'

He nodded slowly, deep in thought.

'Yes. Of course. I was thinking of Rosalind's brother for a moment. I don't quite know why…'

'Justin!' Giles looked puzzled.

'Yes. Who knows what career choices he would have made after the war had he been spared…'

Giles turned away as Matthew lit another cigarette retrieving the telegram that he had received from Paul Crowley inviting him to their party in London prior to them starting at the Slade. He would accept as it would do the family some good to have some distance and absorb the decisions he had made about *his* future, but he knew he also had one other decision to firm in his mind and that it would take time, but if Justin Marriott's story taught him anything it was that life could be cruelly short.

So to commit to Rosalind, as their respective mothers had wished for so long, just for the sake of avoiding a conflict with all the hurt that would come afterwards, when he wasn't sure that is where his heart truly led him, would be to inflict a far harsher fate upon her than having to face up to the fact that their destinies were not irrevocably entwined.

He patted Giles gently on the shoulder as he took his leave, convinced now that there really was no other way.

London – Three Days Later

Matthew Fullerton stood at the window, looking down at a drab grey Fleet Street, while behind him, the editor of the *London News* methodically read through recent samples of his journalism for several Dorset-based papers. He put them carefully in Matthew's attaché case and sighed.

Matthew turned sharply.

'I thought you would be in New York, preparing for the US Open, yet here you are in my office showing me some good journalistic work – I acknowledge that – but it's the kind of writing you can produce five years hence when you have got several titles to your name.'

'If I *ever have* several titles to my name! I want to write, sir. Tennis has been good to me, but I have come to accept that I am average at best. Recently I have been knocked out of tournaments two, maybe three rounds before I should have and it has barely registered as a disappointment. Take Wimbledon last summer, a few years ago a defeat that tame would have seen me sulking for days.'

The editor smiled, indicating the seat in front of his desk. He could easily give Matthew Fullerton a job as a reporter/correspondent and get his money's worth based on the samples of work that he had seen, but he had known Denys Fullerton at university and they had remained friends since so he didn't want to incur his disapproval, by giving his son a job and effectively sanctioning the end of his career in tennis, although he had told Denys that if he didn't give Matthew a job there were other editors who would seize the opportunity.

'Any job I could give you would pay a paltry amount and living in London doesn't come cheap. You have a good set-up at Fullerton Chase…'

Matthew smiled. He had imagined this response in his head. He had used his father's connection to secure this appointment, but he knew that having his request accepted would come with strings attached and that his father may well be pulling them.

'Exactly what Denys has told you already?'

'Almost verbatim…'

'OK. I will consider you. That's all I can offer… I know I run the risk of losing you to one of my competitors, but that's a risk I will take out of loyalty to Denys. And *if* it's a yes, I shall tell him first, I'm not having him hear it second-hand. Where are you staying?'

'With some friends near the Slade School of Art.'

'Fitzrovia, eh? Very classy. Next you will be telling me you have found yourself a wealthy patron.'

Matthew smiled as he rose and said, 'Who knows how things will pan out?'

The editor looked at him with a twinkle in his eyes and jabbing his thumb at the door he said, 'Get the hell out of here, will you?'

★ ★ ★

Chelcombe Place, Chelcombe Lacey

Alicia Savernake pulled the sheet up to conceal her breasts and smiled.

She felt wistful, despite the orgasmic sex that she had just enjoyed with Jack, which had been a pleasant bonus. For her peace of mind, she had felt the need to escape the stifling atmosphere which permeated the family home for the small studio Jack was renting on their estate, given that her father's mood had mostly remained sour in the days since her mother's telegram from the Riviera, and his residual anger at St John Crowley's visit.

Rising from the bed, Jack poured red wine into two enamel mugs, handing one to Alicia. She took one pensive sip, but it didn't taste good.

'I should bring you some decent glassware.'

Jack bowed theatrically and said, 'Apologies, Lady Alicia, that it doesn't come in your family crystal. I don't suppose this label would be found in the Savernake cellar for that matter...'

She shook her head, smiling sheepishly as he rejoined her in bed.

'I shall have to take advice on what wine to serve a lady after sex.'

Alicia punched him gently in the arm.

'Don't you dare!'

She took another mouthful pulling a face as she placed the enamel mug on a dresser. She rolled onto her back as Jack leaned over her, his head resting on his elbow. He pushed a lock of her hair away. It had been an amazing summer here at Chelcombe Place, but like all good things it was coming to an end. He was looking forward to his fresher term at the Slade, but this summer with Alicia had been a blissful idyll, which he suspected he would look back on as one of the best of his life.

The work had been fulfilling, inspiring him for what he could achieve at the Slade, while the afternoons he had spent with Alicia had been incredible. She was an incredibly generous lover and although he was confident their relationship would continue – doubtless flourish – he knew she had her career plans and that her overtures to magazine editors and modelling agencies had been encouraging. Her career could grow faster than his, with the potential to take her further away from him, and he was reluctant to acknowledge how much the prospect scared him.

He felt the softness of her hand on his face as she gently turned his face to hers.

'What is it?'

'I am being foolishly possessive of the time we have enjoyed with each other this summer and conscious it won't be like this again for a while…' He shrugged. '… Who knows, maybe never…'

Alicia bowed her head and she nodded. Looking up at him she said, 'You are right, but it will be different. One thing I am certain of is that we *will* be together. After what we have shared I'm not letting anything come between us, no matter how successful you become once you have enrolled at the Slade.'

It surprised him suddenly, how gratified he was to hear her say that because he had never believed himself to be the person who needed others. He had cultivated the art of self-sufficiency; although to many it rang true, it was also a facade as he always had the Trevelyan money to fall back on, even though outwardly his circumstances appeared slightly more constrained than what Paul and Lynette Crowley might expect from staying at their cousin's town house in Bloomsbury. What they all had was the right to be there this term, and it was a right based upon their individual talents. He understood to some extent Alicia's continuing anguish over her brother's loss. Hugo felt it as well having fought alongside Miles Savernake and many other comrades and he had survived when they hadn't. It was a burden that his elder brother felt constantly, so he was conscious of a duty to seize his opportunity and to ensure that he and the rest of what would be the Class of '25 would make the most of the opportunities the hard-won freedom gave them.

3

London – September 1922

Nicola Fearns still felt that she didn't quite belong among those she described as the elite at the Slade School of Art. As if her presence there was some kind of fantastic dream from which she would eventually wake and discover that fate was *mocking* her. That it must be a cruel joke that she could expect to exist among the brightest and best artists of her generation. Yet as her mother and third cousin tried to remind her, she had won her scholarship on merit. She had confided most of her doubts to her cousin in the weeks leading up to the start of term.

Martin Fearns had been uncharacteristically brusque in telling her that she was at the Slade because she had earned the right to be there and she shouldn't let anyone tell her otherwise.

He had suggested quietly that she paint his portrait in the library of the family home near Bagshot, Surrey, dressed in the khaki uniform he had worn as a lieutenant in the Hertfordshire Regiment. He still bore a slight facial scar from the injuries which had ended his war. It was much faded now, but he had insisted it be included in the portrait.

She was pleased that he liked the finished portrait, but she still found fault with some of its detail and he had said that while there was nothing wrong with being your own critic, she still needed to have a firmer belief in her talent.

She had encouraged him during the last sitting, before she left for London, to talk about his experiences during the war and he been most comfortable talking about a fellow lieutenant who had risen swiftly through to the rank of captain. He was also the heir to an earldom and Nicola could tell from the timbre of his voice that her cousin held a deep and abiding respect for the man who had fallen at Passchendaele. The earldom he said had been his friend's destiny from birth and while he had once feared the burden of responsibility that came with it, he had come to embrace what it could mean for him, only for fate to cruelly deny him that prize.

Nicola smiled now, recalling how he had turned to her and said she should embrace what she had worked so hard for and to seize the opportunities her scholarship afforded her.

★ ★ ★

Jayne Campion had seen Paul Crowley regularly in recent weeks as she had eagerly accepted several invitations to sit for him while he strived to finish her portrait before the start of term. She had teasingly suggested that it might yet become his signature work.

Slotting in sittings between modelling assignments for several Mayfair boutiques had become easy and she was earning a reputation for being one of the most sought after models in London, but she was aware that her friend Alicia Savernake had shown interest in developing her own modelling career and Jayne was determined to hold her ground.

She had been given reason to hope she might soon secure

17

work in Paris, suggesting Paul might follow her and pursue his art there, adding mischievously that he would look the part in a garret on the Left Bank.

'Like the cliché of a struggling artist, you mean? If I am going to starve for my art, Jayne, I would prefer to do it in London.'

Jayne had turned, smiling.

'As you wish, Paul, darling, but you may have to get accustomed to sharing me with the world of *haute couture*.'

Paul smiled his best saccharine smile and lifted his brush as Jayne let the silk robe slip from her shoulders.

'I think I might just about survive your absences… Take a seat!'

'But isn't it some *rite of passage* for an artist to struggle for their creative integrity?'

'I think you may have a very jaundiced view about the kind of existence an artist is supposed to lead. We are not all doomed youths like Thomas Chatterton.'

Jayne exhaled heavily on a cigarette as Paul arranged the pose he wanted her to take.

'I thought he was a poet?'

Paul smiled. 'I believe he was, but Wallis immortalised him in just the kind of garret that you imagine me inhabiting. Although not to meet a similar fate, I trust. I can imagine what St John would make of that…'

'So has he offered you a place to stay?'

'Yes, at his home in Bloomsbury, but I am guessing it's a last-resort option and that he hopes Lynette and I will have alternatives…'

He stood back to look at his work, hoping he was managing to capture Jayne's spirit, the essence of what made her the woman that she was onto the canvas. He was also single-minded about making his mark at the Slade and was particularly looking forward to the life classes led by Henry Tonks, about whom he had heard much.

It wasn't all about being better than his peers, including Jack Trevelyan.

The supposed rivalry between them wasn't anywhere near as intense as some liked to suggest and he stressed that *they* were friends. Not that it would stop him from ruthlessly pursuing his bid to become one of the best artists the Slade had turned out in its long, illustrious history.

'OK, Jayne. You can relax. I am finished for now.' He covered the canvas with a dust sheet as he knew she wasn't averse to sneaking a look when his back was turned. As she rose to a kneeling position on the divan, her red and black silk robe fell open, but she made no embarrassed bid to refasten it. Standing up she went behind a screen to redress and he reminded himself of her qualities, possessing as she did a supreme self-confidence that some of the other young women that he knew lacked. To the extent that in a man, it would be invariably described as arrogance. Her natural charm, however, drew people to her like a magnet.

He wanted her in every aspect. Sexually, artistically and intellectually, he fed off her, though in that regard he feared that sometimes he fell short. He thought he might never succeed in getting her to commit to him. That ephemeral part of her spirit was an elusive desire not to be tied down. He watched with an artist's eye as she emerged from behind the screen in a black and white dress, her dark eyes sparkling behind the deft application of kohl. He lit two cigarettes, handing one to her as she came towards him.

'So as the artist has finished work for the day, does it mean it's time for play?'

He exhaled heavily on his cigarette, creating a blue-grey cloud between them.

'I could be persuaded. What do you have in mind?'

Jayne took two heavy drags on her cigarette and then tossed it into the grate, as her black gloved arms went around his neck and she smiled. Opening her mouth to receive his kiss, she said, 'This.'

They kissed lingeringly for a while and then smiling mischievously she took his hand, leading him into her bedroom. She turned her back to him and he trailed kisses down her back as she arched against him, pulling his hands around her waist as he moved to the nape of her neck. Turning in his arms, she faced him with a mischievous glint in her eyes and began to undo his shirt and for a moment he hesitated, the smile uncertain, but from an encouraging nod, he said, 'You're sure?'

'Absolutely...'

Within minutes she was running her manicured hands along his naked torso which shone, slightly tanned, in the muted light from silk shades as he felt the stirring of arousal.

Jayne lowered herself onto the bed, taking Paul with her, as he let some of his tension subside and although still aroused he let himself submit to the blissful vortex of her desire.

The Crowley Townhouse – Bloomsbury

St John Crowley was not in the best of moods, which wasn't unusual.

He had – he was often inclined to acknowledge – a talent for moroseness and his friend Laurence Naismith wasn't helping.

The novelist was having one of his *crises* of confidence and anyone unfortunate to be in his orbit on such occasions was likely to incur his wrath. He was still smarting from having his request to work at Mercy Campion's villa at Cap St Vincent denied and he had confided to St John, without a hint of irony, that he had no other acquaintance in similarly warmer climes upon whom he could "impose".

'I detest London at this time of year,' he told St John who raised an eyebrow, his patience tested to the limits. Having issued the invitation to his cousins Paul and Lynette to stay with him for the start of the new term at the Slade, he put their initial reluctance in accepting down to Naismith's extended presence. He was aware that his friend was going through a rough patch financially and that his current novel, which he had described as his long heralded "comeback" wasn't going as well as he had predicted and that not for the first time in recent years Naismith's hyperbole overreached the reality. Fortunately, his agent had secured some review work and commissioned several magazine articles, so St John didn't have to subsidise him, which was a relief, as previous loans had swiftly turned into "gifts". That said things couldn't continue. Paul and Lynette would delay their arrival as long as Naismith remained and then he would incur the displeasure of their parents, who had initially been sceptical of how genuine his invitation was. He was looking forward to having them stay long term – even though he had given them the run of the house for the evening – as it would be full of bright, young, artistic minds as it had been among *his* peers during his youth and he found that prospect infinitely more appealing than long autumnal nights with only an increasingly belligerent Naismith – who had thankfully gone to their club – for company.

St John didn't blame Naismith for wanting the warmer climes of the Mediterranean in which to work on his novel. Late September in London didn't hold the same appeal, so he would have to resolve to finding him a warm billet for a few weeks and that was no easy task as most of his peers knew from experience what a difficult house-guest Laurence Naismith could be.

There was a slight tap on his bedroom door and he commanded they enter. He smiled as Lynette poked her head around the door.

'Cousin St John, our guests are beginning to arrive.'

'I am glad, my dear, and I shall be out of their way in due course.'

He looked at his reflection in the mirror, remembering Naismith's garbed comment that he had gained weight and while he had resented it, in that moment, he could see evidence that he had. He turned to her and nodded at her questioning look, resisting the urge to remind her whose house it was.

Gorgeous, vivacious Lynette. Invariably cast in her brother's shadow. A situation she seemed to accept all too readily in his view. She possessed an artistic talent and she had earned *her* place at the Slade on merit, but St John knew she didn't have the raw natural talent Paul had and he felt a tinge of empathy for her in that regard.

'I shall introduce myself and then take my leave. May I enquire as to how many guests?'

'We only invited ten between us, but you know how word spreads?'

St John smiled.

'Indeed. I have told Naismith to stay out until midnight, so you might want to take the party to one of those clubs you frequently mention by then.'

Lynette pulled a face at the mention of Naismith, but nodded, her eyes smiling.

'Hasn't he overstayed his welcome?'

St John looked at himself in the cheval mirror and nodded.

'Typically, but I have a tentative plan to divert him elsewhere. Although you might mention casually to Mercy Campion's sister... she is one of your guests?... that as his plan to stay at her villa was thwarted, we have had to endure him for longer.'

Lynette laughed, nodding.

'Yes, Jayne is invited and she will probably arrive on Paul's arm, so I might not do as you suggest. So does Naismith think that he has a sense of entitlement to descend on Mercy Campion's villa at will?'

St John grabbed his overcoat and hat from the bed and nodded.

'A sense of entitlement is something I fear Laurence Naismith might well have been born with!'

Lynette followed her cousin downstairs as the front door opened and Paul arrived with Jayne on one arm and a stranger following behind. 'I have met a "*waif 'n' stray*" and rescued her – so to speak – Nicola Fearns. My sister, Lynette. She is a fellow student at the Slade.'

Lynette nodded at Nicola. Frowning slightly and taking Paul's arm, she pulled him aside.

'St John is leaving us to it. We have got the run of the place until midnight before Naismith returns, however our cousin is in one of his moods…'

Paul swore slightly, rolling his eyes. There had been moments in the last month when he had begun to wonder whether having the invitation to stay in St John's home was worth the trouble, given some of the baggage that came with it.

He gently pushed Nicola towards Lynette and with Jayne following he made his way to the lounge.

Nicola had strongly resisted Paul's urging to join them as she feared she would appear as gauche and out of place in what she had termed their "*sophisticated*" company as she now felt, when Paul Crowley had found her staring at the Slade School in the gathering dusk. Now she was certain that she should have very firmly declined as Lynette wasn't as welcoming as her brother. One of her biggest fears was being labelled a "*hanger-on*"; that students would point her out and dismiss her thus.

She didn't doubt that Paul Crowley was being genuine with his invitation, however she knew that she wasn't one of them and she could never hope to fit right within their circle. She felt her cheeks suffusing with heat as Lynette Crowley asked to be excused as further guests arrived and she had resolved to slip away unnoticed the first opportunity she got.

She remained in the hallway, hemmed in by other guests as Paul joined her with a drink, which she tried to refuse, but he foisted it on her and she mumbled her thanks as he turned to someone else and Lynette rejoined her, holding out her hand.

'You must think me terribly rude. I'm Lynette Crowley. So tell me, how long have you known my brother?'

Nicola looked aghast, shaking her head. As if a Byronic hero type like Paul Crowley would give her a second look, when he had that goddess-like creature on his arm.

'We only met tonight. Outside the Slade. I was gazing up at the building looking as if I were in awe that I had actually won a scholarship to study there and your brother and his friend were passing by. We got chatting and he suggested I come to this party – well, actually he *insisted* – and now I'm not sure that it was such a good idea.'

Lynette shook her head.

'Nonsense! You will enjoy it. What are you drinking?'

'I think Paul said it was gin.'

'I will get you a cocktail.'

Nicola was going to protest, but she knew it would be futile, as "no" didn't appear to exist in their vocabulary, so she half nodded as Lynette left her and she tried to relax, remembering what her cousin Martin had said. "Believe in yourself and your right to be there. You have earned it and you are studying at the Slade on merit. Some of your peers may look other worldly and more sophisticated to you at first, but they will have their own doubts and they will be striving to conceal them as keenly as you! No amount of money their families may have or what their position or title is *will* change that. Remember that friend I told you about, the heir to the earldom, he was writhen with doubts about his ability to survive the war. All because someone had said he would get his bloody head shot off in the first weeks… I was always in awe of him and yet he had his *own* confidence issues to deal with."

Martin's voice seemed so strong in her conscience that she felt his presence in the house with her in that moment and she wished he was, as Lynette rejoined her with an exotic cocktail and snapped her out of her reverie.

'Were you daydreaming?'

Nicola shook her head.

'Reminding myself of some wise words my cousin said to me about dealing with new challenges in strange surroundings, and as he was in the trenches he knows what he is talking about. Attending a party full of strangers, must be a picnic after that…'

Nicola blushed as she took one long gulp of her cocktail to conceal the rush of embarrassment. Was Lynette Crowley likely to suffer a crisis of confidence about starting at the Slade? Somehow Nicola doubted it.

★ ★ ★

Chelcombe Place, Chelcombe Lacey

Growing up there had been a very close bond between the Savernake sisters, which family friends would comment upon for just how remarkable it was. They shared very strongly and equally with their parents the enormity of the loss of their beloved brother, Miles, during the war, coming to rely even more on each other for support, through adolescence and into adulthood, as their mother's renewed interest in pursuing her art as a form of catharsis grew.

For all that, Laura was sensing a distance developing between her and Alicia, who she had always regarded as the more beautiful sister.

Her own looks were frequently commented upon favourably, however Alicia seemed to her to be brimming with confidence and Laura wondered whether her relationship with Jack Trevelyan might be the root cause.

In a rare moment Alicia had confided to Laura that she was determined to cement the relationship for fear she might lose him to someone else, especially Lynette Crowley, who had never been shy in making her interest in Jack known. Laura had told her with as much confidence as she could claim that she was being emotionally irrational, but Alicia hadn't taken the comment well and the conversation had descended swiftly into a quarrel. Laura was usually the first to endeavour to repair any damage from a sisterly quarrel, but she had determined to let Alicia stew for a while, when her bedroom door opened and Alicia appeared.

Laura half turned.

'I thought you were with Jack?'

'I was but he's been issued with an invitation to join us for dinner, so I have left him to bathe and change… Nothing too formal, I said. Although he does looking dashing in evening dress'

Laura quirked an eyebrow.

'You say that about everything he wears…'

Alicia laughed lightly and said, 'Do I? Yes, I suppose I must. Because it *is* true. I *am* sorry, Laura. I know you were trying to reassure me about the strength of Jack's affections and I was unkind…'

Laura continued applying the kohl to her eyes and then she turned.

'Well, perhaps I should record the date in my diary! It might be a long time before you apologise again…'

Alicia shot her sister a warning look and then smiled.

'You don't really consider Lynette Crowley competition for his affections do you? Jack is crazy about you, Alicia! A star of the art world he may be and therefore likely to attract admirers but it's you that he wants, everyone can see that.'

Alicia laughed slightly.

'What?' Laura asked tersely.

'I am just wondering when my younger sister became *so* wise and how I missed it!'

'Go away if you're being beastly!'

'Beastly? I was complimenting you and I came in to make the peace!'

'That's why I said it was a date to remember!'

Alicia made for the door and Laura turned to her.

'I take it you have slept with him. More than once?'

'Laura!' Alicia's shock was genuine, but she nodded slightly.

'Be careful, Alicia. You want to retain his respect.'

Alicia folded her arms. Laura had a point, although Jack wasn't like that. She had his respect, she was sure of that, but was conscious that he hadn't yet confessed that he loved her. However mindful she was about Laura's concerns that he might move on to other conquests, she felt the urge to defend him.

'Jack isn't like that. He can be sensitive... like Miles!'

Laura stood taking Alicia's hands in hers.

'So you will be off to London when term starts. I will miss you!'

Alicia took a deep breath.

'I didn't think you would be saying that earlier today.'

Laura shook her head.

'We have always quarrelled. Over everything and nothing. It still makes Mama mad and it always amused Miles. I don't think you being in London is going to change much in the dynamic between us.'

Alicia took Laura's arm and said, 'I hope not. Shall we?'

Laura nodded as they made their way down to dinner. For a moment she had briefly glimpsed a return to the younger, less-assured Alicia that she had preferred, however she knew it was a momentary lapse of confidence as her sister had every reason to be confident in her blossoming career as a fashion model and in the strength of her relationship with Jack, but she held back on articulating a tiny fear that events might not always go as smoothly as Alicia hoped.

4

In the first weeks of term, while Paul and Jack were establishing themselves in the life classes at the Slade, Matthew Fullerton was successfully securing himself journalistic work initially on a freelance basis at the *Express*. His failure to convince the editor of the *London News* to take him on had irked him, as he had believed his father's connection with the editor, which had helped to get him an interview, might have led to him securing a job.

He was chafing against his parents enthusiasm for him to continue pursuing a tennis career, along with their sadness at his reluctance to make a formal commitment to Rosalind Marriott. So he had left Dorset under a cloud of parental disappointment and much regret from Rosalind who was taking the blame upon herself for failing to convince him that their future lay together. Despite his efforts to reassure her to the contrary, she hadn't been swayed. Sitting together in the summer house, he had taken her hand.

'Why, Matthew? What is life in London going to offer you, that staying here won't? You have a base here at Fullerton Chase and as the eldest you will inherit. I believed that was *our* future.'

29

Matthew bowed his head, taking a deep breath.

'Why isn't that enough, anymore? Why am I not enough?'

He looked at her and saw the glimmer of tears on her lashes, and it felt like a kick in the stomach that she was so upset because of him.

'That's because it isn't you. It's me. I don't want the life I thought I had wanted any longer. I have given up tennis because I realised I didn't have what it took. I lack the required edge to be a real winner in the sport. As for us, I think we have grown apart and I realise that is down to me as well. I'm sorry…'

'There's someone else, isn't there?'

Matthew shook his head, half turning away from her. He was being a coward, he knew that, but he had never wanted to hurt Rosalind, despite Giles' assertions to the contrary.

'Did we have an understanding or were we simply falling in with what our mothers expected of us?'

The tears came unchecked then. Rolling down her cheeks, as her bottom lip quivered. Matthew couldn't bear to see her so upset, because now he felt like a total heel.

Rosalind angrily wiped her tears away, knowing she hadn't wanted to give into tears when she had suggested they have this talk. She felt badly let down and she had wanted to appear more resentful, angrier, but found that she couldn't. Because there was some truth to what he had said.

The deepening of their relationship had always been actively encouraged.

Her mother had high expectations and she had been especially encouraged to spend as much time as possible at Fullerton Chase when she was invited and she had actively nudged Rosalind – not always so gently – towards the eldest Fullerton brother. Maybe Matthew hadn't fallen in with the plan as willingly as she had thought he had based on what he had told her tonight, and now he was seeking a way out. In which case he should have been honest with her sooner instead of heeding to pressure from his mother as she always had with hers.

Rosalind knew her mother had been heavily motivated by ambition and she didn't dare think *what* the reaction was going be to the news that Matthew Fullerton's interest in her daughter was waning.

'So how long have you felt this way? Have I been holding you back?'

Matthew stood with his back to her, and lighting a cigarette he exhaled heavily.

'Not long... Since I knew that tennis wasn't my future, that waiting to inherit this place wasn't what I wanted. You've always fitted into the picture here. You have said you don't understand the lure of a life in London that is pulling me away from you. Would you have been prepared to come with me, or that I continued to pretend that all was OK and we muddled along whenever I came back at weekends? You deserve better than that, Rosalind...'

'What I wish, Matthew, is that you'd had the courage to end things with me long before I had come to care for you as much I have. Unless...?'

Matthew turned sharply, his expression partially obscured by a cloud of blue-grey cigarette smoke.

'Unless what?' He heard the sharpness in his tone and he regretted it.

'I always *was* your back-up plan. The girl that you could always rely on coming back to when whoever *she* is looked elsewhere...'

'I have told you there *is* nobody else.'

'There is, Matthew. Or there will be. You might not know who as yet, but there will be *someone* for you in London, but remember this, if the life you crave there doesn't work out, don't come back to Dorset for me, pinning your hopes on a second chance. Because there won't be one!'

Matthew stubbed out his cigarette beneath his foot, his head bowed, too embarrassed to look Rosalind in the eye. He'd had a good thing with her, even if the impetus for their relationship had been eagerly pushed by their mothers. Rosalind was still a good catch for someone, but he had come to realise that that someone wasn't going to be him and he felt wretched for all the reasons she had laid out.

He thought his feelings for Paul Crowley's sister, Lynette, were growing stronger each time they met, but he was far from letting them be known, so he wanted Rosalind to believe there wasn't already someone else, but he suspected it wasn't enough for her. That he wasn't for her was what mattered and as he looked up again, all he saw was her retreating back as she left the summer house and *him* to absorb and deal with his guilt.

★ ★ ★

St John Crowley sat opposite Laurence Naismith in the lounge of their club on Northumberland Avenue, which to him seemed to have lost some of its appeal in the post-war years. Subsequently he frequented it more sporadically these days, but it had been Naismith's choice of venue for lunch.

'I half expected old Frobisher to put an appearance in, much the worse for drink. Poor chap! He never did learn the value of pacing himself when it came to alcoholic libations.'

'I understand that he could be a terrible bore to other members,' Naismith said with a sneer. He never saw why St John easily tolerated the company of those that many others in their circle found less appealing.

'Well, I always got on very well with him at Eton and then Oxford…'

He signalled to a steward to take their order and then sighed wearily.

If Naismith was going to persist with his current black mood it was going to feel like a very long lunch.

'So how is the novel going?'

'It isn't. I have been forced to abandon it temporarily and accept some journalistic work. Reviews, etc. and some short fiction. I need to rediscover my inspiration and time away will help. I am still hoping Mercy Campion might let me have use of her villa at Cap St Vincent when it's free…'

St John smiled. He had heard rumours that Mercy was unlikely to offer Naismith her villa on *gratis* terms as she was tired of his free-loading.

Naismith was notoriously tight and he accepted the largesse of friends, almost as if it were a right.

'So have your cousins settled themselves in?'

'Not entirely. I am guessing they will treat the house as their base and come and go as they please. Which is fine as long as I am not confronted by too many strangers… Laurence, I am curious, did you invite me for lunch for inane small talk or is there some purpose to it?'

Naismith pulled a face. He suspected he might have inadvertently offended St John or that his friend was responding to the negative view of him perpetuated by his cousin Paul Crowley, who had never liked him and didn't make much effort to conceal it. It had made life very difficult as he had curtailed his visits to the Bloomsbury house out of respect for St John as their friendship mattered more to him than most and Paul's obvious antipathy was straining it almost to its limit.

'I am sorry if you find my company so irksome suddenly, St John. Has your cousin become more effective in spreading his poison about me that even *you* are taking heed of it now?'

'You are being ridiculous. Paul is far too busy and self-absorbed to occupy himself with rumours about you! No offence!'

'None taken!' Naismith responded in a tone which St John knew meant that offence had most definitely *been* taken.

Their drinks arrived and orders for lunch were taken and as the steward left them, St John lit a cigarette, taking time to look around the club lounge, searching for familiar faces. He saw Edgar Trentham sitting alone in the corner and inclined his head. Trentham looked much older than his years and St John suspected the strain of the war years in the Asquith and Lloyd George Governments was showing on the face of the publisher.

Edgar's brother Charles who they both knew better had commented upon it when they visited Ashburn Park, but now he could see it for himself.

He said something to Naismith which his friend didn't hear or he chose to ignore and St John finished his drink in a gulp, stubbing out his cigarette as the steward approached to lead them to their table.

He didn't think this was going to be one of the long leisurely lunches like they had enjoyed on so many previous occasions, nor did he see any reason to invite Naismith back to the Bloomsbury house. *If* Mercy Campion relented and allowed Naismith the use of her villa for a few weeks that suited him perfectly, as he would be spared the awkwardness of having to make convincing excuses for his absence as Naismith's company was sadly becoming increasingly tiresome.

Mayfair Boutique – The Same Day

Alicia Savernake was thrilled to see her mother sitting alongside her friend Mercedes Campion, but it was the sight of Jack Trevelyan among the patrons sitting in the moderately sized

Mount Street boutique waiting for the show to begin that was most surprising and which caused her a greater sense of alarm, as she couldn't help wondering which art classes Jack was missing at the Slade, but she was grateful nonetheless that he was there to support her.

The modelling assignments she had so far received had been very welcome as the work had kept her in London since term at the Slade began three weeks earlier. The atmosphere at Chelcombe Place between her parents had continued to be a little strained following her mother's return from France but she had been assured that all was now resolved between them.

It was a subtly mentioned offer of modelling work in Paris which had her most excited as it would be a statement of how far she had come so swiftly. Her agent had assured her that it was a significant indicator of how much she was in demand. The designer that she most wanted to model for was Elsa Schiaparelli, however she had also heard great things about Madeline Venniot. Her employer today was a London-based couturier who she had been introduced to by Mercedes Campion.

She turned left and right as instructed, smiling slightly as her gaze locked with Jack's and he winked at her conspiratorially. They had arranged to meet after the fashion show and she hoped that their evening might end with them in bed.

While she was aware her parents hoped the relationship would be a long-term one that might culminate in marriage, she dared not think too far into the future. There was a mercurial quality to Jack's character – she suspected it was probably the same with all artists – which made them resistant to being tied down. So she was going to be patient.

The sex was great – better than great in fact – but she was astute to know that she couldn't build a future just on the physical aspects of their relationship and alone with her thoughts, sometimes she feared that when the mutual desire was exhausted that was all there might be. He had mentioned taking her to Cornwall the following summer to the artists' colony that his mother had established, which her brother, Miles, had spoken of, on his frequent visits to the Trevelyan home.

She was struck by a tinge of sadness as she went backstage for the next dress change as she often did when thoughts turned to her beloved brother. The war cast long shadows for their generation as they had narrowly escaped the horror of the trenches in which Jack's eldest brother, Hugo, had been spared, but it had claimed the lives of her beloved Miles and his close friend Ralph Horton.

She could easily allow herself to imagine a future that was idyllic – where she modelled while he devoted his time to painting, but however dreamlike it appeared, Alicia knew that she was getting ahead of herself.

She dared not risk what Jack was offering her now, by appearing to want more than he was willing to give and by doing so lose him before his heart had been truly won.

5

In the weeks that followed as autumn established itself, Jack, Paul and Lynette found their way easily past the early days of study. Nicola Fearns, however, who had initially appeared so keen to prove herself, was struggling in the life classes. For her just winning the scholarship had come hardest of all and although she definitely had an artist's eye, as some of her tutors and fellow students willingly acknowledged thus encouraging her not to lose heart so soon, the doubts expressed by some senior members of staff had caused her to question her presence there again.

Paul had also told his sister to be nicer, but the kinship that Nicola had wanted to strike with Lynette hadn't materialised and she often felt gauche in her company. Lynette confessed that she found Nicola's wide-eyed admiration a little too much and laughing, she had confided she thought Nicola might declare her love. Paul dismissed that as nonsense, but he agreed that Nicola did need to relax. To assert her personality on them and not appear *so* eager to please all the time, especially around Alicia, who she found particularly aloof. Alicia wasn't enrolled at the Slade and her sole purpose among them to Nicola's mind appeared to be keeping a watchful eye on Jack. When Nicola discreetly mentioned this to Paul, he nodded, laughing gently, and he explained in hushed whispers that it had more to do with *his* current girlfriend, Jayne, who had briefly dated Jack, prior to him moving onto her.

A visit from her cousin Martin Fearns was a boost –albeit a brief one and like Paul, Martin urged her to give the art classes, that she had strived so hard to study at, a realistic chance. Paul, Lynette and Jack were all agreed however that they had to *urge* Nicola to have as little to do with Laurence Naismith as she could politely manage.

That his interest in her was piqued at their first encounter was obvious to Paul and he had been eager to rescue her. Naismith was a close friend of their cousin St John, who they forced themselves to tolerate, but Paul knew how a man like Naismith could charm an innocent like Nicola into submission. When St John overheard them he surprised them by vigorously defending his friend.

'Careless comments like that can seriously damage a man's reputation, Paul, as you well know, and Trevelyan, you are as much a guest in my house as Naismith is.'

St John's tone was deliberately caustic as he felt he had no other choice. Although he hadn't witnessed Naismith being overly interested in the Fearns girl, he knew what he could be like.

'You are being unfair to Jack, St John because I saw Naismith fawning over Nicola at the party you threw for us the other week and she only accepted the invitation at my behest. I know you have been very generous in offering us accommodation here for the first term, but you didn't say anything about having to tolerate Naismith being a caveat…'

St John struggled to marshal his temper, although he didn't blame Paul for his scepticism regarding Naismith's conduct sometimes, given that he had railed against his friend's idiosyncrasies in their presence on sufficient occasions over the years for them to have just reason for feeling as they did.

Although he counted Naismith among his best friends, the man could be *so* infuriating! He treated his hospitality as a given. Most of all, St John *resented* feeling *obliged* to defend Naismith to his family.

'OK, Paul, point taken, but from the little that I saw of her, the Fearns girl looks as timid as a young foal and your instincts to protect her are sound. However, comments like Jack's have to be substantiated by facts.

'With that I will leave you all to it. Try not to be judge and jury to Naismith, as I am sure he meant the Fearns girl no ill...'

As St John turned his back to leave, Jack shook his head, raising an eyebrow, and Paul smiled. Their cousin was being very generous in opening up his Bloomsbury home to them, however much he thrived on being at the centre of things in the artistic world, so Paul imagined it suited St John having them stay here, as much as it did them, but they hadn't anticipated Naismith being part of the deal and he couldn't see himself tolerating that for very long. So very soon St John would have a choice to make.

'Why does your cousin tolerate Naismith so readily?' The incredulity in Jack's tone was evident and he didn't care if St John overheard him as he left.

Paul lit a cigarette shaking his head vigorously and wrapping his arm around the chair in which Jayne Campion sat, drawing her to him. It wasn't a question he could answer, but recalling his father's initial reluctance for them to accept St John's invitation, if ultimatums had to be laid down, he would have no hesitation in broaching the subject.

'The man is a parasite as far as I'm concerned!' Jayne Campion said with as much vehemence as she could be bothered to show.

'He expects to enjoy full use of Mercy's villa for a pittance and then he takes offence whenever it isn't available.'

'Your sister does love the drama though, Jayne, otherwise she would refuse him more readily, just as when she hosted my mother there recently,' Alicia commented as she moved to sit on the floor within the circle of Jack's arms.

As Paul and Jack exchanged looks with raised eyebrows, Jayne exhaled heavily on her cigarette, deciding not to respond to Alicia's barbed comment, as Lynette said, 'Can't we find something better to talk about than Laurence Naismith's latest romantic yearnings?' Paul gave his sister a dark look, suspecting her comment might have been aimed at Nicola, as he poured more wine into each glass.

They were aware of being fortunate in having the run of their cousin's house, but for Paul in particular if that luxury came at a price of having to defend Naismith in any circumstance, then it would be too high and he wouldn't stand by and let Nicola become a sacrificial lamb to Naismith's baser desires, if he had the power to prevent it.

Chelcombe Place, Chelcombe Lacey – Hampshire

Alexander Savernake looked down at the letter and then at his youngest daughter Laura. He sighed heavily.

'I don't suppose there is much point in trying to dissuade you as you are quite determined to go. The fact that your sister is already in London does sway the situation in your favour, Laura, but—' He paused, steepling his fingers and tapping them against pursed lips. 'I am also mindful of the opportunities that are likely to come her way to secure more work in Paris and I would be unhappy about you living in London alone.'

Laura looked at him pleadingly and Alexander knew that he was out of his depth and fighting a losing battle with her. Daphne had given her tacit approval of Laura's plan, albeit with similar concerns to his. She had added that she had been given time to follow her dreams to study art by her father and as it was entirely possible Laura could enjoy the same level of success in modelling as Alicia, they couldn't in all conscience deny their youngest the same opportunity.

Alexander jolted himself back to the present, happy for a diversion before his thoughts drifted onto St John Crowley, which was territory he never wanted to explore.

'Well?' Laura asked him again, the eagerness evident in her voice.

'I must be mad to say this, but OK, you can pursue your career in London, however, I want you to keep in regular touch.'

Laura leaned over and kissed her father on the cheek. He smiled at the obvious delight his decision had given her, although he remained uneasy as she took her leave.

Reaching for the worn photograph of his son, Miles, in its gilt frame on his desk, he smiled, filled with pride that Miles had served in the regiment that had seen generations of Savernake men do their duty.

He swallowed past the lump forming in his throat and said, 'Your sisters are growing up fast, Miles, and alas, away from us.'

He looked around his warmly lit study and realised that with Alicia and Laura spending more time in London, Chelcombe Place would begin to resemble a stately pile more than the family home as he remembered it. He realised that he was being foolish, that it was the natural order of things, however he yearned to turn back the clock to happier times before that fateful day in August 1914, which led to Miles heeding the bugle call of war. He felt the sting of tears, putting the photograph frame back in its place on his desk, gulping against the urge to shed them, at which moment the study door opened and Daphne walked in.

'You have made our youngest very happy.' She came to stand behind his chair, gently resting her palm against his temple. She realised how big and significant a decision it had been for him, saying yes to Laura.

'I know you were annoyed that I missed Miles' memorial, but I cannot bear it, Alex. I just can't! Even now, four years after the Armistice, the carnage of it haunts me still. I didn't abandon you and the girls. I merely took refuge for myself.' Daphne Savernake bent to kiss her husband's head, relieved that he didn't flinch or move aside, as she had feared he might. She knew that St John's sudden arrival had infuriated him more than her absence had.

'It didn't help that I had to suffer Crowley turning up uninvited. He knew that you were not at home. I could tell from the expression on his smug face… He brought that obsequious author with him as well. Wretched creatures, both of them!'

Daphne wrung her hands and took a deep breath.

'Shh. You never had anything to worry about where St John Crowley is concerned. I would never have chosen him even if my father had a mind to sanction a union, which I doubt. Besides which, he only succeeds in getting under your skin because you allow him to. I will take responsibility for many things, Alex, but never again will I apologise for the bizarre behaviour of that man!'

Daphne squared her shoulders and looked at her husband with steely determined eyes.

He moved to stand by the fire, half turning to face her. He nodded.

'Fair enough! I respect your position on the matter of Crowley… I will try not to mention him again.'

Daphne smiled. She would have a word to her friend Mercedes Campion as she was someone Crowley took notice of. He always claimed that the portrait of her on the landing was one that he had commissioned, which only served to add to her husband's anger, but she knew that it was given to her, as an engagement present by the artist who some had speculated was Augustus John, but she knew to be Nate Gilbrandsen.

'So what now?' He shrugged.

'We have this large house to ourselves, with the estate to run and we are here whenever our girls need us. As they *will*… Perhaps when they have dazzled London enough and have grown tired of being dazzled by it. Chelcombe Place will be here for them to return to, as it has always been. Have no fear.'

Daphne approached her husband and he took her into his arms. He had never liked quarrelling, but Crowley *did* get under his skin like few men ever could, but he had vowed not to dwell on him and he would keep that promise. He hadn't had many interested suitors before her and the few there had been made little or no impact on him. Daphne Milford, however, had swept him away from the first and he had told his closest friends and his siblings that he meant to marry her, and so he had.

He freely admitted that he had never regretted it for a single day since.

6

Having severed ties with Rosalind in Dorset, Matthew Fullerton was keen to establish himself at the *Express* and to swiftly reconnect with Paul Crowley and Jack Trevelyan. Having previously met Paul's sister, Lynette, briefly on a couple of occasions, he was keen to get better acquainted. On meeting Alicia Savernake, however, he felt an instant and strong tug of primal male desire. A reaction that he was embarrassed to realise had been very noticeable, not least by Paul who felt obliged to inform him that Alicia only had eyes for Jack these days, and so she should be considered out of bounds as any interest he had made known was likely to be swiftly rebuffed.

Jack had noticed Matthew's initial reaction to Alicia and had been amused by it because Alicia had done everything to convey to their group that she could be blissfully contained within their relationship, to the exclusion of others. With his journalistic eye Mathew quickly observed that while Alicia commanded the respect and affection of her peers, Lynette Crowley was slightly jealous of her.

They chatted quite amiably but Matthew noticed there was a distinct edge to their discourse. That if Jack ever fell foul of Alicia or committed any action likely to incur her wrath, then Lynette would swiftly seize upon any frisson in their relationship. When Matthew attempted to engage Lynette in conversation, he saw that her attention was easily diverted towards Jack.

Paul took the trouble to quietly inform him that his sister was smitten with Jack. It helped Matthew to better understand the various dynamics at work within their group, as it fuelled his wish to get to know them better. Suffice to say he found them intriguing and he felt comfortable in their company, thus easing any residual sense of guilt that he had felt at severing his ties in Dorset *so* abruptly.

Turning to Paul he had said, 'Lynette is beautiful. Engaging. She won't want for admirers, surely.'

Paul had shrugged nonchalantly, smiling as he handed him a drink.

'That would depend on whether she can get over him...' They both looked across at Jack and Paul continued: 'You know what they say about first love, surely.'

Matthew nodded silently, having been determined to keep his tone neutral so as not to give Paul anything to think about and to get it wrong. The process of breaking up with Rosalind had been painful for both of them, despite Giles' accusations to the contrary, so he wouldn't be rushing into forming any rash attachments for the foreseeable future.

'Do you see Jack as your great artistic rival?'

'It's the kind of backdrop that you journalists relish, isn't it? The slightest hint of resentment. An implied edge to our friendship fuelled by a desire to do anything just to be the best? The threat of relations turning sour if one of us enjoys swift early success, but the other doesn't. As it is our freshman year at the Slade, I'm not too worried. We both have a lot to learn about art, our instinctive natural talent notwithstanding, and from what I have heard there are some in a position of authority there who will relish knocking any cockiness out of us the first glimpse they get of it...' Paul paused to drag heavily on his cigarette before continuing. 'Besides, there is a lot to admire about Jack and I like him genuinely. I apologise if that doesn't make good copy for you, Fullerton, but it's how it *is*... For now, anyway.'

'I could do a piece on you both. How your friendship works so well, what drives you both to be the best and how you think it might impact that friendship going forward?' Paul laughed slightly and Matthew was embarrassed. 'I can see why you are keen to make an impression in one career having just bravely abandoned another, but I doubt you could convince an editor that such a piece on two art students would be newsworthy... yet. Let us produce something of note and then I will give you the nod. I can't speak for Jack, of course, but I suspect he will feel the same... Unless?'

'What?'

'You are interested in interviewing his mother? From what I know of Margot Trevelyan she never declines free publicity. It would involve a long trek down to Cornwall.'

Matthew was a little unsure whether Paul Crowley was being slightly mocking as he took his leave to rejoin Jayne Campion, but Matthew knew he wouldn't be seeking an interview with Margot Trevelyan, although he knew of her by reputation, having done his research as any good journalist would, but no! He had come to London to assert his journalistic credentials among his peers in artistic and literary circles and this was where he meant to make *his* mark.

Nicola Fearns by contrast was still struggling to fit in. Her artistic studies, as far as they went, were providing her some satisfaction, but she had fallen victim to a degree of censure from some of the tutors who felt she wasn't quite ready for life classes at the Slade School of Art and they didn't feel obliged to spare her blushes by saying so. Jack was encouraging on the occasions that their paths crossed, having told her that from what he had seen of her work, she had every right to be studying at the Slade just as he did and that she shouldn't think she was taking a place that should have gone to someone else. He suspected there was an element of snobbery at work, although he chose not to share that with her and he had doubts – although here again he chose not to share them fully – whether it was wise for her to demonstrate such a slavish devotion to Lynette. He feared for her sake that if he had noticed it then the others would have also and from what he knew of Paul's sister, she wouldn't take kindly to what had appeared to him at least, as Nicola's cloying attention.

'Don't force the issue. The friendship has to develop naturally if it's going to last,' was all that he had been willing to say from a neutral point of view and Jayne Campion had nodded vigorously as Jack spoke.

When Paul took Lynette to task about Nicola later, he accused her of being a snob, to an extent even their cousin St John would have been proud. Lynette had bristled at the suggestion. 'Why is she so keen to be friends with me, anyway? I don't see her going to the same lengths with Jayne or Alicia. I don't want to be anyone's heroine, Paul, and she needs to learn that nobody likes a hanger-on.'

Paul half nodded accepting that Lynette had a point, however he knew that Jack had been nervous of tackling Nicola on the subject, other than to gently urge caution. 'I understand Jack has tried to clarify the situation with Nicola by advising her to let any friendship develop naturally, but with your attitude, Sis, I wonder why she would even want to be friends. It's the sort of behaviour I would expect from St John and most definitely from Naismith – especially if he felt his romantic attentions were being rebuffed. But not from you…'

Lynette bowed her head slightly and then she looked up.

'OK! I will give her a chance, but I'm warning you, Paul, and you can pass this on to Jack, as he appears to have elected himself Nicola's champion, I won't be anyone's *crush*!'

Paul had doubts about whether that was what Nicola wanted, but he chose to let it slide, having made more progress with his sibling on Nicola Fearns' behalf than he ever anticipated doing. As Paul took his leave to return to Jayne's side, he saw Lynette look in Nicola's direction and smile. Nicola smiled back. It was a start. He had known that a comparison with St John on the issue of snobbery would make Lynette bristle with indignation, but it would also give her cause to think. However their friendship might develop, like Jack he feared Nicola might remain on the margins for the whole of her freshman year and that she would have to strive harder than others to make her mark and impress the tutors.

He had fallen foul of them himself on some of the finer points of life drawing, but he hoped she would begin to flourish.

Along with Jack he was going to see she would get her chance to shine.

★ ★ ★

Laurence Naismith felt comfortable in Nathaniel Gilbrandsen's company.

The artist attached great importance to a hermitage existence at his home in Northern Spain. Especially when he was in what he described as one of his wild flurries of frenzied painting, when he worked on several canvasses simultaneously. Although Laurence felt exhausted just watching his host, preferring to adhere to his set daily target of writing 2,000 words, he found the atmosphere more conducive to work, as unlike St John, Nate Gilbrandsen encouraged silence and he was content with it.

Those who had always admired Gilbrandsen's work still coveted a new canvas, although for some he had fallen out of favour and although he hadn't intended for his home in Spain to be perceived as a form of exile, his choice to remain there had prompted rumours in the arena of artistic criticism that he was past his best; beside the fact that Northern Spain wasn't especially warm in late October and as the sunset descended, an autumnal chill permeated the air as Gilbrandsen cursed at losing his precious light for the day, and the fire was lit and the wine uncorked.

'So how is it going with the novel?' Gilbrandsen nodded at the scattered pages on the desk that he had allocated to his guest, having noticed without remarking on it that Naismith never required much encouragement when it came to finishing his work for the day. Naismith grimaced and shook his head.

'Better than it was when I arrived, but that's not much of an endorsement on my part. I do appreciate your hospitality though. St John could have been more sympathetic regarding my bout of writer's block and those cousins of his were a nightmare sometimes.'

'Young artists can be impossibly arrogant. I can vouch for it. I have heard some great praise being lavished on Jack Trevelyan...?'

Naismith was intrigued that his host had made particular mention of Jack but he didn't give the fact away, but he had picked up on the idle rumours thanks to St John and Mercedes Campion.

'He is a real talent, but he still has a lot to learn yet. To his credit he doesn't tend towards the arrogance that Paul Crowley and his sister, Lynette, find it easy to show and they both have a poor opinion of me. Based upon nothing much more than idle tittle tattle.'

Gilbrandsen raised an eyebrow, noticing how irritated his guest had become. He sipped his wine gently, watching Naismith without appearing to do so. He knew Naismith too well not to realise he was covering.

He didn't pay too much heed to the gossip which did reach him, but he knew his guest had an eye for a pretty girl and although he liked Naismith he wouldn't trust him with a god-daughter or niece of his.

'So who is she, Laurence?'

'What are you talking about?' Naismith had coloured slightly and Gilbrandsen pressed on.

'I think you know. There is a young woman who has caught your attention. Is she part of St John's coterie and impossibly young?'

Naismith coughed slightly on a mouthful of wine, which he had to acknowledge was a particularly fine red, however he could feel the intensity of his host's gaze and felt it was better to come clean.

'I wouldn't claim any interest as such, but her name is Nicola Fearns and she is as timid as a doe. I think my attentions were misinterpreted.'

Gilbrandsen nodded. 'It happens… Where does her romantic interest lie?'

Naismith shook his head. 'It's hard to tell, although I think she had developed a slight crush on Lynette and I am not alone in that view so don't accuse me of being sour.'

Gilbrandsen smiled taking a long gulp of his wine and holding his hand up in surrender. Having told Naismith he could stay for as long as he needed to finish his novel, he wasn't going to risk incurring his wrath and have to suffer a sullen guest for days, perhaps weeks.

'So you haven't made a clumsy pass at her yet?'

'No! Absolutely not!'

The vehemence of Naismith's denial had Gilbrandsen wondering.

'You do want to seduce her?'

'My god, Gilbrandsen!'

'You're prevaricating! Even if her interest lies elsewhere that doesn't deny you have desires… What do you know of her background?'

Naismith shook his head. 'As much as she has divulged which is little. She is on a scholarship to the Slade, so I am guessing that any money in the family is scarce. She's hopelessly *gauche* and when it suits her, she can be a hopeless wallflower, but if the right person pays her heed, she will respond in kind. I am certain of that. Otherwise, she's barely worth more than the attention that I have already paid her.'

Gilbrandsen nodded thoughtfully, murmuring his ascent. Naismith knew his host too well to believe he would let the matter rest. That would do young Miss Fearns a far greater disservice than any ill-founded rumours could do to him as Gilbrandsen's interest in Nicola was definitely piqued, and because he knew his host had a reputation as a player and that his appetite for collecting young biddable artistic muses was legendary.

Paris – November 1922

Alicia Savernake was nervous. She didn't usually suffer from nerves prior to a modelling assignment, however the vendeuse of the hiring boutique was especially critical of what she saw as young, beautiful, but inexperienced models in general. However, in Alicia's view, she was outrageous in her demands and she had caused Alicia to start doubting her abilities and that wasn't something she was accustomed to doing.

Ever.

The opportunity to come and work in Paris had been offered to her so swiftly that she found it alarming, while the timing of the assignment had prevented Jack from joining her. While Paris was consolidating itself at the apex of post-war European fashion, Alicia's reputation as a sought-after model was growing with each assignment. She was still slightly annoyed that her father was placing so much responsibility for looking after her sister upon her shoulders. She was pleased that he had allowed Laura to leave home and try to establish herself in London, but not as she saw it at the cost of *her* freedom.

She was missing Jack with a growing intensity and that alarmed her as she wasn't accustomed to over-relying emotionally on anyone, but what she readily acknowledged feeling for Jack was stronger than she had ever felt before.

Then her thoughts slid easily onto her beloved brother, Miles, who Jack had known well from his many visits to the Trevelyan home in Cornwall as one of his eldest brother Hugo's best friends. Thus the link between their families had been forged and then strengthened and it would endure if, as she hoped, her love for Jack was as strong as she believed it to be to sustain a relationship, which might yet lead to marriage.

She was forced out of her reverie with a sharp rebuke to hurry up by Veronique, who wasn't a woman to make an enemy of in the close knit arena of Parisian *haute couture*, but from whom a positive reference was a gift that any model who had experience of modelling in Paris, valued beyond price. She looked at the vendeuse and nodded, her mind focused once more, as she was determined to make her mark among the elite fashion buyers of Paris and from there who knew where her talent might take her?

7

The extent of Jack Trevelyan's independent financial means became apparent to his peer group when he announced shortly before the Christmas recess that he had taken a service flat in Gresse Street, which enjoyed close proximity to the Slade. Alicia was the first to know that he had acquired the flat as he had sworn her to secrecy while showing her around one wet late-November afternoon shortly after she returned from Paris. He had decided on the interior decor with an artist's eye and said he hoped to be moving in before Christmas which he would be spending in Cornwall, while she was expected to join her family at Chelcombe Place – which she was happy to do, albeit in the hope that Jack could be there with her. She had teased him gently about marking the flat as his, in their own way, and he had smiled mischievously at her suggestion, his arm around Alicia's shoulder as he had said he was taking it unfurnished so that he could design it firmly in *his* image, so she would have to wait to share *his* bed there.

She feigned a crestfallen pose at that, but although intrigued, Alicia was too polite to enquire whether he could afford such a luxurious place, but her curiosity was piqued later by the extent to which both Lynette and Jayne appeared determined to know.

'All I can say is that you are evidently well endowed financially speaking, you Trevelyans!'

Jack had smiled as she kissed his cheek, amused by her attempt to keep her tone neutral, pretending that she didn't care about his answer to that when it was obvious to him that she did.

'Well, I shall have to take you to Cornwall soon, so that you can see our ancestral pile for yourself. I'm sure Miles must have told you what it was like from his visits. I hope you are not expecting anything as grand as Chelcombe Place. So what do you think our friends will say about my soon to be "bachelor pad"?' He mimicked the quotation marks with his fingers as he said the words and taking Alicia's hand, led her into what he planned to be the master bedroom. She smiled mischievously.

'At the risk of repeating myself, it's a shame there's no bed yet.'

Jack nodded, wrapping his arms around her waist and smiling. He kissed her forehead and said, 'Well, I shall have to overstay my welcome in Tavistock Place, won't I, to slate your insatiable urges?'

She punched him lightly in the arm. 'Careful, you will damage my parents' view of you as a respectable suitor with talk like that and I refute that my urges are insatiable. I just have a healthy view when it comes to sex…'

Jack nodded. 'As often and as much as I can offer…'

Alicia smiled back, kissing him on the mouth, then with a swift look around her she said. 'OK! Well, you're failing to satisfy my needs, so your first purchase should be a bed in here, or I won't be coming back until it's fully furnished.'

'Is that right?'

Alicia nodded.

'OK! Consider it done.' He bowed theatrically as she led him down in the lift. She bit her bottom lip nervously, deliberately avoiding his gaze, as she knew how scared she became on occasion with the pace with which their relationship was progressing, fearing she could become too emotionally dependent upon him and aware of how swiftly his relationship with Jayne withered once he had made his interest in *her* known.

Given their family's shared history, there was an air of inevitability about them getting together, but Alicia knew that Jayne had been deeply hurt by Jack's rejection and was as determined as she could be not to suffer the same fate.

Alicia tended to look upon her parents' marriage as the best example of what she wanted for herself, of what a thriving relationship should be, but she feared she might be setting her sights too high and would have to play second fiddle to his art, along with the nagging question of whether any woman could become as important to him as that. She knew their friend Jayne had similar concerns about Paul Crowley as she'd had about Jack, which she had shared with Alicia without betraying the residual bitterness that she was entitled to feel at having lost Jack to her.

'It's the price we pay as their muses. Wanting to be allowed in. To get close enough to these brilliant men.' Alicia remembered the conversation now and the wistfulness that had permeated Jayne's tone.

She considered herself a pragmatist, willing to accept that some distance was a price that she could pay, for being in love with Jack Trevelyan, but how much distance and for how long were the important questions, to which she wished she already had the definitive answer. So many young women had in the last decade suffered the ignominy of being described as a "spare" woman having lost their man to the war. How glad she was to be spared such a plight. Theirs was the generation to have had luck on their side. Jack looked at her quizzically as they climbed into the taxi he had hailed, as Alicia remained lost in her thoughts.

'You OK? You looked lost to me for a while and you're shivering.'

Alicia nodded. 'It's getting colder and I'm ready for tea.'

Jack pulled her to him in the back of the taxi, kissing the top of her head. He sensed she was stalling him, but chose not to pursue it.

He imagined she might be thinking about Miles, who he was aware she had looked up to, but he worried sometimes that she might expect him to fill that void, which was a lot to ask as he knew Miles Savernake would be a tough act to follow.

★ ★ ★

St John Crowley was in the foulest of moods. Standing in the hallway of his Bloomsbury house, he ripped open the telegram, reading its contents with a furrowed brow. Laurence Naismith was returning to England in late November, which was earlier than he had planned. He swore under his breath. Having received his friend's previous telegram which he had read with surprise to hear that Naismith was staying with Nathaniel Gilbrandsen, and trying to complete his novel, now he was intending to return and doubtless expecting to be put up once more in Bloomsbury, but that wasn't going to be possible. Paul and Lynette had said they would move out and that would involve him incurring the wrath of his cousins, their parents, who had readily accepted his invitation for them to stay as an act of financial expediency.

He threw the telegram onto the fire. Naismith hadn't formerly asked if he could stay, but St John knew him too well and that wasn't his modus operandi. He would subtly hint at it, and then sulk when the invitation wasn't forthcoming. St John had been surprised that Gilbrandsen had willingly provided Naismith with accommodation as he wasn't aware that the artist knew Naismith so well and he was known to be a reluctant host at best – a fact to which both Mercy Campion and Margot Trevelyan would attest – so why had he made an exception for Naismith who, St John knew, was never the easiest of guests? He didn't like being put in the position of having to offend Naismith by refusing him in order to placate his cousins, but that was the position they had placed him in and he knew they weren't bluffing.

Having heard about Jack Trevelyan's new flat he could guess that's where their hopes were being pinned which meant they had a choice, which limited *his*. He had offered Paul and Lynette the run of his house for the whole of the year and that was up to next summer. He had no intention of incurring the wrath of the wider Crowley family, so the choice was simple. Naismith would have to make alternative arrangements and although he could suffer his sulking, the premise to Paul and Lynette's objections were based upon idle rumour. The Fearns girl was a timid "mouse" and he knew Naismith was a hopeless flirt, and that he could be boorish about it when rebuffed, but *he* wasn't aware that she had made any complaint, so Paul was probably using Nicola Fearns as a scapegoat for the fact that he and his sister didn't like Naismith and they felt no compulsion to conceal it. He swore under his breath and was about to ring for tea, but glancing at the clock he decided to have cocktails and dinner at his club instead.

Chelcombe Place, Chelcombe Lacey, Hampshire

Alexander Savernake had felt slightly lost and ill at ease of late, describing his feelings thus (but only after having been pushed into doing so, by his wife): like the walls of their vast house were closing in on him.

Which he knew had Daphne worried and although he had played no part in her decision to plead with their daughters to come home for the weekend, he was glad that she had. He stood gazing down at his son, Miles', grave as the taxi turned in the curve of the gravel drive where she stood awaiting their arrival. Every time he came to the grave, his memory flashed back to an image of Miles in the moment of bravery, which had cost him his life. "A total waste!" was how Daphne described it.

He could hear the guns and the mortar fire as if they were happening here and now and he closed his eyes tightly against the horror of that memory and in that moment the rear door of the taxi was slammed shut, as his daughters alighted and he was back in the present, the moment of anguish gone until it resurfaced again as he knew it would.

It helped him to understand a little better why Daphne struggled to mark such dates and over the years the grieving process hadn't got much easier, nor did he expect it would.

He turned at the sound of voices, relieved that it was just Alicia and Laura; although he had half expected Jack to be with them, he was glad that he wasn't here. He wanted it to be just family this weekend.

He raised his arm in greeting as Alicia approached him just as Laura accompanied her mother inside the house. He clicked his fingers as Hector, his springer spaniel, sat obediently although he wagged his tail furiously in anticipation of Alicia's arrival as she bent to stroke his ears, then she received her father's perfunctory peck on the cheek.

'No Jack?'

Alicia shook her head. 'No, he's on a duty visit to Cornwall. He will drop by on his way back and we will travel back to London together. So how are you?'

Alexander shook his head as they turned towards the grave. Alicia and Laura adored their brother, but Alicia had been the closest to him and she, Alexander knew, felt the loss just as keenly. Whereas Daphne dealt with the grief by withdrawing from it into herself, so that sometimes he couldn't reach her for days, Alicia felt it raw as he always had.

'It's cold out here.' She shivered slightly and Alexander smiled. He knew what she was doing and that it had been prompted by a quiet word from her mother.

'You should dress for the outdoors in November then and not for one of those Paris boutiques.'

Alicia nodded, knowing her father hadn't been fooled, as she linked her arm through his and he clicked his fingers for the obedient Hector to follow.

'So how is Hugo? Does Jack mention him?'

Alicia shook her head. 'Not much, or Adam for that matter and he is based in London.' She tended not to pry too much into Jack's family life as she knew he didn't share the same close relationship as they all did. Miles had commented on the dynamic of the Trevelyan household when he returned from his occasional visits and he had said it was nothing like what he enjoyed at Chelcombe Place, while Ralph Horton and his sister, Sybil, always preferred the long weekends and holidays they had spent in Hampshire to the ones in Cornwall.

'He did mention that Sybil had been a frequent visitor of late. We know she is a good friend of Hugo's wife, so it's not surprising, but Jack was quite hesitant about it at first, and keen that I shouldn't hear of it from anyone else.'

Alexander shrugged, frowning slightly. 'I can't understand why she would resist coming here. We have told her she is always welcome – as she should expect as Miles' fiancée.'

Alicia knew that her father had spoken in the present tense, but although she couldn't be certain that it wasn't accidental, she chose not to draw his attention to it.

Alicia nodded. Sybil Horton, the woman who would have become her sister-in-law, was very attractive, and she had always been vivacious and gaily extrovert, but losing Miles had been the third tragedy she'd had to endure. Having been orphaned in her teens, she had lost her brother, Ralph, and her fiancé in quick succession and the latter had hit her especially hard as it had shattered her dream of a happy marriage.

She hadn't coped, turning her back on those who knew her, to volunteer as a VAD tending the needs of the surviving wounded, and she had gone to France. Alicia hoped that her recent visits to Cornwall would have helped her in the healing process but she would like to see Sybil again here at Chelcombe Place, where she had so many memories to cherish – just as she knew her parents would.

As they entered the drawing room together Alicia thought about the telegram their mother had sent her, which had been awaiting on her return from Paris.

Your father isn't coping too well. He would love to see you both!

She bent to give Hector a sliver of fruit cake as he was taken to his basket, ignoring her father's shake of the head as he said, 'You always spoil him whenever you come home!' Alicia smiled as she took her seat by the fire. It was a gentle rebuke but a rebuke nonetheless, to which she nodded defiantly.

★ ★ ★

Laurence Naismith arrived home from Spain, via France, on an overnight boat from Calais, docking at Dover in drizzly rain. He felt chilled to the bone and in foul spirits. Gilbrandsen had proved to be a diffident host at best as the weeks wore on and although the artist had listened to *his* tales of woe, about the hostility that St John's cousins had felt towards him for the most part, Gilbrandsen had, in the last week of his stay, become even more withdrawn, speaking only when he had to, working ever more feverishly for longer hours and so Naismith had begun to feel almost invisible.

His farewell when it came was greeted with a dismissive grunt and now he had to put himself to the task of finding somewhere to live, as his hopes of returning to St John Crowley's house had been reassessed and he had no hesitation in blaming St John's younger cousins for freezing him out. His only hope of a reprieve was the Christmas recess at the Slade which would begin in a couple of weeks, so he expected Paul and Lynette would be going home and then he wouldn't have to give another thought to the wretched Fearns girl. While he couldn't be sure their temporary departure would lead to him being invited back, he remained hopeful, even though he had telegrammed from France the time that he was docking and St John hadn't sent the car, so he would have to catch the London train. He lit a cigarette and pondered his next move.

Truth be told he bitterly resented the animosity that Paul and Lynette displayed towards him and he had wondered on numerous occasions how much St John might see his cousins if he hadn't got the Bloomsbury house to offer them. Naismith realised it had been an error to point this fact out while in a bristling mood to his friend prior to leaving for Spain and St John had responded by saying in a caustic tone that *he* had "filched" free accommodation off him for too long, adding that he tried the same trick on their friend Mercy Campion.

Wincing at the harsh words which had been exchanged on both sides and fearing the threat they posed to a friendship of long standing, he finished his cigarette and stubbed it out with his heel and raising his arm to summon a reluctant porter to take his trunk to the Victoria train, he snatched up the worn leather valise containing the finished draft of his novel. He smiled. Gilbrandsen's late-night brandy-fuelled indiscretions had been an inspiration to him and he considered the novel which he had practically reshaped to be his best work of fiction in years.

Although it pained him to admit it, he desperately needed the novel to achieve the success that he believed it had the potential to, as he had been forced to surrender his flat in London when his previous novel had "bombed" with the critics and he just couldn't afford another flop. His agent – bless her – had been keen to point out as subtly as she could that she doubted his career would survive another setback.

8

London – December 1922

Martin Fearns had taken great care in his choice of venue for lunch with his cousin Nicola, who was, he knew from her mother, in great need of a boost to her confidence, amid a very real threat to abandon her studies at the Slade School of Fine Art after just one half term.

He didn't know yet what had prompted this latest crisis of confidence in Nicola, but he was determined to find out. He rationed his trips to London these days and whereas he would have once lunched at the club on Northumberland Avenue which his friend Daniel Swiffen had first introduced him to and with much coercion urged him to become a member, that wouldn't have been a viable choice today given its policy towards guests of the female gender. Besides, it held too many memories that he had no wish to resurrect, so he had tentatively suggested a quiet place on Coventry Street and was confident it would provide him with the privacy he needed to persuade his cousin to stick with her studies.

He doubted he could rely on her father and knew that her mother – who had been most pleased by Nicola's admittance – was over-wrought with worry.

He laid the portrait she had done of him on the seat beside him, as a not too subtle reminder of just how talented an artist she was and that, he hoped, would serve its purpose and convince her to continue with her studies at the Slade beyond the Christmas recess. He was convinced for himself, aside from her mother's concerns, that Nicola's instinctive talent shouldn't be wasted. His cousin, who preferred to be called Simon rather than his given name, Clifford, was worse than hopeless in these situations, so he didn't expect a positive outcome for Nicola to come from her father. While he doubted that *his* words alone would do the trick, he was going to give it a damn good try.

Nicola arrived as he was on his second gin and tonic and that had been sufficient to calm his nerves as she smiled wanly, taking the seat opposite. She launched into a demand for him to explain why his invitation to lunch had come as a direct consequence of her mother's intervention, which she confessed had been her initial suspicion.

'Well?' she prompted and Martin smiled.

'What can I say? Other than that I plead guilty to sharing your mother's concerns. So you have rumbled us, but our concern comes with your best interests at heart – well, as we see them at least and yes, I have been handed the task of trying to convince you that you have worked hard for this opportunity; that you are at the Slade entirely on merit...'

Nicola sat back with her arms folded across her chest, as she arched an eyebrow at the canvas resting on the spare seat.

'Is that why you have brought that? I expected better of you, Cousin Martin! You say that I am there on merit, but am I compared to artists like Jack Trevelyan and Paul Crowley? You want to look at what they are producing if you're *critiquing* artistic talent!'

'Do you *need* to set yourself against them artistically, or is it that you want to feel that you belong in their *clique*?'

Nicola turned her head sideways and for a moment he feared he had lost her. She buried her head behind the menu as the waiter hesitated to approach them and Martin discreetly shook his head and then took two tentative sips of gin.

'You are at the Slade to become a better artist and if you don't belong in that movement you spoke of, perhaps you could become the leader in your own. Listen, this isn't my bag, this artistic world, but I would hope that I know you enough and that gives me an edge, some advantage in *urging* you to make the most of this opportunity!'

'Because that is what men like you fought a war *for*?'

Nicola kept her tone light for fear that she might have caused offence, but as Martin's face broke into a smile, he summoned the waiter who had retreated with some discretion at his behest.

Martin perused the menu and ordered for himself and a second gin.

Nicola declined a drink, ordering a plain omelette. Martin felt more relaxed, having feared he had lost his hand by underestimating his cousin's intuitiveness, but whatever decision she came to, he felt he had done his best to convince her that quitting her studies after one half term would be a colossal waste that she would likely come to regret.

Nicola watched Martin with an artist's eye, however she admired him for so much more. He had always been fond of her mother and she suspected he resented that his cousin got "in" with her first. She had no doubt that is why he had accepted the request to speak to her on her mother's behalf – or should that be plead? Either way he had done his best and whatever decision she reached it would be up to her.

Their meal finished, Martin ordered a cognac and out of politeness she agreed to join him. She nursed the brandy glass, taking tentative sips, unsure of whether to gauge her cousin's opinion on the issue that had troubled her from the very beginning of term.

'How do you define admiration of another, especially someone of the same gender, without it slipping into something more serious which makes the object of that admiration feel awkward?'

Martin took a long breath and then an even larger gulp of cognac and looked at Nicola with wide-eyed bewilderment. It wasn't as if he didn't understand what she was getting at, because he did understand it all too well. He had witnessed it first-hand. He tried not to think too much of old comrades these days as it usually always left a lingering sense of survivor guilt. There were a few however who invaded his thoughts more robustly than others and one in particular, was Daniel, the Viscount Swiffen. He was not the kind of man you could easily forget and nor would he ever want to. He gulped slightly and said, 'One of your fellow students I take it?'

Nicola, bowing her head, nodded. A gesture so imperceptibly subtle that he almost missed it.

'Has this admiration had any bearing on your thoughts about quitting your studies?'

Nicola bit her bottom lip nervously, determined to stem the flow of tears and nodded.

'Does this person know how much you admire them and are they comfortable regarding the extent of it?'

Nicola shook her head. She imagined Lynette had some idea. How could she not?

'I feel *so* gauche around her sometimes because of it and she comes across so classy and sophisticated by comparison, so even if she were fully aware, how could she be even remotely interested?'

'I think she should be flattered to be the object of your "crush", I believe is the term?'

Nicola smiled. How could she have underestimated her cousin's astuteness even in this regard, which must be so far out of his range of experience, she couldn't imagine.

'Because her brother is *so* attractive and so artistically brilliant she could be excused for thinking that my interest lies with him, but in that regard I should take my place at the back of a very long line of admirers!'

Martin looked at Nicola and felt his heart tighten for her. He had seen hero-worship for himself so he knew how painful it could be for anyone who felt their feelings were being rebuffed or worse still ignored. Yet his invitation to Nicola to join him for lunch had been motivated by a wish to encourage her to remain in London and continue her studies. Her scholarship to the Slade had been too hard won to risk throwing it away so recklessly.

'I would urge you to use the Christmas recess to carefully consider your options in every regard. That is the best advice I can offer...'

He stubbed out his cigarette, giving Nicola an encouraging smile and she smiled back. Martin had always been adept at making her feel better about herself and she wondered how she could have thought it would be any different this time.

Gresse Street Flat – Later

Jack Trevelyan removed his arm from around Alicia's shoulders, reaching for his cigarette case, as she snuggled into the warmth of his body.

He lit one for each of them and looking around he nodded satisfactorily, pleased with how the flat looked now the interior decor was exactly what he wanted. He thought it could become a permanent London base after he had finished his studies at the Slade. He was aware that Paul and Lynette had been a little envious when he first showed them around, realising he had his own pad while they were still guests of their cousin St John in Bloomsbury. He had assured them they could look upon Gresse

Street as their home from home, especially since Naismith had returned from Spain in an irritatingly ebullient mood.

'Are you sure a party is such a good idea? I want you all to myself.'

Alicia nudged the sheet aside and her mane of brunette hair fell across his bare chest as she kissed him hungrily on the mouth.

She smiled, biting her bottom lip provocatively as her hand travelled down and Jack barely flinched as she continued her foray beneath the sheet.

'Go on. I *dare* you!'

She kissed him again, removing her hand, and laying down against the pillow she asked, 'How was Cornwall?'

'Tense as usual. My parents are almost living separate lives in that enormous house. They are totally absorbed with their own interests, to the exclusion of everything else. I don't know how Hugo and Caroline tolerate the atmosphere between them. They are entirely civil to one another, but it lacks emotion and I even said to them both that a good quarrel would do them good.'

Alicia smiled. 'And?'

Jack shrugged. 'Nothing.'

'I guess being heir to your father's estate makes up for it, as far as Hugo is concerned.' Jack smiled ruefully, nodding. He stubbed out the cigarette and glancing at the clock, he raised an eyebrow, before leaning in to kiss Alicia on the cheek, but she raised a hand to hold him at bay.

'Did you see Sybil?'

Alicia reached for her silk robe and was conscious of how quiet Jack had suddenly become.

'Well? Was she there visiting Caroline mainly?'

Jack had seen her, but only briefly and Hugo had revealed something that he expected the Savernakes would take very hard and *he* didn't want to be the bearer of bad news on the eve of his flat-warming.

'I did see her, but I got my dates wrong and she was at the end of her visit. Someone had told her we were seeing each other and she seemed pleased. She sends her love to you all.'

Alicia smiled wanly as she shrugged herself into her robe. Jack was withholding some news from her, she could tell that much, but she was at a loss to understand why.

'Will I get to see her?'

Jack half nodded. 'She said she would be seeing Adam while she is in London, so he may bring her to the party as his date, if not otherwise committed. You know Adam!'

Alicia smiled. She did know the middle Trevelyan brother, all too well, so wouldn't be surprised, but she wanted to see Sybil, her brother Miles' one-time fiancée, as she was convinced it was the only way she would find out what Jack was holding out on her about and more importantly *why*?

He leaped out of bed and Alicia let her admiring gaze rest on the beautiful man that Jack Trevelyan was, even naked. Although that didn't alter the fact that he knew something that *she* ought to know and yet he couldn't muster the courage to tell her for whatever reason and that unnerved her.

★ ★ ★

Nicola Fearns left her cousin after a long, leisurely lunch, resolved to return to her studies after the Christmas recess. She would be spending Christmas with her family, and felt compelled to admonish her mother for having got Martin involved. She still hadn't found a way to reconcile her initial reaction to Lynette Crowley which would enable them to move forward amicably so that she could remain part of their group. She had felt like an outsider from the moment she had enrolled at the Slade, even though Paul and Jack had made the effort to include her, while Jayne Campion had been very generous recently in fulsome praise of her art and had offered to sit for her. In her darker moments however, she still felt she was being tolerated at best. It was also noticeable in life classes that tutors could be cruelly condescending of her without even meaning to. Nicola was convinced it was motivated by snobbery and she attributed it thus, while Martin had pointed out over lunch as subtly as he could that the opportunity to study art and nurture her talent *had* been derived from a freedom that men like him had fought to preserve, for her generation.

Although he was too kind to spell it out explicitly, she came away with the sense that she had a duty not to waste the opportunity or the artistic gift she had been given. Not – and the thought caused her to shudder – for a misunderstood attack of heroine worship.

She was also determined to attend the party at Jack's Gresse Street flat, which she had been told was very stylish in terms of decor. Matthew Fullerton had invited her, but to override her hesitancy, he had told her Jack had intended to issue the invitation himself, but when Matthew suggested she be his plus one she had accepted demurely. She was more taken aback when he announced that he had a journalism assignment in Paris fixed for January as he had been talking about it for weeks and she could sense in his absence that others were growing sceptical. He wanted to interview an English-born artist and he saw the potential of securing such an interview would be quite a coup. After he had expressed his frustration at not being able to convince either Paul or Jack to grant him an interview about their art, someone had suggested in jest that he should approach Naismith, but he had been less than impressed, stating the less he had to do with the novelist the better.

For Matthew the evening would be dominated by Paul revealing his much-anticipated portrait of Jayne Campion and *if* he could yet secure an interview on the basis of public reaction to that, it would be another credit that he could claim to his family in Dorset, still concerned by his decision to quit the tennis circuit.

They had parted agreeing to meet outside the Slade and head to the party together. Nicola felt her mood was much lighter now than the melancholy she had been feeling prior to lunch, but her cousin and now Matthew had played a part in lifting her spirits. As much as she knew about Matthew's background from what he had imparted and what she had learnt listening to others, he had suffered a broken engagement prior to settling in London and although she couldn't guess at what his ex-fiancée was like, Nicola knew that if she were fortunate enough to land a jewel like Matthew Fullerton as her betrothed, she would do everything within her power to keep him.

The Crowley Townhouse – Bloomsbury – Same Evening

St John Crowley had greeted his friend Laurence Naismith's return as evenly as he could, his mood distinctly lacking the pre-Christmas joviality.

Shortly afterwards, Paul had informed him that he and Lynette would be attending Jack's "flat-warming" party in Gresse Street, which was expected to last until the early hours, so they would be staying there.

'As you wish.' His clipped tone had been distinctly not friendly as he resented his cousins' belief that they had a right to influence who he invited into his home, however they had chosen to make their absences so obvious. He would readily admit that Naismith could be a difficult man and his secretive demeanour since returning from Spain had become maddening.

Paul sighed and with hands on hips he raised a quizzical eyebrow.

'We are grateful to you for opening your house to us since we started at the Slade. Neither Lyn nor I would want you to think that we have taken your hospitality and kindness for granted.'

St John raised his hand and smiled slightly.

'We are family after all and I promised your parents this would be your home once you had enrolled, so as much as your gratitude is appreciated, it isn't necessary, as I *made* the offer. However, I also understand you find Naismith's presence *intolerable!*'

St John stood by the roaring fire, rocking slightly on his heels as he looked at his cousin. He felt he deserved their candour on the subject if nothing else.

'I do find his attitude intolerable. It's almost as if he expects his friends to offer their hospitality as a right. Jayne has told me that Mercedes finds his expectation to stay at her villa in France an imposition sometimes.'

St John smiled. 'So why doesn't she say so? I believe the last time Laurence asked to stay there, Mercy was entertaining Daphne, Alicia's mother. So I think some of these complaints which are usually made behind his back could be said directly to him. Hasn't Lyn been slightly guilty of appearing to tolerate the Fearns girl, whilst bitching about it?'

St John quirked an eyebrow at Paul who smiled, as he had wondered whether Lynette's initial coolness towards Nicola had been widely noticed and now he had his answer.

'Yes, she has and I was first to tell her. I think Nicola's fault has been an over eagerness to fit in and so her demeanour can appear *gauche*.

'Naismith is not out of place in these circles and yet he still manages to be irritating and I think, St John, that includes you!'

Paul watched as his cousin re-lit his cigar and then shrugging his shoulders, he said, 'Well, if Laurence is being entirely candid, which I admit is open to doubt, regarding the potential success of his latest novel, I think he may be in a position to be making his own accommodation arrangements in due course. So if you find his mood when melancholy less than appealing, I know from experience that when he thinks he is doing well, his opinion of his talents can be even more intolerably inflated…'

Paul fished in his pocket for his cigarette case which he found half empty. Cursing, he smiled as St John lifted the lid of the lapis lazuli box on the coffee table and said, 'Help yourself.'

Paul filled his cigarette case from the large rectangular box and smiling sheepishly he said, 'Thanks, St John, I will replace them tomorrow.'

He rose and went into the hall, shouting up to Lynette that she should hurry or he would leave without her.

St John smiled to himself, and rocking on his heels, he murmured, 'Of course you will.' Then exhaling heavily on his cigar, he said, 'I understand you are planning to unveil your portrait of Jayne at Jack's party this evening?'

St John quirked an eyebrow at Paul, who was growing restless.

Lynette was always notoriously slow at getting ready for social events and to his mind Paul should be accustomed to that now, although he never was. Paul nodded. 'That's right.'

St John half smiled. He had every confidence in his cousin's artistic talent and he had even gone as far as to remark that he would probably flourish in the art world without having studied at an institute as prestigious as the Slade.

'Are you pleased with it?'

'I am. Hope Jayne will be.'

'You like her, don't you?'

Although St John's question took him by surprise, he wasn't embarrassed by the strength of the feelings he was starting to have for Jayne Campion, even though she had been interested in Jack before they had started dating. But now, he was satisfied that she had reconciled herself to having lost Jack to Alicia. For himself he was content to see how a relationship with Jayne might go, but he accepted that she might want to see a more formal commitment from him soon.

'I think you have chosen an excellent subject in Jayne. She has the same quiet beauty that Mercy possessed at that age… I am surprised Jack didn't rush to capture her on canvas when they were dating.'

Paul shrugged, unwilling to answer. He didn't know where St John was going with that remark, but he wasn't following. As he thought the rivalry between himself and Jack to be so over-blown, there wasn't the need, but he also knew his cousin would encourage him to be a little more selfish, even ruthless, if it came to exerting himself in the bid to become the most outstanding artist, not just of their class at the Slade, but of their generation.

St John knew Margot Trevelyan enough to be certain that is what she would be urging Jack to push for and Paul knew his cousin wanted the accolade for *him*. St John had pointed out more than once since term had begun that one day Paul would have to be willing to sacrifice his friendship with Jack for the sake of their art, but St John wasn't yet sure that *he* had reconciled himself to that reality.

He was about to provide St John with an answer of sorts when he saw a reflection of Lynette descending the stairs, in a black and cream silk gown, which looked to him like it had been designed by Schiaparelli and he was genuinely stunned by how beautiful his sister looked when she set her mind at making an effort. St John wolf-whistled at the sight of her, as she offered Paul her gloved hand, with a twinkle in her eye.

'Have you rustled up a taxi?' she asked.

'No, because I didn't know how long you were going to take.'

'So who have you set your cap at tonight?' St John asked, not caring if he had embarrassed her.

Lynette shrugged. 'I shall take my opportunities wherever they land, but I have heard a rumour that Adam Trevelyan is hoping to put in an appearance so hopefully there will be someone other than my dashing brother or our host to spark my interest. Who knows what other handsome stranger will be on hand to tempt me…'

St John smiled, as Lynette sashayed her way to the door. He had never doubted she could attract the attention of any man that she chose to dazzle with her charm, or land herself an eligible husband when the time came. He sighed heavily as he watched them. What it was to be young like Paul and Lynette and the others in their circle. Theirs was the generation lucky to have escaped the horrors of the trenches and they appeared absolutely determined to make their mark, yet while he would caution against their restlessness, he felt this was their moment; the decade where they would reach their zenith. But they would also be wise unlike Icarus not to fly too close to the sun. He possessed the wisdom that came with experience, but St John smiled as he heard the front door slam, knowing that he would swap that in a heartbeat for the exciting vibrancy of youth.

9

Adam Trevelyan looked around him, nodding admirably. He could see that his younger brother had brought his artistic talent to the fore in the decor. He smiled to himself, raising a quizzical eyebrow in the direction of the easel in the corner of the room, covered with a dust sheet, waiting for the "big" reveal later. It had been the main topic of conversation since he had arrived, although Jack was tight-lipped about what Paul Crowley's masterpiece might reveal.

The awkward moment he had feared had not materialised despite Jack's initial misgivings over his choice of date as Adam hadn't expected Sybil Horton to be in London and the only alternative to not asking her to be his "plus one" was to absent himself from the party, but his mother's telegram had been explicit. He had to support his brother.

As the middle son of Gervaise and Margot Trevelyan, he had always been conscious of the need to follow his own path and he had been pleasantly surprised at how satisfied he was that it had led him into the Civil Service. Hugo would inherit the estate while Jack had his art, as their mother so succinctly phrased it, always with immense pride.

She had never shied away from telling them that her own ambition to study art had been thwarted by her father and so she had taken Gervaise as a husband almost as a means of escape as she hadn't quite possessed the courage for outright rebellion and all that would entail financially had she continued her relationship as muse to Nathaniel Gilbrandsen.

He lit a cigarette, exhaling heavily, and was thrust out of his reverie by a jolt in the arm as someone pushed past him. The offender smiled her apologies and he recognised her as Jayne Campion, the younger sister of Mercedes, one of his mother's artistic friends who had been a guest of theirs in Cornwall, but not he noted for some years.

Aside from her, he was on nodding terms with several guests, including the Savernake sisters, their respective families having been friends for many years as Hugo and Miles Savernake had been close throughout their years together in academia and had fought bravely alongside each other during the war. As had Ralph Horton, which brought his thoughts back to Sybil. Adam scanned the room for sight of her. He couldn't rationalise why he felt responsible for her, although Hugo and Caroline had urged him not to appear overly attentive.

At that moment Jack approached him with a bottle and refilled his glass.

'I can see where some of the family money has been spent. A tad too plush for the role of the struggling artist, isn't it?'

'Don't be jealous,' Jack chastised gently, knowing when he was having his leg pulled. 'I seem to recall your pad was well appointed when you first set up in London. Besides, I wish you had forewarned me about bringing Sybil as your date. I could have prepared Alicia for meeting her again.'

'Why so nervous? Sybil is at her shining, brilliant best and she turned up out of the blue, before Hugo's telegram had arrived, asking me to entertain her and I felt pressured into inviting her to dinner. Then I remembered my invite to your party. As our mother was insisting I do *both*, I had no choice…'

Jack half nodded, smiling empathetically. 'She is as stunning as ever, although still emotionally fragile. I got the sense when I was in Cornwall that she was holding something back.'

Jack frowned as he moved on to another guest. Adam blushed slightly as he was at an advantage of knowing what she was withholding as she had pleaded with him not to spoil the surprise as she wanted to tell Alicia and Laura Savernake in her own time.

Adam drained his glass as Paul Crowley passed him by.

'So when is that artwork going to be revealed?'

'In good time. Once the press are here.'

Adam half smiled. He had to give Crowley his due, but he wished Jack appeared more outwardly ambitious. He didn't want his younger brother to be left in the slip-stream of his rival's success. He had said as much earlier. It was a rivalry that Jack was quick to eschew, but Adam knew it would exist anyway, if the artistic press had their way, and it would grow with them stoking the flames. Divide and conquer tactics made for good copy and it would be in their interest to drive a wedge between them. Jack had said firmly, 'We are friends, so leave it at that, Adam, please…'

'Yes, but you want to be the star of your year and so does he. Paul is not short of ambition, you can be certain of that…'

Jack had stormed off at that point and Adam feared he had taken it too far. He knew however that his point had hit a raw nerve in Jack because his brother knew that he was *right*.

★ ★ ★

Sybil Horton looked very different to Alicia from the last time she had seen her at Miles' memorial service at the parish church in Chelcombe Lacey; when their shared grief had still felt very raw.

Of course Sybil had suffered a double blow, in having lost a brother and a fiancé. There had been a kind of inevitability that when the orphaned Hortons first came to stay at Chelcombe Place, Miles and Sybil should fall for each other in the way that they had.

Tonight she looked more like a flapper, with her hair short cropped and the dark eye make-up which combined to great effect with the midnight blue of her eyes. When she had first arrived on the arm of Jack's brother, Adam, Alicia had felt for a nano-second as if she were frozen in time. As if she were staring at a ghost and not the beautiful, vibrant girl who had made her beloved Miles happier than she had ever known him. She had hero-worshipped Sybil from the moment they had first met and while it had been awkward to begin with this evening, once they had embraced, it was as if the years had melted away. There would always be the shared anguish of loss, of grief acknowledged and then set aside.

'How are you parents?' Sybil had asked and Alicia nodded.

'Coping. Anniversaries still hurt. They mark them in their own way, but I wish they could find common ground to share the experience...'

Sybil nodded. 'I understand the modelling is going well. I saw your *Vogue* cover and the *Tatler!* Loved them.'

'Thank you, Sybil.' Alicia put a hand to her mouth and stifled a sob and then she felt Sybil's firm grip as she squeezed her arm. She scanned the room, looking for Jack, but she felt wretched that she had made Sybil feel uncomfortable. She had thought she could meet the woman Miles had wanted to marry and that it would be all right for a while – hell, just for a few hours of one evening was all that she asked – but the truth was she wasn't that brave, cliché, though it may sound. She was lucky as she had Jack and he, like Adam, had escaped the horrors of war, while Hugo had survived to bear the scars and to feel the loss, but for Ralph and Miles the lottery of survival had not been in their favour.

She knew she owed it to their memory to be the best version of herself that she could. be. Miles had always believed in her, and she knew that Jack did, so it was down to her. Whether she made her mark on the covers of *Tatler* or in the plush boutiques of Mayfair, she had to prove that the values her brother and Ralph Horton had fought and died for had been worth it. That their sacrifice had not been in vain.

Alicia felt the salt of welling tears and tried to stem them with a deep breath. She angrily brushed them away, but Sybil caught her hand and wiped the tears for her, smiling.

'It's OK, Alicia. It will always be OK to feel sad sometimes… to miss them. I know I do. Yet we have the opportunity… perhaps an obligation to strive to be happy… Tonight is one of those times.'

Sybil took one long gulp of champagne and squeezed Alicia's hand.

She looked across at Adam and he came to stand beside her. Sybil took one lingering look around the room, nodding her approval. 'I am guessing Jack had your input in his design for this place, didn't he?'

Alicia nodded. 'I put my points across.'

Sybil kissed Alicia on both cheeks and then turning to Adam, she said, 'You're ready to leave?'

Adam nodded.

Alicia said. 'I hope you are taking care of this woman, Adam, as you know she is very precious to all of us…'

Adam let his gaze span the room, looking for Jack, and then he saw Paul Crowley approach the easel and stand to one side of it, while Jayne stood on the other. He threw the sheet aside to gasps and a ripple of applause and for a nano-second it felt like time had stood still, but to his ears the response was positive and Jayne smiled.

She looked across at Alicia who nodded. Paul had captured her brilliantly. Alicia's gaze scanned the room looking for Jack to see his reaction to Paul's masterpiece and Adam's gaze followed hers and yet Jack was nowhere to be seen. Which left Alicia perplexed and Adam wondering if the instinctive artistic rivalry would trump their friendship after all.

Adam found Jack at the front door of his flat.

'You missed Crowley's big reveal?'

'I saw it from a distance. Very impressive!'

'Said with genuine feeling, Jack!'

Jack rolled his eyes.

'Will you always be content, applauding on the sidelines while he absorbs all the accolades or are you going to claim some for yourself?'

'This again, Adam, really?'

'Yes,' Adam said firmly as Sybil smiled ruefully at Jack as he opened the door and Adam took one last look at his younger sibling, throwing him a look that he wanted Jack to take as a challenge. A throwing down of the gauntlet, because Adam feared the friendship only went *so* deep for Crowley. That in the bid to become the best artist of their generation there would be the impetus to drive them apart.

10

Adam Trevelyan sat in the back of a taxi nearly an hour later, with Sybil beside him. She moved closer, taking his left hand in hers.

She smiled and he said, 'I accept my humble flat doesn't enjoy the *avant-garde* decor that Jack can boast of, but you are welcome to my spare room.'

Sybil laughed. 'I have seen your flat, remember. The decor is more than adequate. You have no reason to be envious of Jack.'

He could hear the slight admonishment in her tone, even though she was laughing.

'His incredible artistic talent aside…you mean. I'm not envious, but I am concerned. I fear his friendship with Crowley is perhaps more important than it should be. I was watching Crowley's expression after he had unveiled the portrait and he was soaking up the praise. It was like he was feeding off the applause. Basking in the reflective glory of his peers. I am convinced he is set on projecting himself as the undisputed star of the artistic world and my instinct tells me Paul Crowley won't let anything stand in the way of that ambition, including maintaining a friendship with Jack.'

Sybil made a moue with her mouth but she remained silent. From what she had seen, Jack was confident enough of his talent to be able to compete with Paul Crowley, although she didn't know Crowley well enough to comment on the extent of his ambition and she suspected that went for Adam as well.

'I appreciate the offer, Adam, but I think my hotel on Albemarle Street will suffice and it is no reflection on your decor.'

Adam smiled as he removed a bottle of champagne from the inside of his overcoat. Sybil gasped, laughing. She had always had an infectious laugh he remembered from her visits to Cornwall. Alas, there had been too much tragedy in recent years than there had been cause for joviality.

'How did you filch that from under Jack's nose?'

'I took my chance while he was mesmerised by Crowley's portrait... Besides I doubt Jack would begrudge his older brother one bottle!'

He produced two glasses and filled each, before wagging a finger at her.

'Now, why didn't you mention your Canadian fellow?'

Sybil bowed her head, taking a moment to compose herself. She looked back at Adam and smiling she said, 'Because my Canadian fellow as you refer to him wants to be as completely fit as he can before we go public with any announcements! Then there's Alicia.

'You must have noticed how seeing me there affected her. Yes, it was initially shock, but the grief she still feels for Miles is too raw and I am a reminder of that. We were going to be sisters-in-law and my moving on is going to be painful for her... I wanted to spare her that. For tonight at least.'

Adam put his glass down and took both Sybil's hands in his, and kissed them.

'You are very kind!'

She laughed, wondering whether he had got drunk, but she could see from the earnest look in his eyes that he meant it. She waved the compliment away but he shook his head.

'No! I'm not having you under-value yourself… To make light of your humility.'

Sybil shook her head. 'I don't, Adam, truly. I just remember how the Savernakes took us into their home, enveloped us into their family just as you Trevelyans did when the only family that Ralph and I had was each other. There was a strong element of fate, I imagine, that Miles and I should fall for each other and Alicia was our biggest champion.

'Not that his parents needed much convincing about the idea of "us". At first I thought it was because she worshipped her brother, but it went deeper than that. So I'm not prepared to trample all over her feelings by making a rash announcement about my future… Not until *she* is ready to hear it and my "Canadian fellow" is ready for us to be officially announced as a couple…!'

Adam nodded. 'She has got Jack now and they appear solid.'

Sybil nodded. 'I am glad for both of them, but please trust me when I say I know that biding my time is the best option for all concerned.'

Adam nodded, sipping his champagne. He gazed at Sybil over the rim of his glass. It was no surprise to him that Miles Savernake had fallen hard for Sybil. He imagined Hugo might have done so also had he not already committed to Caroline. When he saw her glass was empty, he said, 'More champagne?'

Sybil shook her head.

'I am heading off to France tomorrow or the day after so I guess champagne might be on the menu then.' She smiled as the taxi came to a halt outside her hotel on Albemarle Street and she attempted to alight. She stepped out and two young men passing by whistled their appreciation for her as she dipped into her evening purse.

Adam shook his head. 'I've got this. Goodnight, Miss Horton. There are not many tasks entrusted to me by my mother that I enjoy quite as much as I have enjoyed accompanying you tonight…'

Sybil offered him her hand, which he kissed and she smiled. 'Thank you, Trevelyan Minor!'

Adam laughed, his eyebrows raised.

'You know only Hugo gets away with calling me that… but I will let you off. Have a good Christmas and don't be a stranger for so long next time…'

Sybil waved as she pushed the door shut and the taxi backed away.

She could see Adam watching until she disappeared into the hotel.

★ ★ ★

Gresse Street Flat – Same Evening

Alicia Savernake found herself a moment of much needed solitude in the bedroom she had shared with Jack many times over the last few weeks.

Seeing Sybil again had been a shock and she needed to readjust.

Suddenly there was a rap on the door and Lynette Crowley appeared.

'You ok?'

Alicia nodded. 'Come in, join me. I am snatching a moment or two for myself.'

Lynette nodded, smiling. 'Being the hostess can be tiring…' Lynette sat down on the bed and lit a cigarette.

Alicia nodded. 'I hadn't thought about that, but you're right, it is. Paul must be delighted with the reaction to his portrait. What does Jayne think of it? Have you had a chance to ask her?'

'I think she is overjoyed. She said he has immortalised her in oils… I can't help wondering what Mercy will think about her younger sister stealing some of her thunder…'

Alicia smiled. 'Sibling rivalry. I think we all know about that.'

'That woman who was with Jack's brother? I don't think I have met her before.'

Alicia shook her head. 'You won't have. Her name is Sybil Horton. I have not seen her in more than three years as she has been nursing in France; a follow-on from the war when she was in the VAD. If fate had played a different hand to my brother, Miles, she would have become my sister-in-law!'

Lynette fell silent as she could see the tears welling in Alicia's eyes.

'Sybil and her brother, Ralph, were orphaned in their adolescence and as he went to the same school as Hugo and Miles, they divided their holidays between us at Chelcombe Lacey and at the Trevelyans in Cornwall!'

Alicia felt her bottom lip quivering and she turned her head, but Lynette merely tightened her grip on her hand and said, 'Should I fetch Jack?'

Alicia shook her head. 'Why the interest in Sybil?'

Lynette smiled and took a long drag on her cigarette. 'She intrigued me. I rarely see such beauty and level-headed confidence combined. She had both and there wasn't a trace of arrogance! I am guessing you were close?'

Alicia nodded. 'I felt like the younger sister with her and that was a rare treat for me. I have the sense that she is moving on, but that she wasn't ready to tell me with what or with whom. That her reticence is for my sake rather than her own!'

Lynette nodded. 'You don't think it would be with Adam?'

Alicia smiled. 'You're interested in him?'

Lynette shouldered her good-naturedly, resisting a smile as she leaned over to stub out her cigarette. 'I thought there was spark of interest from him, before Miss Horton joined us. I could just be clutching at straws and Adam might have just been polite.'

'Don't rule it out. I know Adam is very career-orientated, but I am sure he has other interests…'

Lynette smiled. 'OK, but make sure any queries are casual…'

Alicia linked arms with Lynette as they stood poised to rejoin the party.

'So how are things between you and Miss Fearns?'

Lynette shrugged. 'We have reached an understanding of sorts. I never wanted her to quit her studies at the Slade, but I understand that she was considering it, which would have been a waste as she has the talent… I know she had something of a *crush* on me, no matter how much she tried to deny it, however she came with Matthew tonight and they have barely been apart all evening so perhaps there's something developing there…' Lynette nodded in their direction and Alicia smiled.

'She will have to work fast to establish anything with him. I hear he is off to Paris in January to interview some of the artists of the Left Bank…'

Lynette shrugged. 'From what I have learnt, Matthew Fullerton has a tendency to fluff his opportunities. That his family wanted him to pursue tennis as a career and they were happy to continue supporting him, financially, but he claimed he lacked the necessary instinct for winning and apparently he took defeat far too casually…

'There was also some understanding with a girl he had been seeing in Dorset. Almost on the verge of a formal announcement, but he called it off…!'

'So Miss Fearns will have to act fast to make sure he is for keeps…!'

Matthew Fullerton had been watching Nicola Fearns from a distance for most of the evening aside from when they were together, and looking across at her, he let a small smile curve at the corners of his mouth.

Sighing softly, he took a long gulp of his drink and seeing her standing alone, he felt a sudden protective urge that came unbidden, from where he didn't know, but he acknowledged his feelings for her were altering ever so *subtly*. He couldn't rationalise these feelings as he couldn't recall ever having had the same protective instinct for Rosalind. He suspected that Nicola had a tendency to feel out of place in certain company and it was a confidence issue, that she admitted to with him, albeit with some reluctance. She had confided in him, about the "pep" talk she had been given at luncheon with her cousin that afternoon and he hoped it would have the desired effect. Raising his hand, he caught her attention and she smiled as he began weaving his way through the throng of guests to her side of the room.

'A great party, don't you think?'

Nicola nodded. 'Jack must be very pleased with his flat. He's done superbly with the decor. Paul must be ecstatic about the reaction to his portrait unveiling. It's good that Jayne is pleased.'

Matthew nodded. 'It helps to have such a beautiful model to work with. What about you, Nicola? You are very generous with your praise of others, yet strangely reluctant to accept it about yourself!'

Nicola bowed her head, blushing, and Matthew feared he had upset her.

'I'm trying to appear more positive, Matthew, but it takes time…'

Matthew nodded. 'I am just glad your cousin – Martin, isn't it? – managed to convince you to continue at the Slade next term. In fact I would like to write a piece about you! What inspired you to pursue art as a subject, what a challenge it was to secure the scholarship to the Slade, etc., etc. Would you be willing?'

Nicola looked terrified at the prospect, but she didn't say no.

'Wouldn't Paul or Jack be more suitable subjects for an article than me?'

'I tried to convince them early in the term and neither thought it was the right time, although judging by the reaction to Paul's unveiling, I think he's going to get more attention than he bargained for... but no. I want *you* to be my subject. I believe you need it more than they do.

'It would be my words on the page, based on what you tell me, so my interpretation of your experience, but I would give you prior approval, before it went to print...'

'I will think about it, but no promises.'

'I can't expect more than that as I did kind of spring it upon you! Let me refill your glass...' He took it from her and felt a frisson as their fingers touched ever so fleetingly and Matthew could only hope it had ignited the same sensation within her, that it brought him.

It surprised him to realise just how *much* he wanted a relationship with Nicola to work, as he hadn't given romance much thought after his break-up with Rosalind, which had affected him more than his brother Giles had believed. It suited his brother to portray him as thoughtless – even heartless – as he could then play the role of gallant knight.

Rosalind deserved the best, so if his brother fit that role for her, then good luck to them. He had moved on. Yes, he had insisted on it being a swift, clean separation, which he admitted ruefully gave substance to Giles's charge of him being inconsiderate of Rosalind's feelings. A view shared by their parents. When he had been quietly informed that any romantic interest that he had in Alicia Savernake or Jayne Campion would be a fruitless pursuit, he had put all his efforts into work.

Journalism had become his focus, but he was seeing Nicola Fearns in a different light. She *intrigued* him! Her quiet demeanour was as unusual as it was a part of her charm, and the modesty that she expressed about her artistic talent – while it frustrated him – set her aside from most of her peers studying at the Slade, along with other artists that he knew. He poured her another red wine and then glanced in her direction. He didn't know to what extent others within their circle had noticed the interest he was showing in Nicola, but he gained satisfaction from not caring a damn about their opinion. He made his way back through the assembled guests, oblivious to their chatter, and finding Nicola alone, he put her glass down and found his arm snaking around her waist. Then he kissed her, swiftly and very hard but then broke away, scared that she might resist the overture, or worse resent it completely and over-react, but she did neither, she simply bit her bottom lip and smiled, unsure of what the gesture implied and how she was expected to respond.

'I wasn't expecting that!' she said, hoping her voice didn't sound wobbly.

Matthew smiled. 'I didn't realise I was going to seize the moment to kiss you until I had done it. I am glad you didn't pull away…'

Nicola smiled, and leaning in, she kissed him fervently, then she wound her arms around his neck, and leaning into him, she nodded encouragingly that he should kiss her again. That she wanted him to kiss her *again*. That she was learning to heed his advice to take what she wanted when the opportunity arose, as it tied in with the advice that Martin had given her before they had departed after lunch. He had confided that he had regrets about not acting on impulse and she was sure Matthew must have had and although a similar experience had yet to test her, she didn't want to fight against the urge to follow her heart when the opportunity came for her to test feelings, that hitherto she had not had reason to adhere to. Matthew may not possess the Byronic good looks that Jack Trevelyan could claim, but he was a very attractive man and letting herself be swept along by whatever might develop between them was a new and exciting adventure.

11

Jack Trevelyan woke in the early hours, having finally got to bed after the last guests staggered out of his Gresse Street flat into the cold December air. He hadn't bothered looking at his watch as he bid the last guest goodnight, wishing them the compliments of the season, and now unable to sleep he leaned his head on his hand and gazed at the sleeping Alicia beside him. Utterly beautiful in repose, he had been wanting to paint her for weeks, but her modelling commitments had made it impossible for her to sit for him. There was a slight fear for him, that he wouldn't be able to capture her beauty in the same way that Paul had captured Jayne Campion's and he wanted to do Alicia justice in oils, just like the portrait of her mother, Daphne, captured at a similar age which hung on the landing wall at Chelcombe Place.

He bristled slightly, recalling Adam's suggestion that it should be impossible for him to remain such good friends with Paul when they should be rivals. Pushing the thought aside he looked again at Alicia as she stirred slightly. It was worth noting of course that Alicia and Jayne were very different creatures in looks as well as temperament so it was unfair to compare them too minutely, but Paul had the advantage of Jayne making herself available to him for many hours at a time. He smiled imagining Alicia being able to relax for that long. He always admired the models who sat in life classes at the Slade, although he hadn't planned to paint Alicia in the classical way.

Alicia moaned slightly, curving herself into the space beside him in bed. Jack was aroused suddenly, recalling the last time they had made love. Sex was as good as it had always been for them, but he felt that she had been emotionally distant recently and he had been reluctant to ask her why. Seeing Sybil Horton at the party tonight must have stirred up memories of Miles, and he wished Adam had telegrammed him in advance that Sybil would be his "plus one" even though he knew that Adam was bringing her at their mother's behest. As the youngest Trevelyan, he had admired Sybil Horton from afar as an adolescent and he could admit to having had a crush. Given that Ralph Horton had been as close a friend with Miles Savernake that he had been to Hugo, it was inevitable that the connection remained strong, but knowing what he did from his recent visit to Cornwall, that link was going to be broken even more than it had since Miles' and Ralph's passing and he wasn't sure how Alicia would react when Sybil told her. Only that he had to be there for her, to be the emotional crutch she may need.

He leaned in to kiss Alicia on the mouth, applying the right amount of passion, but careful not to wake her and turning aside he welcomed the blissful oblivion of sleep and succumbed to it readily.

★ ★ ★

Laurence Naismith had much to be pleased about that night as well.

Dining at his club on Northumberland Avenue with Edgar Trentham and Austin Westmacott he was ironing out the terms of his publishing contract, which he was convinced would favour him considerably in financial terms and in helping to re-establish his name as a major force in post-war English literature. He lit a cigarette and smiled. Austin looked nervous as usual, but Edgar was relaxed and as cunning as his years of experience had taught him to be.

'The terms you have laid out are very generously one-sided, Naismith, which I find interesting given that you haven't produced even a modest success in recent years…'

Naismith bristled slightly at the insult and took a long gulp of cognac.

'I could have approached any number of publishing houses with this one, which is my best work in years.' He leaned forward, jabbing at the manuscript with his finger and looking Trentham directly in the eye.

Having demanded that Trentham be here tonight had been a risk on his part, but he was tired of having to deal with feckless over-promoted office boys. Even the fact that Austin bore the firm's name carried little weight with him, as he was as skittish as a young foal and never able to make a decision without consultation.

Edgar Trentham smiled his best avuncular smile and said, 'So why have you come to us? Our house hasn't published a new Naismith in years. Even when I was focusing on political matters and Austin's father was running the show…'

Naismith gulped slightly, and said, 'I realise I was one of Cedric's authors, but that doesn't alter the fact that in my prime, I earned good money for your firm.'

Naismith was determined to keep his composure, conscious of St John's advice on how to negotiate with Trentham. He knew he couldn't afford to concede ground or to appear like he was pleading, but Edgar Trentham had cunning. He was an astute businessman, who would take advantage of any sign of weakness.

Edgar Trentham took a long, considered sip of his whisky and soda, trying to read Naismith's body language without appearing too obvious in the task. Naismith was nervous. He could see that, but even as a young man Laurence Naismith had invariably been highly strung. With the kind of temperament that meant he could never have survived in the political arena. Trentham only hoped for his sake, he wasn't *so* desperate.

'A lot of what you say remains to be seen, Laurence, but from what I have read and judging from Austin's report, I am quietly confident that with the right promotion, we can enjoy a modest success of your latest tome.'

'Modest? What does that mean?'

Naismith could hear the heat in his tone, while the irritated looks of other patrons told him of their displeasure at his raised voice.

Trentham steepled his fingers and paused. 'A more modest advance is what I am thinking… sadly…' Pausing he pulled a sheet of folded paper from the inside pocket of his jacket and slid it across the table towards Naismith, who snatched at it swiftly. Digesting the figure, his complexion paled.

'For that I might as well give it away…'

'Or seek another publishing house. It is unfortunate of course that you recently dispensed with the services of your agent as you are now having to do the negotiations yourself!'

Trentham took another long sip of whisky and soda, then turning to Austin he shot him a look which said "listen and learn". He hadn't wanted to come tonight as he had always found Naismith an irritating man, with an exaggerated view of his literary talents. He was glad that he was one of Cedric's literary "finds" but he wasn't going to pay over the odds for a very modest tome and he had feared Austin might be swayed by Naismith's celebrity. The advance that Naismith was demanding was unrealistic based on average sales of his most recent books and he didn't consider him an especially vital name to have on the company's list.

'I am seeking another agent to represent me, but I wanted

a deal that would show that I am back in the game. You have to admit that with this one, the old Naismith literary touch is back...' He said it with more hope than confidence. Trentham checked his watch. The lateness of the hour irritated him as he had plans to head to Dorset for Christmas now that the Commons was in recess.

He thought of his brother, Charles, an acquaintance of Naismith through St John Crowley and Edgar knew that even Charles who could be prickly when it suited him found Naismith hard work when forced to endure his company.

'The real test is of course whether the reading public still crave the old Naismith, as you so put it. I fear you may be considered too old-fashioned. A product of the post-Edwardian era which was sadly shattered by the horrors of the war. I include myself in this Naismith – we cannot realistically aspire to be part of the demi-monde.'

'Absolutely not! Nor do I wish to!' Stubbing out his cigarette, Naismith turned on Austin angrily. 'I blame you for this. I was led to believe the deal was all but done. That he was semi-retired from the day-to-day running of Trentham & Westmacott... That my terms were acceptable!'

Austin Westmacott looked at Naismith open-mouthed, feeling his throat going dry, as he began to perspire. Of all the authors that his father had off-loaded onto him, Laurence Naismith had proved himself the most challenging. Taking a long sip of his wine, he was about to offer an explanation until Edgar Trentham laid a reassuring hand on his arm.

'Alas, Austin does not have the authority to endorse such an advance, so even if all the elements of your deal had been complete he would still have had to consult the board... That is the point at which I came into the negotiation. My advice to you, Laurence, is find yourself another agent and swiftly. He will be... less emotional in the process and so be able to secure a deal that you can be happy with.'

Trentham checked his pocket watch and rose, as the lounge bar clock struck eleven. Trentham smiled as he offered Naismith his hand. It was a benign smile, but it had the veneer of a man who knew that he had won. Naismith felt sick. He had over-played his hand against a man who had been more than adept at tricky political negotiations and that had been a grave error of judgement.

'I suggest we resume our negotiations after Christmas, when I am sure after some reflection, we can achieve common ground, although I am inclined to offer you the time to secure the services of another agent.'

Naismith offered Trentham his hand with only a brief nod, and he watched them take their leave. Resuming his seat, he lit another cigarette which he smoked quietly alone. Stewards who were eager to see patrons leave so they could close the club for the night, busied themselves with the clearing of tables while throwing furtive looks in his direction. He now had the erroneous task of having to tell St John what a disaster tonight had been from his point of view. That all of his previous optimism looked like it had been built on foundations of sand. That his spirit of bravado about his latest novel wasn't widely shared by the publishing world which had, as much as it pained him to admit it, seen too many Naismith "flops" in recent years to be convinced that his latest was the renaissance novel that he had "pitched" it as.

Nathaniel Gilbrandsen had been a genial host for the most part and especially in his cups had been candid about certain romantic escapades in his past, some of which Naismith heard second-hand over the years and he had used them in his manuscript. Was that why the publishers were spooked? Or had he been played? Laid a trap into which he had been pushed by the force of his ego? Because he believed he was achieving a coup. He shook his head. Too much of what Gilbrandsen had said was too personal for him to have made up to spoon feed to his guest in a fit of spite! He was convinced that what Gilbrandsen had told him was largely the truth, spoken unwittingly perhaps when imbued with cognac. He cursed under his breath, requiring the steadying hand of a nearby steward as he rose to leave and wobbled on his feet.

Smiling weakly he left the lounge-bar, ignoring the disapproving looks of other patrons who didn't know him so well. He wouldn't like to guess how many of his readers were among them, but what did they know of the mark of good literature? Nothing, he ventured, as he went out into the sobering cold reality of a December night.

12

Chelcombe Place – December 1922

Alicia and Laura Savernake returned to the family home for the Christmas holidays in entirely different frames of mind. Alicia knew she should have been happier than she was, given how well her modelling career was progressing. She had adorned the covers of *Tatler* and *Vogue* in recent weeks to great acclaim and was swiftly becoming much sought after in London and Paris. Laura however was much less satisfied with how her attempts to establish herself in modelling were being received, however, personally she was very satisfied with life, although struggling to remain quiet about her latest romantic interest, who had insisted on being introduced to her at Jack's flat-warming party. She had genuine fears that her father, unimpressed that her modelling career wasn't taking off, would insist that she return home just when she had most reason to remain in town. She wanted to be sure her sister would remain an ally in that regard, having implored Alicia to make the case for her remaining should their father insist on her return. On the train down to Hampshire, Alicia had quietly acquiesced, but Laura knew Alicia was troubled and that Sybil Horton's appearance at the party was the root cause of *her* distress.

'Sybil's appearance at the party doesn't have to be a prelude to her having something important to tell us. I guess it was a shock seeing her there… I was quite surprised, but she looks well.'

'I know there's something she is holding back, and that I – *we* as a *family* – probably won't like, but I also accept Jack's point that she needs to move on. It's that severing of the link with the past… the link to Miles, that I am dreading…'

Laura nodded without speaking, biting her bottom lip to stem the threat of tears. She reached out so that her fingers touched Alicia's.

Alicia smiled. Sybil's appearance at Jack's party was only one aspect of why she felt melancholic. Jack was the other. She had invited him to spend Christmas with them at Chelcombe Place, but he had said his presence was expected in Cornwall.

On arrival at Chelcombe Place, Alicia suggested a walk with her father, to which Alexander Savernake readily agreed. She squeezed her sister's hand as Laura headed indoors to greet their mother, as they exchanged a conspiratorial wink.

The frost underfoot was crisp and startlingly white, but the snow that had usually come to Chelcombe Lacey by Christmas was strangely absent, as Alicia tucked her arm into her father's and they walked with his ever-faithful Hector at his heel.

'What is it, Alicia?' He suspected Laura wasn't doing so well career-wise but he wanted one of them to tell him, although the look which had passed between them as they parted hadn't fooled him.

'I was thinking of Miles. I have been a lot recently and not just because it's Christmas and that he loved this time of year, but Jack hosted a flat-warming party the other night and his brother Adam came with Sybil as his guest…'

Alexander tightened the grip on his daughter's arm, bowing his head.

'She is doing fine and looks well, but I could tell there was something she is withholding... She owes us nothing. I accept that, but I prefer that she was honest with me, us, that she has met someone. *If* that is what has happened.'

Alexander turned to face Alicia, placing both hands on her shoulders.

He smiled and said, 'I never doubted that Sybil would be a good wife to your brother. Sadly fate denied them that happiness, but I want her to be happy however she may attain it. It is what Miles would have wanted for her. It's what she deserves. Miles will always be dear to us and I shall miss him for the rest of my days, but Sybil and her brother, Ralph, had already lost loved ones when they came to us and now Sybil only has herself to think of and I am sure she will want the same happy ending for you and Jack as we all once wanted for her and Miles...'

Alicia choked back a sob, as she could see her father also marshalling his emotions as he often did when the conversation was focused on Miles. She knew every word he had said was true. *Poignantly* so. That there had very likely been developments in Sybil's personal life that she wasn't yet ready to share. That it would have been unfair to expect Jack to betray a confidence had there been any that he had been included in, which she doubted.

She leaned her head against his shoulder as they began strolling back towards the house.

'How is your sister doing in London?' That had been the question she had been dreading and her father, astute as ever, had decided to get it out of the way.

'The work could be more frequent, but I did warn her there would be times when she wouldn't be in demand. I know she is worried that you will demand she returns home...'

Alexander nodded. 'It might be her best option in the short term. I know that she will miss the bright lights of the capital, just as I realise that Chelcombe might be dull by comparison with just me and your mother, but we will need to discuss her options. It was conditional upon her getting the bookings you are enjoying. Couldn't she sit for Jack? If he could make a splash publicity-wise from painting her, that might do her some good!'

Alicia nodded. 'Or Paul Crowley, but a portrait takes time and Laura needs more urgent results…'

Alexander nodded. 'Yes, I heard from your mother that Mercedes Campion's sister sat for Crowley and that his portrait has caused quite a stir…!' He squeezed Alicia's shoulder. 'I am glad you have your sister's best interests at heart and I won't insist she comes home immediately, but her work situation will have to improve…'

Alicia smiled.

'Thanks. It will mean Laura can relax and enjoy the festive season.'

Alexander nodded.

'I take it Jack couldn't accept your invitation to spend Christmas with us?'

Alicia smiled, shaking her head. Sometimes her father's intuitiveness could be quite galling. This was definitely one of them.

'He was keen, but Margot Trevelyan insisted she had all her offspring with her in Cornwall.'

Alexander nodded, smiling, as he led his eldest daughter into the house.

★ ★ ★

St John Crowley was at his wit's end with Naismith and he refused to let his friend cast a gloomy pall over Christmas with his melancholy.

They sat opposite each other in the lounge-bar of their club on Northumberland Avenue on the day before Christmas Eve.

Naismith was nursing a Scotch.

'I am *so* glad Trentham isn't here!'

'Really! You do surprise me!' His tone was dryly matter-of-fact and he knew his friend was piqued that he hadn't enquired about where he was spending Christmas. In a gesture of goodwill he had said he could stay at the Bloomsbury townhouse as long as he knew the servants would be away as he was spending it with Paul and Lynette's parents.

'I had believed that I could rely on your support, St John, in my dealings with Trentham given your friendship with his brother, Charles…'

'I said that he was an acquaintance, Laurence, maybe a casual friend at best and Trentham senior can be as tedious as Edgar has proved, however it is a business relationship that you have with him as a publisher and he *is* entitled to have confidence that your novel is the best you believe it to be.'

'You read some of it, St John, and you said that I was back to my best… as did Nate Gilbrandsen when I was staying with him in Spain. I was humiliated the other night! That Austin Westmacott is wet behind the ears and I think Edgar Trentham was more interested in denigrating my credentials as a novelist than he was in cutting a deal.'

St John slammed the leather-bound menu down on the table and said, 'For goodness' sake, Laurence! Why did you dismiss your agent and so make life that more difficult for yourself? Edgar is a shrewd man. He knows that without representation you are vulnerable and so any publisher in London will believe that you are fair game for a bad deal…Which, based on what I have read of the manuscript, is less than what it deserves… Besides which, publishing isn't my area of expertise. You would be better asking Mercy Campion for her opinion!'

Laurence Naismith looked as wounded as he felt. He summoned the steward and ordered another Scotch.

'I don't know why you invited me for luncheon, St John, if

only to humiliate me over the meeting with the publishers. It went as badly as it is without your input!'

St John sighed heavily. He took a long sip of his martini and then hid his face behind the leather-bound menu, taking a long, deep breath.

'I don't recall inviting you, Laurence. I mentioned that I was having lunch at the club as it closes this afternoon and you decided to join me. I trust you have sufficient funds to pay…?'

Naismith blushed crimson.

'My god!! How bloody typical!'

'I can leave now, St John, but I understood it to be an invitation…'

St John detected the petulance in Naismith's tone as he half rose to leave.

'No, stay, Laurence – but when your advance comes through in the New Year you owe me a luncheon – or three at an establishment of my choice…!'

He lit a cigarette and studied the author from across the table. He only hoped for Laurence's sake that given all his hype the novel was as good as his friend was claiming it to be, as he summoned a steward and ordered lunch.

★ ★ ★

Across town in the first-floor office of Trentham & Westmacott on Henrietta Street, Edgar Trentham lit another cigarette and exhaled heavily. He was not in the best of moods, having planned to be on the train to Dorset by luncheon. His partner, Cedric, who was semi-retired and taking a reduced role within the firm that he had helped to nurture, was keen to reach a decision and close for business until the New Year.

'So a more modest advance than what the author is demanding and a commitment to publish, is that what you are proposing, Cedric?'

'I can tell you have doubts, Edgar?'

'I find Naismith petulant. Arrogant and conceited. If he still had an agent to negotiate for him, and they had come to us – which I doubt – we could have wrapped this up weeks ago, but this is where we are at. The novel is good and it shows touches of the Naismith of pre-war days, but I don't think it merits what he is demanding!'

'Can we afford to see the best Naismith in years go to a rival house?'

Cedric Westmacott was an old man. He was as cunning as they came in business, but he looked every inch a Victorian.

Edgar and Austin Westmacott shared a look that said they could easily see Naismith go to another publisher, but they feared they could still regret losing him and that Cedric wouldn't let them forget it.

Edgar Trentham steepled his fingers and with pursed lips, he thought for a moment.

'It concerns me greatly why he dispensed with the services of his agent. We don't even touch most authors without representation, but Naismith has a reputation behind him, although his work has been well below par in recent years. We have to acknowledge that, reputation aside – we are taking a risk!'

Cedric banged his fists on the arm of the chair.

'Has he had other offers?'

Austin shook his head. 'He told me he could come to us first out of past loyalty… Whether he would have pitched that line to his agent while he still had one it's impossible to tell. It could just be hype, knowing Naismith!'

Cedric smiled. His son still had much to learn about the art of negotiation, but under Edgar's tutelage, he would make a first-rate publisher in time.

'Do the deal, Edgar, according to your judgement. Past successes won't count for much if the new book doesn't have potential, but I can see we are taking a gamble, but maybe not as big a gamble as Naismith is taking as he cannot thrive on past glories forever…!'

13

Cornwall – Christmas 1922

Margot Trevelyan had made it abundantly clear that she wanted her two younger sons home for Christmas in her customary style, which didn't sound like an instruction, but was taken as such, so Adam and Jack took the Great Western train to the station closest to the Trevelyan estate where they were met, not by one of the staff as they had expected, but on this occasion by their elder brother, Hugo. They embraced each other warmly before getting into the car, Adam claiming the front seat. Jack in a reflective mood, was happy alone in the rear, having indicated on the journey from London that he would have preferred to accept Alicia's invitation to spend Christmas at Chelcombe Place.

Sybil's appearance at his flat-warming had affected her deeply, even though she had denied it when prompted. Adam had felt a little guilt as well, telling his younger brother that he'd had no choice.

'Some forewarning would have been helpful,' was Jack's only response on the subject, which Adam acknowledged with a nod. Jack had spent most of the journey from Paddington, sketching.

'How are things at home?' Adam asked hoping to keep his tone neutral.

'Much the same. Our parents now tend to communicate directly only when they have to, or through me, which infuriates Caroline. You know that Pa takes most things in his stride, but our mother's idiosyncrasies become more strident with age, so I fear that a policy of swift surrender to her whims has become the best policy for him. Although I believe he has his limit and she knows not to push him to it...'

Adam huffed with indignation. Since leaving university to commence his Civil Service career he had become less tolerant of his mother's domineering ways. Her bohemian instincts to which she had always adhered in the interests of the artist colony that she had established, with her husband's acquiescence, was the characteristic that most people who knew her well enough most admired. She did dominate some people in the pursuit of her students' careers, however, and those who weren't swift enough to notice usually came off worse. Gervaise was sufficiently wise to know that a path of least resistance suited him for peace of mind, but they all knew who was really in charge in their marriage and Margot was sufficiently cunning to pick the battles with her husband that she knew she could win.

As Hugo drove through the gates, the house looked starkly imposing in the weak wintry sunlight, prompting Jack to comment. 'I want to paint the house just as it is now... in all its savage beauty!'

'So do it, Trevelyan Minor. You have been promising to do so for years...'

To Adam it looked like a Gothic mansion in a Dickens' novel, with fog slowly descending. It was still home and like Hugo he felt a surge of pride as they alighted the car. Hugo laughed gently at Adam's use of the "minor" tag as he recalled how Adam always hated it being attributed to him.

'I will let that barb go this time, but you will be wise not to refer to me as minor again…'

'He hated it when Ralph and Miles used to taunt him with it, so I am intrigued as to why he has resurrected it now.'

'It was Sybil who mentioned it the other night after we had left your party.'

'How is she?' asked Hugo.

Adam and Jack exchanged looks and Adam said, 'She's fine.' Hugo didn't need them to elaborate, and he knew that she was yet to share her news.

Adam and Jack proceeded into the house, but Hugo held back, so Adam turned to him. 'Are you coming in?'

Hugo smiled as he held up his hand and watched as his siblings entered the house. Doubtless they would be summoned to see their mother within the first quarter hour of arrival and he smiled, trying to shake off memories of Miles and Ralph. Normally reference to them didn't affect him so much these days, although Hugo had endured his own share of survivor guilt and for him the wounds were internal. He looked up at the window of the room that his father, Gervaise, used as an office and waved. Nodding gently he thrust cold hands into his trouser pockets and made his way into the house.

He hated keeping secrets from his brothers, but most especially from Jack. He wished his father had never shared his suspicions, but once told, he couldn't not know something which would probably never be confirmed – at least not by his mother – as on the only occasion he had been bold enough to raise it with her, she had dismissed him with a wave of her hand and Hugo knew his father had been blamed for sharing his concerns with him. Margot Trevelyan's icy disdain was legendary and none had been on the receiving end more than her husband and on that occasion Hugo understood something of what his father had to endure.

He had hoped ever since being told that the enormity of it, should it ever be confirmed, would be something that Jack could endure, that his bright future as an artist wouldn't be affected in any way. There were worse things that a man could endure and he had seen the physical scars of war to know that. Seeing Sybil Horton always had an effect on him, as much as he liked and admired her. She was of course one of his wife's closest friends, but the searing memory of all that Sybil had been forced to endure caused him to feel sick and sometimes hollowed out inside and that was a legacy he feared he would never be released from.

Margot Trevelyan was still considered a beautiful woman at nearly fifty years old. Her once bright blonde hair looked more silver in a certain light, but her violet eyes were as keen and as vibrant as ever. She told her Maltese terrier to hush its barking as Adam and Jack entered her bedroom.

'Jack, come and sit here,' she commanded patting the empty space on the chaise-longue beside her.

Adam went to stand by the window, and half turning he said, 'Is Hugo OK?'

Margot was only half listening and she waved her arm dismissively. She was content that her three sons were close to each other, but there was no secret among them that Jack was her favourite.

'What? I suspect so. You know how your brother is. I believe Sybil's visit had an effect on him; you know he starts dwelling too much on stuff he would be better off not thinking about… If you see what I mean.'

Adam shook his head and went to warm his hands by the fire, as the Maltese terrier jumped down to greet him and he scooped him into his arms.

'My god! He doesn't usually let anyone do that. He's rarely that submissive.'

As Margot returned her attention to Jack, Adam said, 'No surprises where he gets that from!'

Margot arched a critical eyebrow at her second son as Jack stifled a snigger.

Adam set the dog down on its feet and said, 'I will leave you both to it and go and greet Pa.'

Margot half acknowledged him with a nod that he took as a dismissal and Adam, smiling, headed for the door, giving Jack a conspiratorial wink as he left.

14

Until the evening of the Gresse Street flat-warming party, Matthew Fullerton acknowledged what he described as a "surrogate" older-brother relationship with Nicola Fearns. He felt an urge to protect her. From what he wasn't always sure, only that the instinct existed, but when he had watched her standing alone in the corner of the lounge observing events as they unfolded around her, he felt his feelings change, ever so *subtly*. Suddenly it wasn't that of an older brother. Now he realised with a feverish desire, that he wanted to become her lover. Whether she was ready for such a change in the dynamic between them wasn't something that he stopped to consider but he could feel it inside him nonetheless and was inclined to think the newfound confidence that he had about his journalistic career, enforced by the fact his forthcoming trip to Paris had been approved by his editor, meant he felt he could be bold in other aspects of his life. He spent most of the evening chatting with Nicola, pleased that lunch with her cousin had gone well and that she was determined to return to her studies at the Slade after the Christmas recess. He had seen first-hand the effect on Nicola of the crush that she had developed for Lynette Crowley and was pleased this had been resolved. To his mind there was no better way for her to demonstrate that she had moved on than to take up with him, but he was conscious not to force the issue. Nicola had to be handled gently, otherwise she would be "spooked" and then his chance would be lost, perhaps permanently.

He didn't know yet how long he would be in Paris, so there was wisdom in not declaring his hand as yet, but he was conscious of not wanting to ruin his chance by prevaricating and not saying anything.

Nicola was *very* attractive, so if she began realising that for herself while he was away, he could return to find some other young buck had claimed her and that whatever she might have felt for him wouldn't compete any more if she was in love with another. For all he knew there might already be someone that she hadn't wanted to share by inviting them tonight, or worse, she just didn't see him in that way.

'I'm glad that you are staying at the Slade. You have worked so hard to get in, to abandon it after one half term would have been a shame, especially if it were based on a misunderstanding.' Nicola blushed slightly and Matthew cursed himself for having embarrassed her, but she shook her head.

'My decision was never based on… that. It was always about talent as an artist… or my lack of it.'

'What you lack is self-confidence.' He said it gently and she smiled.

'That's what my cousin said.'

'Then he deserves to take some of the credit when you are a rich and famous artist.'

Nicola half shook her head. 'You mean *if…*'

'It will happen for you, Nicola, I am sure.' Matthew spoke firmly and she left it there, looking across the room to where Lynette Crowley was standing, grateful she had her back to them as there was still a residual tension over the "misunderstanding" as Matthew had chosen to describe it. She doubted anybody would ever truly understand the nature of what she had felt for

Lynette, which was entirely sexual, she was certain of that. An absence of closely-aged siblings growing up might have been a contributing factor. She had been an "unplanned" child, coming some years after her brother. He was preparing for university when the war came and it had looked as if he might have come through unscathed until September 1918 when the telegram came to report that he had died in action. Suddenly her entire world was tipped upside down, and an already distant father became ever more distant, lost in the fog of grief, alongside a stoic mother who just wouldn't allow herself to cry. Thankfully there had been Cousin Martin. Then as he was now, faithful, reliable; a *confidant*.

Suddenly Matthew was jolting her out of her daydream, asking if she wanted a drink, and she was back in the present and he was looking at her in a way that he never had before. She nodded and smiling he disappeared into the throng. Jack came over to chat and as the evening wore on, the alcohol had a relaxing effect on her. Imbuing her with a courage she didn't usually feel, when Matthew leaned in to kiss her the first time, she pulled away, but only slightly, so he tried again and she responded, kissing him back, but only tentatively, fearing that she wasn't doing it right, but Matthew deepened the kiss and suddenly Nicola felt no inhibitions, as if she didn't care that other guests might be watching. She wanted this. She wanted Matthew.

Although acknowledging it shocked her, it was in a good way, because suddenly she wasn't so concerned by propriety; she wanted this. She wanted to feel *loved*.

The following day travelling by train to Dorset, Matthew looked upon the forthcoming Christmas holidays as an unwanted obstacle in the path of his fledgling relationship with Nicola and he could only hope that she felt the same as she travelled to the Surrey-Berkshire border, hoping she didn't regret their first moments of intimacy and that the alcohol didn't just stem her inhibitions in the moment only to leave her in a sense of remorse at her actions now.

He had to think about how seeing Rosalind again for the first time since he had broken their engagement might affect him, especially as he had been led to understand that her closeness to his brother, Giles, had developed very swiftly. That was a fledgling romance that could cause him to feel awkward, which he had no right to claim, but which he had no doubt, Giles would exploit to the limit. He had left her bereft as she hadn't wanted to finish things with him, so he had felt like a heel, but he wanted the best for her, so if she was going with Giles to spite him, Rosalind was only setting herself up for heartache, and sibling rivalry aside, Giles also deserved more.

Cursing under his breath, he sat on the platform at Fullerton Holt waiting for the car to pick him up, thinking what an awful bloody mess he had left at home and why it was *vital* that he made a success of his new career.

He sat alone in the large conservatory at Fullerton Chase, and lit a cigarette. He had remained neutral during courses at dinner when the conversation landed on his fledging career amid his father's less than oblique references to the forthcoming tennis season. He knew that even if he were to make a "splash" with his article on the artistic scene in Paris, that it would cut little ice with his father as the only impact he could make would be on the clay court in the French Open to win any respect from him, but his family had to realise that his tennis days were firmly behind him.

The conservatory door opened and he looked up to find Rosalind standing there in a silk dress in dark green. He wanted to curse, but held his tongue.

'They sent me to fetch you. For charades I think… if your mother has her way. Or cards. Although I think bridge is a little too heavy for Christmas…'

Matthew laughed.

'We had better make it charades then... Quite fitting given how we are all dancing around, trying to avoid treading on each other's feet. Aside from Father, of course. He is being very deliberately direct. What about you, Rosalind? Are you OK?'

Rosalind looked at him with level eyes and nodded. 'Yes, I am. I did insist they told you I would be included in the Christmas invitations and I assumed they had...'

Matthew smiled, shrugging his shoulders. He stubbed out his cigarette and stood up. 'Oh, I think they wanted me to look and feel awkward when I saw you. It's part of my punishment, for choosing journalism and a life in London rather than devote my life to tennis and to life here.'

'Don't... Matthew, please. I was always very content with the promise of life here with you, once you had retired from tennis. You chose to walk away from it...'

Matthew nodded silently.

'Yes, I did, Rosalind, and you deserved better from me. I acknowledge that much. You should get back to the warmth of the lounge though, before Giles comes searching... Let the charades commence!'

He could hear the sarcastic tone in his voice and he grimaced, but he couldn't help it as he grabbed his cigarette case and lighter from the wrought-iron table, following Rosalind now, with the bitter-sweet memory of what had been blissful Christmases past, swimming in his mind.

★ ★ ★

Gervaise Trevelyan enjoyed the Christmas season, but for reasons he didn't understand his wife Margot had been spoiling for a fight for days. His daughter-in-law, Caroline, felt the tension most acutely and he was sorry for that, urging Margot to talk to her, although it wasn't as if Caroline hadn't witnessed many a bust-up between them over the years. He had told Adam and Jack the day they had arrived that he had an idea why his wife was being *so* combative, adding that he wasn't overly concerned as she didn't have to induce an argument, potentially ruin the Christmas holidays and then play the martyr, acting as if she had sacrificed something important just to placate him.

He had waved his arm expansively at this point.

'She can go to London, see the damned man if she so pleases, even take luncheon with him.' As long as she didn't expect *him* to accompany her.

'Who?' said Adam.

'Nate Gilbrandsen. Apparently he is coming home from his so-called exile in Spain for a retrospective exhibition and she wants me to go with her. A show of unity, she calls it. I see no reason for me to tag along and so your mother has misread the situation, implying that I don't want her to go either – as if that would ever stop her! Especially if one of her students was exhibiting, she would have a reason to go and I have always accepted the life your mother had before we were betrothed. I also accept that she gave up a lot, largely at her father's behest, as he found her artistic inclinations louche and amoral. I never have…'

Adam slumped into the leather chesterfield and lit a cigarette. 'So why does she think you will object?'

Gervaise shrugged. 'Because she always leaps to the wrong conclusion about Gilbrandsen and me. I knew him, but she was his muse and very likely his *lover*. He had a great many. I believe the mother of Jack's current girlfriend may have been another… What's her name? Daphne Savernake…

'If your mother had her way, she would have stayed with Gilbrandsen, but her father wouldn't have it. So she was encouraged to walk out with me. I would have had a much quieter life if she'd had the courage to defy her parents and chosen Nate.'

'You would have hated a quieter life. You thrive on the fights as much as she does.'

Gervaise nodded. 'Yes, although I found that easier at the beginning, but she doesn't consider the impact on you and your brothers, especially Hugo and Caroline, who see most of it first-hand. Worst of all are the silences after we have had a fight, which stretch longer than before, when we used to make up in bed…' He paused to see if Adam was blushing before adding, 'That's where Hugo's skills are most useful, as he brokers the peace between us. As much for his own sake as ours.'

Adam exhaled heavily. 'My god! How do you stand it?'

Gervaise shrugged. 'The management of the estate keeps me occupied and your mother has her artist's colony. We co-exist as best we can, but I am *not* going to London for the sake of show. The people who know your mother well, the ones that matter to her, will see through the charade. I am not subjecting myself to that. I trust your mother, the longevity of our marriage is testament to that. So she can sulk all she likes.'

Adam bowed his head and taking a last drag on his cigarette, he stubbed it out. Looking up at his father, he smiled slightly. 'Where is she staying in London?'

Gervaise shrugged. 'With Mercedes Campion, I guess. Unless she has plans to descend on you! I suspect Mercedes will be her likely option, so you can relax. Enjoy Christmas and continue as you always do here.

'Your mother's storm of wrath, which is directed at me, will sweep itself away in due course.' Gervaise put a reassuring hand on Adam's shoulder, squeezing it gently as Adam half rose smiling. Gervaise returned his attention to some papers on his desk and Adam sat watching him in silence, imbued with a surge of newly found admiration.

He had been led to believe that there was a mercurial quality to artistic men like Nate Gilbrandsen. He saw some of the same

118

qualities in Jack and Paul Crowley and he understood how women would be attracted to that. His father appeared safe by comparison and that was what his maternal grandfather, a man of puritan instincts, wanted for Margot. The idea of running off to Spain as the casual *muse* and lover of an artist would have appealed to Margot Phillips in her late-teenage years, having not quite made her mark as a "deb" – a process which Adam knew his mother considered frivolous. Yet his mother for all her rebellious instincts had done as her father had bidden her and taken Gervaise Trevelyan's hand and she had enjoyed much more freedom than many a wife of her generation and class might have expected, but Adam wondered if his mother was still entirely happy with her choice.

15

Laura Savernake had another more clandestine motive for wanting to return to London after the Christmas holidays which she hadn't revealed even to Alicia. She had been very pensive on the train down to Hampshire as her sister quizzed her about life in general, but more particularly her stalled career as a fashion model, especially given how much the *Tatler* and *Vogue* covers had boosted hers. Given how much Alicia was invested in her relationship with Jack and how happy it made her feel, Laura felt she should be sharing details of her recent romantic interest with her sibling. It had happened at Jack's flat-warming party while Paul Crowley had been waiting to reveal his portrait of Jayne Campion, that the gorgeous Spaniard had caught her eye, just as he seemed unable to take his off her. He had been standing in a corner of the lounge most of the evening, occasionally accompanied by another very handsome man, who – she was later informed by Matthew Fullerton – was Christopher Stretton, usually known as "Kit", the youngest son of the Earl of Broxbourne.

The Spaniard, according to Fullerton, was Antonio Viaz, a junior diplomat attached to the Spanish Embassy in London. He exuded self-confidence that probably came from being high-born, Laura thought, which had the effect of making her feel slightly gauche in his company, but there was no denying his charm and she had an inexplicably sinking feeling when he bid her goodnight long before the party was over and along with "Kit" Stretton he took his leave. Matthew had, she believed, noticed her reaction to the Spaniard, but he had been discreet in telling her that "Kit" Stretton was not someone to get too heavily involved with, as he had gained a reputation that he doubted her parents would approve of, but as to any interest she had shown in the Spanish diplomat, he made no mention and thankfully among her sister's friends he had been the only one to notice.

Laura stood in the drawing room at Chelcombe Place, her mother's voice diverting her from daydreaming, to the extent she was shocked by how much her thoughts were focused on Sênor Viaz. Her mother who was never the fussy type didn't like to pry, and she seemed troubled by a letter she had received the previous day, containing an invitation to an artistic soirée in London as the guest of Mercedes Campion. Her mother seemed distracted as she had read and reread it twice, so when their maid Elsie brought the afternoon tea tray in, Laura excused her with a smile, offering to pour, to which Daphne waved her hand expansively with an air of dismissal, grateful to be relieved of the mundane chore. Laura handed her mother a cup and said. 'What is it? That letter bad news?'

'Not bad news, dear, but an awkward situation as it means I will have to make a decision that someone will be unhappy with. Although given it's from Mercy and it concerns Margot, it's probably more of an instruction!'

'Margot? Jack's mother?'

'The same. Although of course I always think of her as Margot Phillips, even after all these years. I should go to the event as it might benefit me as an artist, but I know how your father will react...'

'Why?' Laura's brow was pleated with confusion.

'Because St John Crowley is going to be there! You were here the last time he turned up unannounced and uninvited. Your father was fuming for days… Then if I decline to placate him, both Mercy and Margot will be put out… Although if Nate Gilbrandsen does put in an appearance Margot will be glad if I am not there! She was consumed with envy when I agreed to sit for Nate, for that portrait that is hanging on the landing.'

'Were they lovers?' Laura's eyes were dancing with intrigue and her mother sighed.

'Laura, really… You shouldn't be asking that, but yes they were, although being faithful wasn't in Nate Gilbrandsen's nature and Margot suspected he might have wanted something to happen with me, while I was sitting for him… and I am *not* saying anything more on that subject so you can wonder all you like.'

Daphne laughed tapping Laura softly on the end of her nose with the envelope as she replaced the letter inside and put it on the mantlepiece above the fireplace.

'Your father and I shall discuss it after Christmas.'

'You have to go, Mama.'

Daphne took a long gulp of tea, sighing heavily. 'Oh Laura… If only it was that simple.'

Laura smiled, offering her mother her hand. She couldn't understand why it wasn't so simple, but suspected that it was a luxury of youth, but that one day she might.

★ ★ ★

Alicia left her father as he returned to the house and she took the path down to the studio Jack had been renting prior to starting at the Slade and she entered the rotunda, wanting now to feel close to him in the space he had occupied. Where they had slept together for the first time, tentative, excited, explorative in their approach, but also fearful of being discovered. She felt his absence very keenly now and she *so* wished he could have said yes to her invitation to spend Christmas at Chelcombe Lacey. Gazing around, she smiled, taking in the scene, imagining him working at his easel where he could capture the best light.

He had left some of his materials here for when he returned once the first year at the Slade was complete. Alicia did one more lap of the studio and in her mind's eye she could see them naked between the covers on his makeshift bed, Jack's arms around her, enveloping, making her feel safe... and *loved*. She had lain in his embrace for what seemed like an eternity after the first time they had sex and biting her bottom lip mischievously, she wondered if Miles and Sybil also had their first sexual experience in here, as it had always been a favourite bolt-hole on the estate.

She took a sudden deep breath angrily wiping away stray tears she felt against her now cold cheeks. It was time to join the family indoors, she thought, and taking another lingering look, her imagination brought Jack to mind standing at the easel, gazing at her furtively and then softly she said, 'Stop it...' and the moment was lost, then she walked out, making her way back across crisp, frosted grass to the house.

16

The New Year was heralded in and Paul Crowley welcomed it in a buoyant mood, hopeful that the influential art critics he had invited to see the unveiling of his portrait of Jayne were sufficiently impressed to feature either him and/or it, in one of their future articles. Jack had known what he was up to and had shrugged it off nonchalantly.

Paul admitted to having had a few qualms, but they hadn't lingered for long. He claimed Jack understood when Jayne quizzed him about it and he suspected that she wouldn't have been unduly concerned had the occasion been any other than Jack's party, given their history together.

'You could have used St John's Bloomsbury house for the event…' she had said more pointedly than he had expected, but all had seemed well when they parted for the Christmas holidays.

He needed readers to have the same reaction to his portrait that Jayne had, the critics on the night had, along with the rest of their friends. He had returned to London, from the Crowley family home, two days after Christmas as the mood was soured somewhat from a quarrel between his father and St John. He and Lynette were concerned about how the quarrel might impact on their current lodging arrangement, but despite his foul mood St John sought to reassure them that he wouldn't punish them for their father's boorishness, combined with the long-running apathy that he had towards his cousin, which he said meant it was unlikely he would endure another Christmas with them.

Paul knew it wasn't entirely down to St John and their father not getting along, as St John had been angry about his luncheon with Naismith the day before Christmas Eve.

'So why do you tolerate him, St John? The man is a parasite.'

St John was struggling to retain his irritation. 'Do I tell either of you who to be friends with? No. I admit to having had my fill of Naismith, at times, but he is still a long-standing friend and he will *still* be welcome in *my* home!'

He gave Paul and Lynette a warning look and took a long drag on his cigarette, before continuing. 'As for him being a parasite, I am guessing that comes from Jayne and I don't doubt Mercy might tell Jayne the story she wants to hear, but then she might still do the opposite when the time comes, as she has done hitherto! I have known Mercy many years and I like her. Her artistic soirées are legendary, but I know that she loves a *drama!*

Paul and Lynette exchanged a look, bemused by what their cousin hadn't said as they knew that he and their father always had a difficult relationship and that they tolerated each other at best, largely for their mother's sake, who St John adored. It was important to them that their cousin was happy for them to remain in his Bloomsbury house for the duration of term at least and for that they needed to keep him on side.

As for Naismith, he could go hang for all they cared, but if his current displeasure with St John meant they would be seeing less of him at the Bloomsbury townhouse, they would be very grateful for that.

Lynette chose to remain silent, but Paul said, 'OK, St John, point taken as far as Naismith is concerned, but what is intriguing us is that he has got you so mad; what motivates it?'

St John sighed heavily. 'The publishers mainly. He claims they are taking advantage of him because he's not represented, even though he decided to part company with his agent, which he did in a fit of pique. I will admit that he can be his own worst enemy sometimes and he has to accept that his last few books haven't captured the heights of his pre-war work, and while I don't think Trentham & Westmacott are trying to get his book cheaply, he is much mistaken if he thinks that my acquaintance, at best with Charles Trentham, will carry much weight. He needs to find fresh representation who can negotiate a deal on the merits of his work rather than trying to scrounge a favour through friends. Besides which, I just don't believe that Edgar Trentham does business that way!'

Lynette covered her mouth with a black kid-leather-gloved hand to stifle a laugh as St John finished his tirade.

* * *

Nathaniel Gilbrandsen was a giant bearlike man standing at over six-foot, possessing a permanently tanned, weathered complexion, derived from his many years of self-imposed exile in Spain. He rarely returned home, especially since the war and so when he did, to the artistic world it was an *event*. He had begun his trip on 28 December and he was exhausted, feeling chilled to the bone on arrival, with a large steamer trunk of canvases at his side, belying the claim that he liked to travel light.

It was his first trip to England in over five years and alighting the boat train from Dover at Victoria in wintry rain didn't help with the foulness of his mood. Instructing a porter to load his luggage into a taxi, which he sent on ahead to the

Charing Cross Hotel, he paused to light a cigar, wondering whether he should send a telegram to Mercedes Campion who was assisting as the curator of the exhibition and she would be liaising as his hostess. More importantly, he knew she would be his best option for making contact with that damned novelist Laurence Naismith, to whom he had played host for weeks in Spain, while Naismith finished his damned novel. Gilbrandsen admitted to having been less than discreet over several cognacs and several bottles of moderately drinkable red wine each night, but damn it to hell! He hadn't expected some of his most lurid tales to find their way into Naismith's fiction.

No wonder the man had left him so abruptly. Gilbrandsen cursed, stubbing out his cigar. He climbed into another taxi with his worn brown leather valise under his arm, instructing the driver to take him to the Charing Cross Hotel.

Growling under his breath, Gilbrandsen was determined to make Naismith pay for any of *his* indiscretions that found their way into the published text. He had been warned about Naismith and he wouldn't ever host him again and Naismith may live to wish he hadn't called upon his hospitality that autumn. The issue of the publisher's disclaimer form still had to be resolved and it would be to his satisfaction, even if that meant a partial rewrite of this damned novel!

It irked him to know that if it hadn't been due to the diligence of an employee at the publishers sending a telegram to the postal office in Spain which handled his correspondence he would have been none the wiser. Naismith would have succeeded in using sensitive information as fodder for his fiction. Mercedes had warned him that Naismith was struggling with the latest novel but it wasn't until he had been informed by his housemaid-cum-cook that his guest had left suddenly that he began to understand the rationale for Naismith's rushed departure. He hadn't wanted to run the risk of his host seeing anything that he would insist be removed from the manuscript.

Then there was Margot Phillips – Trevelyan, he reminded himself with a curse. The best muse he had ever had. Damn it! The best sex he had ever had, but he had lost her to Gervaise, because he had not been husband material in her father's eyes. Damned shame it was, as although he had always liked Gervaise Trevelyan, he had doubts whether he could handle a woman like Margot.

He had told her that she would shrivel at the damned estate in Cornwall.

Which of course she had taken as a challenge and she had achieved just the opposite, thriving with that artists' colony she had established.

He retrieved his cigar and relit it. Frowning, he speculated on how he would feel seeing Margot again and strangely he couldn't begin to guess on how he would react to seeing his old model, his *muse*, his all too brief lover, no longer in her prime, of course. He had enjoyed her in her youth, but so much promise had been lost to him. Wasted on Gervaise.

Gilbrandsen leaned back, shaking his head sadly, and taking a long drag on his cigar, he said, 'Damn! Damn! Damn!'

At least he could bask in the glory of being at the centre of the London art scene again. He had been persuaded to come to London because it was to be *his* retrospective. He could deal with Naismith via a solicitor, if necessary, as he doubted the man had sufficient backbone to resist a threat of legal action, and if he could sell two or three of the canvases he had brought with him, he could return to Spain with his pockets full.

Grimacing he took a swift glance out of the taxi window. London looked so wearily drab to his eyes in its grey wintry garb. Alighting the taxi, he instructed the hotel porter to take the rest of his luggage with an imperious wave of his hand and taking one long look of weary contempt at his surroundings, he strode inside the hotel.

17

Matthew Fullerton spent his last night in London prior to setting off for Paris with Nicola, as their relationship had, with the few opportunities that their schedule allowed, blossomed since the night of Jack's party.

Matthew was concerned that she might have become too clingy, too dependent at first, but he had been forced to acknowledge that she had developed a much stronger resolve recently and he wondered whether the change could be contributed to advice given by her cousin Martin to a greater extent than it could to him. She had become far more adventurous in love-making since their first clumsy attempt and although still instinctively shy, he felt she had come to enjoy sex. The possibility that this newly acquired attribute to her character would be entirely down to him brought a broad smile to his face. He lay in bed, sated from making love and he turned to her, aware that his forthcoming trip would be a wrench for her as he couldn't be definite about how long he would be gone. She had also shown no interest in his previous girlfriends which had been a relief as he definitely *didn't* want to discuss Rosalind, but she accepted happily that he was more experienced in that aspect of things and it was a relief to know that he could tutor her in the physical aspects of their relationship so that she would come to know what he liked. Lying within the circle of his arms, he turned to her, running a finger gently down her forearm from the delicate curve of her shoulder. She looked at him, with the deep brown eyes that were like a window into her soul and he almost melted in seeing the strength of her desire reflected there combined with the growing respect and affection that he was coming to have for her.

His assignment in Paris was relatively straightforward: To arrange an interview with the English artist, Christopher Wood, but also to engage with as many of the artists of the Left Bank as he could find who would be willing to speak to him.

'Is that what your editor is expecting?' asked Nicola.

'At the very least. Which is understandable as the newspaper is financing the entire trip. I am not guaranteed the interview with Wood but I will try my best, but I understand my editor said he wants me to capture the atmosphere and colour of the city's artistic community as much as anything... The city has become a melting pot of nationalities since the war: Americans, as well as British; many Russians who flocked there to escape the tyranny of the Bolsheviks, some of them with little more than the clothes on their backs and fortunate to have escaped with their lives! I want to capture it all...'

Nicola nodded, smiling encouragingly. She snuggled deeper into his embrace, as he wrapped his arms tighter around her. He acknowledged an easiness with her that had developed over recent weeks that he couldn't recall ever having felt with Rosalind, who had seemed keen at adhering to propriety and an observance of boundaries that he would have equated more to their parents' generation. He smiled slightly, wondering how his brother Giles would react if his relationship with Rosalind didn't develop in the way that he hoped it might and whether Rosalind's mother showed as much enthusiasm for a union with the second Fullerton son as she had always encouraged her daughter to have with *him*.

He smiled more broadly and Nicola raised her head from his chest to look at him quizzically. 'What?'

Matthew shook his head. 'It's nothing important. Just something that was mentioned at home at Christmas which I think my brother Giles might struggle to accept.' Nicola smiled and laid her head down again, drawing circles with her index finger on the broad expanse of his chest.

'I hope you are not going to be distracted from your writing by some of the exotic women that you are likely to meet in the melting pot you call Paris…'

Matthew looked at her with furrowed brows. It was the first time that she had said anything that suggested she felt insecure and while he wasn't unduly worried, he wanted to placate her. 'When I have you to come home to?'

Nicola laughed nervously as Matthew reached for his cigarettes, lit one and passed it to her. She dragged on it heavily and coughed so, smiling, he took it back. For a moment he feared she might say something like "come back to me" and that would have confirmed her insecurity, but thankfully she had erred on that and he was grateful.

He kissed the top of her head and smiled.

'I'm not sure I will have time for romance, Nicola, but I am guessing that your head could be turned by any of those models who go to life-drawing classes at the Slade.'

She shook her head with a grimace. 'Not with some of those I have seen recently.'

Nicola blushed slightly and feeling suddenly very gauche she turned away, but Matthew placed a finger beneath her chin and brought her face to face with him.

'I'm sorry… I'm just very new to this.'

'So there hasn't been anyone?'

'None that mattered as much as I fear that you are coming to matter.'

He reached for her as she pulled away and then she was out

of the bed, naked and feeling even more exposed.

'I didn't want us to part like this.'

'Like what?'

'On a quarrel.'

Matthew suppressed a laugh, shaking his head. 'We're not. At least I hope not. I am just struggling to understand.'

Nicola shrugged nonchalantly and Matthew got out of bed, taking his shirt with him, which he wrapped around her shoulders, nodding encouragingly as she shoved her arms into the sleeves. It smelt of him in a good way, and she looked at herself in the cheval mirror, wearing only his shirt, and bit on her bottom lip. She smiled, enjoying the sense of wantonness which swept over her. She rarely felt as she did now.

Sexy, decadent and never before she had got with Matthew.

It shocked her to feel excited, but the fact she didn't care was the best feeling of all.

She half turned realising he was looking at her with desire in his eyes.

'I'm guessing that look tells you that you like feeling the way you do now?'

'In what way would that be...?' she asked fluttering her eyelids.

'Sexy, desirable, utterly *unchaste*...'

Nicola nodded as Matthew reached out for her hand and as she gave it to him willingly, he smiled back as he pulled her back into bed.

Matthew knew she had to be treated with kid gloves, that he would have to move at a more sedate pace, but they had been caught in a whirlwind of desire since Jack's party and he hadn't factored in the tail-spin effect upon Nicola, remembering her words.

"None that mattered as much as I fear that you are coming to matter."

For reasons that Matthew hadn't even come to rationalise those were words that he should have been overjoyed to hear from

Nicola and yet they struck fear into him as well. They confirmed what he had dreaded most, that she had already invested so much into the idea of them as a couple, so much that should he walk away now, or at some time in the near future, the greatest fear of all hitting him was that the reality of it would break *her*.

★ ★ ★

When he left his flat, Nicola was still asleep, so Matthew scribbled a swift note stating what she should do about his flat, then he took a taxi to Victoria to catch the boat train to Dover. It was raining heavily and London looked very bleak in its misty winter garb.

Strangely he felt as downbeat as the weather and setting his concerns about Nicola aside he tried to focus his mind on the journalistic assignment in Paris.

He arrived in the French capital to find its skies as grey as in London, but he set about making contact with Christopher Wood, either directly or via one of his acquaintances as swiftly as possible. There was, as he had expected, a genuine buzz around the city and he was eager to absorb its vibrancy, to drink it in and he knew it would mean him having to produce the best writing of his journalistic career thus far, to capture the essence of that atmosphere on paper.

The Campion Flat – London – Same Day

Mercedes Campion threw the telegram into the fire and angrily slammed her hand against the mantelpiece, cursing loudly. Daphne Savernake looked up at her, startled, but knew her hostess well enough to remain silent and to wait for whatever storm she was raging against to abate.

She returned her attention to her sketch pad. Alexander had

been against her coming to London for the exhibition, but had relented eventually as he often did, but had remained adamant that he wasn't going to join her, even though she would be spending some of the time with their youngest daughter, Laura, while Alicia was on a modelling assignment in Paris.

Mercedes took several long drags on her cigarette, pacing up and down the lounge of her spacious flat. She liked entertaining and she basked in her reputation for giving some of the best artistic soirées in London and on occasion at her villa on the Riviera. She had been married once very briefly to an older man, and she could have secured a very lucrative divorce, when both parties realised they weren't really suited and she had remained loyal and had inherited a much larger fortune on his death, some of which she now used to support the burgeoning careers of writers and artists, whose talent she considered worthy of her largesse.

She raised a quizzical eyebrow at Daphne, who looked over the top of her sketch pad and smiled.

'Well? Aren't you even at least a bit curious as to who the telegram was from?'

Daphne smiled. 'Well, judging from the heat of your wrath I would guess at it being either Naismith or Margot Trevelyan?'

'Naismith actually, although I don't know which of those two is worse at the moment. While he was staying with Nate Gilbrandsen in Spain, it appears that Naismith benefited from a morsel of gossip which he has put into the book, and his potential publishers are playing hard about the size of his advance, and because we both know how difficult Nate can be when the mood suits, I now find myself potentially in the middle of a three-way fight between the publishers, Nate who is a good friend and Naismith. Well, say no more. The publishers asked me to read the first draft of Naismith's novel and pen a positive blurb, which I did, and reported back that revisions were required unless they wanted to risk legal action, so they are stalling and wretched Naismith is trying to *coerce* St John to put in a good word for him with the publishers Trentham & Westmacott, by the way. Luckily for me Naismith has no idea that I advised them to seek revisions and I understand his pride has been wounded. I won't be surprised that if St John doesn't buckle, Naismith will seek me out to put in a word. I haven't seen Cedric Westmacott in years. I believe he has all but retired and it's his son, Austin, running the firm and leaning on Edgar Trentham for support... Hell, is it too early for a gin?!'

Daphne shrugged as Mercedes went to her drinks cabinet and poured two double gins which were to Daphne's taste very light on the tonic. Gazing at the clock, she smiled – just before two in the afternoon, so it must be bad.

18

Deauville France

Lieutenant Hayden Ballard smiled at the young French nurse who had tended to him daily, ever since his relationship with Sybil Horton changed. As the nurse completed her morning duties, Sybil arrived discreetly and stood at the back of the room, as she usually timed her arrival for when the nurse had finished.

He looked far out to the sea, which was violently choppy in winter.

Despite all that he had suffered here during the war, he had come to develop an attachment to France and the life that he was cultivating here, although he suspected his family would have been shocked – even horrified – at the idea that sometimes he felt more European now than North American in his outlook; although there were times when he felt homesick and wished that he was already back home in Canada. His letters from family were full of questions and pleas for him to come home, thus far, however, he had kept them at arm's length, waiting partially for the time when Sybil felt she could fully commit her future to him as he had to her. He had been candid from the start. His long-term future lay in Canada, and she had to be certain that she saw hers there for them to build a life together. He had hoped her visit home to England before Christmas might have helped her reach a firm decision, but it had appeared to him to have created more doubt in her mind. Although he had tried, Hayden didn't understand what still anchored Sybil so firmly to England, as he knew she had no blood ties there now, only memories of her brother and the fiancé she had lost in the war; Miles of whom she had spoken *so* adoringly. A man that he had hoped she would think of less often now that she had come to have such affection for him.

Then there were his physical injuries. His legacy of war. The nurse told him they were healing, that physically at least he was almost fit again, despite only having partial vision in one eye. She couldn't allow for the mental anguish that he still suffered from though, because she wasn't qualified, any more than the physician who used to visit.

So it wasn't just Sybil keeping him here. He was reluctant to return home until he was fighting fit in his mind. When he could stand up from the chair in front of the mirror and stand without the aid of the nurse or have to use his stick. When he could walk up the gangplank to board the liner, with only Sybil on his arm for support.

Then he would make plans to return home. So if those factors brought her the time she needed so be it. They both knew, however, that some day she would have a decision to make.

'Sybil?'

'I'm here.'

She moved to stand behind him as the nurse prepared for her exit.

Hayden offered his hand which Sybil took. 'I set out at the same time, so the nurse was running late...'

'I think she was, but no matter. So what do you want to do? I would like a promenade by the sea...'

'Are you sure? It's very cold.'

'I understand that but I am tired of these four walls and you must be yearning to do something stimulating.'

Sybil smiled and he could see in the mirror as she kissed her hand and then laid it against his cheek.

'Maybe after lunch, when it's warmed up…'

He slammed his fist on the arm of the chair and said. 'As you wish… You generally get your way.'

Sybil jumped slightly. Grimacing, she exchanged a rueful look with the nurse as she made her exit, both of them hoping he hadn't seen the look that passed between them. The silence hung heavily between them. She hated the sudden flashes of temper that Hayden succumbed to, as she was never sure how intense they might become, but she knew he was a very proud man and he hated the weakened state he was in. He resented the time it was taking him to completely recover, but when he was in the mood to be placated she reminded him gently that because she hadn't known him before he was in the American Hospital, she had no knowledge of the fit, virile Hayden Ballard he had been, the one that she had faith he would come to be *again*.

Sybil had learnt so much about his background from talking to others, among fellow patients and the medical staff, at first and then later by talking to him. For some veterans the scars of war were totally invisible.

Psychologically, they manifested themselves via nightmares. For Hayden there were also the physical scars to accompany the horrific memories.

There had been times when his frustration had been unbearable and she had borne the brunt of it. It was a relief to her that Ralph and Miles had been spared such an ordeal, but the flip side was that their fates had been sealed in moments on the battlefield thus denying her the chance to say goodbye. With Hayden though she felt as if she relived the horrors of the trenches to such an extent that sometimes she felt like the war had never ended. She knew those instincts lay at the heart of her hesitance to move on, to commit to a future with him, in his homeland, close in proximity to, if not among his kin, more than it had to do with wanting to spare the Savernakes any more hurt. She knew in her mind that she had moved on from Miles and she knew that they understood. Without Hayden, though, she couldn't imagine any future she wanted to move on to and she had felt that way for a while, before she had met him and since. So he was helping to make her feel whole again by offering her a future so different to what she had experienced before that it was like starting anew. She wouldn't make the mistake of deciding in haste, though, out of some misplaced sense of obligation or worse, come to realise she didn't love him enough to stay and thus break his heart and his *spirit* all over again.

After luncheon she acceded to his demand for a walk. The sun had been out since mid-morning and it had burnt the mist away, and although weak, it was warm against their cheeks as Hayden smoked a cigarette, and he looked up at Sybil to see that she was quiet and withdrawn.

He cursed himself under his breath, as he knew that he was responsible for the shift in her demeanour. That she had been the unintended victim of his sporadic flares of temper too often for her to forgive him so easily.

Not that he deserved it. He knew that much. Hayden had asked her once if her former fiancé had ever made her feel scared as he knew he had and he had demanded the truth, and she had looked at him directly and boldly said 'No'. It had been a sobering moment for him, as he realised he had to show her more kindness or risk losing her. When the doctors and nurses had been victim to some of his violent outbursts, they had known how to deal with it because he knew he was just one of many such cases they had to treat and they had been trained for it, but Sybil Horton was different. As a volunteer she was here because she had chosen to be. Ever since her brother's demise had been confirmed after the rumour surfaced that he had survived and might have been admitted to the American Hospital proved untrue, she had kept coming back and Hayden came to understand that each time she was coming back for *him*.

He was in love with her. That in itself was new to him, because there had been girls in Canada before the war who had caught his eye just as they had taken a fancy to him. He had been more attracted to some of them when he had regularly been described as dashing and truth be told the compliments had gone to his head, but looking in the mirror now he wouldn't call himself dashing. Mildly presentable was about the best he could hope for now. How would the young women who had been daughters of his mother's friends, and regular dance partners at soirées in Toronto react now? Would they turn their gaze away at the sight of him? Make any excuse not to seek him out and engage in conversation? That is something he hadn't seen Sybil do even once.

His mother told him in her numerous letters that his friends, both male and female, were keen to see him again. To remember the carefree days before the war ruined everything. Yet he couldn't be sure it wasn't just her maternal instinct at work trying to make him feel better; that he had something positive to come home to, when he was ready. How many of those young, coquettish girls would have looked on without flinching when his bandages had been removed and he had still cried out in agony, just as Sybil had done. Her smile had lit up many a ward and she had been everyone's favourite VAD. With a shaking hand, he took the last drag on his cigarette and then he tossed the butt out to sea. She placed her hand gently on his right shoulder and her touch was like a soothing balm. He reached for her hand as it dropped from his shoulder and took it in both of his, squeezing tight as in a whisper on the wind of a wintry day, he said, 'Sorry…'

Paris – January 1923

Matthew's frustration was growing with the time it was taking to make contact with artist Christopher Wood. He had come across some very fascinating people whose experiences of being a working artist in Paris he could use to fill column inches, but he was conscious that his editor was growing impatient with the delay in securing the journalistic coup that he had been promised. Matthew had been busy visiting the bars and cafes that the artist frequented and one time he had only just missed meeting Wood's friend and mentor, the Chilean-born diplomat Antonio Gandarilas.

He was missing Nicola as well, aware that for their burgeoning relationship this assignment couldn't have been more ill-timed.

Not that he was lacking the opportunity or the means to indulge in romantic adventure. There were always plenty of alluring young women in the bars he frequented each night in the hope of seeing Wood. There would be no necessity to visit a brothel, yet he knew it would be a distraction that he didn't want or need. Paris had lived up to its reputation as a vibrant post-war melting pot for refugees from several corners of Europe and as a not so temporary bolt-hole for self-imposed American expatriates, drawn to its relaxed cafe society.

He had assembled a flow of contacts, some of whom demonstrated a genuine desire to assist him and others who would offer a random bit of useful information, be it a name of an acquaintance or a venue for the price of an absinthe or two. He could only hope that he hadn't been misled into thinking that Christopher Wood was as eager for the exposure that would come from an interview, as *he* wanted to achieve a journalistic coup by presenting him to a wider public, but he knew also that he couldn't expect it to be his biggest priority. He was acutely aware though that failure wasn't an option. Having discarded tennis as a career he had to make his mark in journalism.

He sat alone in a crowded bar, which one of his more reliable sources had told him that Wood did frequent on the rare occasions that he could be dragged away from his work. He sat nursing his third cognac – as he hadn't yet developed the Parisians love of absinthe – and he had incurred the Gallic contempt of several attractive young women who had come over to his table hoping to have a good time, or at least a drink and had been quietly ignored. He could distinctly hear several languages being spoken aside from English and with his limited command of French he admired the city's ability to absorb every nationality that flocked here without it losing its essence and its identity. It was that aspect of Paris that he planned to insert into his article, because aside from its artistic history, he wanted to get right to the core of what motivated the English-born Christopher Wood to move here to pursue his art. He took one sweeping glance around the bar, and fearing he had been badly misinformed, took one last drag on his cigarette, forcefully stubbing it out as a mark of his growing frustration. Then draining his glass of cognac, which suddenly tasted not so palatable, he recalled how both Paul and Jack had been reluctant to offer him exclusivity, and although the brief conversation he'd had with the Spanish diplomat Viaz, who had first tendered the name Gandarilas as a likely source at the Gresse Street party, which had sounded so promising, he could only hope now that the optimism with which he had approached his editor on this project wouldn't amount to more than just alcohol-imbued *hubris* on his part.

Cursing under his breath, Matthew rose, his head raised as suddenly he saw the effete, beautiful young man with the piercing blue eyes and he knew instinctively that it was Christopher Wood, as the artist ordered his drink and then lit a cigarette with slightly trembling fingers. Smiling broadly, Matthew straightened his back, and with confidence he moved to greet his prey.

19

London – January 1923

Nathaniel Gilbrandsen was not in the best of moods and although his suite at the Charing Cross Hotel was more than adequate – he wouldn't say further than that – he missed the comforts of home.

London in January held little appeal for him and he knew he couldn't contemplate resettling in his homeland. Earlier in the week, he had succumbed to the urge to make his usual trip into the City. Via the Strand he trudged down Fleet Street, past St Paul's and into the tiny streets of the Square Mile, until he came to the imposing building which once housed the monolithic insurance company that had given life to the Gilbrandsen Trust, which still furnished him with the monthly income that had allowed him to pursue his artistic career. Although he only had to rely on it now during those rare lean times, his paternal grandfather had always been scathingly dismissive of his artistic ambitions and wouldn't, he knew, have taken kindly to the trust furnishing him with the means to pursue it.

Nathaniel stood, gazing up at the building for several minutes and recalled the nervousness that always assailed him when summoned to visit the gigantic, imposing man that had been his grandfather. He hadn't inherited the old man's drive just to make money, but he had benefited from the same height which meant that if he were still alive, Nathaniel would be shoulder to shoulder with him and thus he could stand his ground. With voices from the past echoing around his head, he had shook his head sadly and hailing a taxi, he instructed the driver to take him back to his hotel.

Leaning back, he had cursed Margot for dragging him to London in winter. His career didn't need the boost that he suspected some artists exhibiting would get from the event or that the exhibition would prosper from the kudos of having him there. He suspected that Mercedes Campion also had a hand in it as the exhibition curator. There was a reason he didn't bother coming to such events and he hadn't attended an exhibition in years, and that was because there were too many bad memories here and he didn't want to have to confront them. He had smiled ruefully, acknowledging that his elusiveness added to the clamour for his attendance.

Mercedes had been bold enough to say that some artists and critics had even speculated that he must be dead. 'You can't be that much of an anti-social hermit and expect any other reaction', had been her barbed response when he had said the work did his talking for him.

'That sounds like one of Naismith's lines, aside from the fact his work has fallen away considerably since the war and I know he was struggling with his latest while he was staying with me. My canvases however are as sought after as ever, whether I am based in London or on the Spanish coast.'

Mercedes had no answer to that, as the validity of his argument had been confirmed on the basis that ticket sales had soared once word had got out that he was attending.

'My life is in Spain now,' he said bluntly and Mercedes conceded the argument had nowhere to go. They had fallen into an uneasy silence, as Mercedes knew the origins of his discontent; that he had lost Margot Phillips to Gervaise Trevelyan at her parents' insistence, because they hadn't approved of him as a suitor. Although it had happened a long time ago, Nathaniel hadn't completely reconciled himself to it, and damn Laurence Naismith had, for his own ends, laid Nathaniel's anguish bare.

'Damned Gervaise won! He was a friend and he got the girl. My best muse. My lover…'

'Damned Laurence Naismith I say, for dredging up these memories. Does he know how much damage he has done or could still do?'

Gilbrandsen waved her concerns away. 'I don't let Naismith's assertion worry me, because he will cave into legal pressure…'

Mercedes looked at him, making silent appraisal. Mentally he was as sharp as ever, but looking at him, she saw that although middle-aged Nathaniel now looked like an old man. His excesses hadn't helped, but the youthful dynamo that she recalled was a fading memory now. Vibrant, wildly energetic, he had once believed he would conquer the art world; become a serious rival to the likes of Augustus John.

Mercedes wouldn't attribute his wild passion for Margot as the reason that some of his early potential had been blunted, but the dismissal her parents had encouraged her into had definitely broken him. 'I know this isn't what you want to hear but Gervaise is a good man, and he has remained a loyal husband, even when Margot didn't always deserve it!'

Nathaniel Gilbrandsen snorted at this, waving his hand dismissively. 'God rot good men. Margot has grown tame to placate him. When she sat for me she was wildly impulsive… Is she still impulsive now?'

Mercedes smiled. She wouldn't betray confidences about Margot with him as it wouldn't sit right with her, but she had come suddenly to the conclusion that Margot's frustration at her husband's reluctance to join her in London might be a blessing after all.

'I take it Margot will be coming to London alone?'

Mercedes smiled. 'I would think so.'

Nathaniel smiled. He hoped Gervaise would remain on that estate of his in Cornwall. His small kingdom. He had only had to suffer them together a few times and not since they had married. He wanted Margot to himself, he wanted her to sit for him as well, so that he could capture her on canvas now as he had in her glorious youth, when each sitting had been interrupted by wild sex. They hadn't been able to keep their hands off each other and yes, the physical aspects of marriage must have been good between her and Gervaise to have produced three sons. He grew misty-eyed, but he wouldn't succumb to being maudlin. There had been other lovers of course, but none had even come close to *her*.

Charing Cross Hotel – Three Days Later

Margot Trevelyan and Mercedes Campion stood anxiously in the foyer before going up to Gilbrandsen's suite. Mercedes had shared how sombre his mood had been, and Margot had bristled with indignation at what her friend had to impart. He was no banked fire. He still possessed the ambition to be the beating heart of Fitzrovia and had the talent to achieve it, even from his bolt-hole in Spain. There were numerous rivals to his claim as such, many of them younger, more energetic and Mercedes knew her friend would make the case for her son Jack, just as robustly as St John Crowley would for his cousin Paul. Gilbrandsen had a rare quality, though, which the artistic journalists always loved. There was the air of a "King Across the Water" about him and Mercedes had to smile, as the exhibition had not only been Margot's idea and she had provided the impetus, but she had wanted Nathaniel to be invited and as a centrepiece make it largely a retrospective of his work.

'It could all be so much easier between us if only he could leave the past alone,' Margot commented wearily and Mercedes nodded. Although she had her opinion on who was largely to blame for dredging all that up, she decided to keep her own counsel on that until the matter was resolved.

'He has always been self-absorbed by his work. It's a flaw that can affect a genius I am told…'

Margot smiled. 'By whom? Nate?'

Mercedes smiled as well and they went to the reception desk, asking for the number of the suite Nathaniel was staying in, then they rode the lift to the seventh floor. 'He wants you to sit for him again. So he can capture you as you are now, a little tamer perhaps then you were, and he blames Gervaise for that as well…'

Margot snorted. 'He blames Gervaise for anything when it should have been my father he blamed. Honestly, Mercy, Gervaise is no better and they are like two rutting bulls… Their pride is their undoing and I won't be the prize in their juvenile contest…'

As the lift doors opened and they walked to the door of the suite, Margot looked around.

'What is it?'

'I thought St John would be here…'

'You have me for moral support, not that you need it. Shouldn't we knock?' The door opened suddenly and Nathaniel Gilbrandsen filled the space, with his height and bulk. Smiling, he offered Margot both his hands and she took them.

'So Gervaise stayed away…?'

Margot nodded. 'You knew that he would, Nate… It's good to see you. The Spanish climate evidently agrees with you as you look well.'

'Pleasantries, is that all you have for me, Margot Phillips…?'

'It's a long time since I have been her. Don't make a scene, Nate!'

He stood aside as they stepped into his suite. Mercedes followed her friend into the suite and her thoughts switched to Jayne. Would her younger sister sustain her romance with Paul Crowley, or would he not prove to be the one? She didn't know Paul so well, but there were similarities in character with Nate, which could prove destructive.

The opposition that Margot's parents had towards a union with Nate had a lot to do with their perception of the artistic community and class, but she would encourage Jayne to follow her heart wherever it took her, but she did realise that like Nate, with Paul the work would always come first.

'Is St John Crowley not coming?'

Nathaniel shook his head. He had engaged a member of the hotel staff to pour the drinks, so that he could mingle. Margot raised an eyebrow in surprise and Mercedes cursed under her breath.

'So what is St John doing? He prides himself on having influence in the art world and yet he cannot turn up for an event like this? Will he even turn up for the exhibition?'

Margot could see that her friend was beyond angry. She shrugged.

'If you ask me, I think St John is losing his edge. His only interest lies with Paul and from what I hear, his cousin doesn't really need it!'

'That is an issue I have always had with critics, patrons or... whatever they chose to call themselves. They hang their reputations on the coat-tails of the artists, well-intentioned as they maybe, but they lack the natural talent to do it themselves... Besides, I think we all know the reason that St John isn't coming to my little soirée is that he doesn't want to appear like he is taking sides between myself and Naismith!'

Margot exchanged a look with Mercedes as Nathaniel

turned his back on them. He was right of course, as loyalty to Naismith was an issue for St John, even if he was as infuriated with him as they frequently were.

They took a seat as Nathaniel bid them and he lit a cigar, drawing heavily on it.

'So aside from promoting me, how many of your students have you managed to get exhibited?' he asked suddenly.

'I'm not sure, but if all those I encouraged did so, four or five said they had work they were confident of showing. Have no fears, Nate. Your work will claim centre stage at this event!'

'What about Jack?' he asked bluntly.

Margot smiled uneasily. 'No. He is focusing on his classes at the Slade, and a tad too much on his relationship with Daphne's eldest…'

Nathaniel sighed. 'Ah yes, dear old Daphne! Does she still have my portrait of her centre-stage at the Savernake pile… Where is it again?'

'Hampshire and yes, she does.'

'Good! Very good. One of my best portraits that one… well at least where the sitter has most of her clothes on!' Nathaniel laughed loudly and raucously until it started a fit of coughing. Mercedes was slightly embarrassed out of loyalty to her friend, but Margot suppressed a smile.

'You know Augustus John wanted Daphne to sit for him, even tried getting his sister Gwen to persuade her, but I got to her first!'

'Was Daphne another of your muses then?'

'Not like you were, Margot, and I always admired your capacity to rise above petty jealousies back then, so please don't disappoint me now!'

Margot slammed her glass down on a side-table and it almost shattered and she waved away the waiter who moved to assist her.

'Leave it! That is the kind of remark I should have expected. Fidelity was always going to be beyond you, wasn't it? Knowing Daphne, I don't suppose that she would have succumbed to your charms, but you always have to insinuate. Like none of your models could have resisted the invitation into your bed. You are still punishing me even after all these years, because I lacked the courage to disobey my parents and abscond with you…!'

Nathaniel rose swiftly and his champagne flute did fall and smash at his feet.

'I loved you, goddamnit!!'

'For what it's worth I believe you, Nate, but I would never have had you all to myself. I saw how you worked, and *loved*. We quarrelled about it incessantly and yes, the making up was equally satisfying, but your very nature meant you would have hurt me somewhere along the way. Not intentionally or with malice, you wouldn't have been able to help yourself…'

Margot resumed her seat and Nathaniel took his, grunting irritably.

He hated being caught in a scene, but he recalled how fierce Margot could be in her defence and she had lost none of her fire…

Drawing heavily on his cigar, he let the uneasy silence continue awhile and then he said, 'So I guess this means you won't want to sit for me again…?'

Margot glared at him angrily and he smiled, hoping to spike her ire.

She was right to remind him that they had quarrelled as often and as fiercely as they had made love and the quarrels mostly were about his models. Especially the ones who slipped in and out of his bed.

He would have led her a merry dance as a lover or as a husband and although it would never have been dull she doubted it could have *endured*. Like a glorious Catherine wheel it would have burnt out eventually. He remembered the youthful exuberance that had been blunted with the passing of the years, but Margot would always remain his best girl, so talented, so alluring and yet *so* frustratingly *forbidden*.

20

The Savernake Flat – London

Laura Savernake smiled to herself as she carefully slid out of bed, determined not to wake her sleeping lover, Spanish diplomat Antonio Viaz. She bit her bottom lip nervously, still grateful for the fact that she had managed thus far to keep her relationship secret – albeit mindful of the fact that mostly it had been achieved more by chance than design as he had been forced to conceal himself on at least three occasions when her sister, Alicia, had stopped by to collect something en route to another modelling assignment. It had been by mutual consent that they had kept Alicia's frequent stays at Jack's Gresse Street flat a secret from their parents, who expected Alicia would be staying with her, at the flat near Tavistock Place, as they had stipulated that Laura's remaining in London was only sanctioned by what their father saw as the guiding hand of Alicia's presence.

The four days that their mother was in London, supporting Mercy Campion with her exhibition, had been particularly difficult for Laura as she rarely saw Antonio, who had insisted it was too soon for their relationship to be made public. Laura was frustrated by his reticence on the matter, but careful not to alienate him into leaving her, but she wanted to tell everyone that the gorgeous Spanish diplomat was her *lover*. The speed with which her attachment to Antonio had grown scared her. It had after all been a brief snatched conversation at Jack's party and initially she feared he had only felt sorry for her, as at the time, she had been standing alone. Since then however they had spent every moment they could together and most of that time was spent in bed.

As a lover he was insatiable, but it concerned her deeply that their liaisons were dictated solely to suit him. If she was not available when it was convenient for him, they didn't meet. It was as simple as that. The nature of his role at the Spanish Embassy was all the justification he gave, minus any details, for not contacting her, and for cancelling a rendezvous at short notice. Her sister would have been horrified, urging her to assert herself, which Laura instinctively knew was right, but she was in *love*. The realisation made her blush, but it was the truth and another truth was that she would rather adhere to his terms than to lose him altogether. She knew from the little hints that he gave her that it was a very real risk and one that she simply wasn't prepared to take, so if that hand made her appear weak, *so* be it.

For now, she would accept that it was the hand he was dealing her.

Laura half turned at the sound of him stirring. She gazed admiringly at his naked, bronzed torso, just visible beneath the snow-white sheet.

She smiled at him, how magnificent he was in his physique. Facially he looked beautiful. She had never met anyone like him, nor would she have expected to, were it not for the move to London. Men like Antonio Viaz didn't idle the time away in quiet semi-rural settings like Chelcombe Lacey. She was apprehensive, however, as if the rate of her modelling assignments didn't pick up, she would be forced to return to Chelcombe Place to live. Her father had stipulated that shortly after Christmas and her mother had gently reminded her, during her stay in town. She would have to declare her relationship with Antonio and plead for mitigation and possibly be damned for it, and likely have him abandon her with ruthless speed as she couldn't imagine him dutifully catching the train down to Hampshire each weekend to see her. She could easily wail with the unfairness of it all. She had been tempted to ask, or even plead with Jack or his friend Paul Crowley to paint her portrait as a means to force her way into public attention, but a portrait, like the one he had done of Jayne Campion, had taken several weeks and time was not on her side. She lit two cigarettes and as she heard him stir again, she gently placed one cigarette between his lips, having first kissed him very swiftly and passionately. He laid an arm around her neck, pulling her closer. He liked the contrast of her pale milky skin, against his bronzed complexion and as they laid down again and her hair spilled across his chest, he prepared to make her *his* again.

★ ★ ★

Nicola Fearns was feeling restless. Her problem was an absent lover who was, she had convinced herself, enjoying his sojourn in Paris a little too much. Matthew's letters when he took the time to write were long and full of news and information about some of the fascinating people he was meeting in the French capital. He had secured an interview with artist Christopher Wood, who had initially been reluctant to commit, and by chance he had met the American poet Ezra Pound, and on a particularly late night drinking Pernod in a bar, he had met Diaghilev. In herself she was more confident about her studies at the Slade than she had been the previous autumn and whether this positive vibe had been imbued by the sense of bliss she felt about her relationship with Matthew she wasn't as yet sure. She had, with encouragement from Paul and Jack, decided that she wasn't going to be bullied by the tutors who were inclined still to question the legitimacy of her scholarship, although she remained careful not to fall foul of some of the esteemed members of the Slade hierarchy such as Professor Henry Tonks, whose reputation demanded the respect that she conferred, but who still managed on occasions to fill her with fear.

Paul encouraged her not to always see constructive criticism as some kind of threat, but to absorb the positive points and balance them against the negative. She pointed out quite boldly, that it was easy for him having produced a portrait of such quality as that he had done of Jayne Campion and although he smiled without blushing at her compliment, he had responded, 'So my next portrait will have to be deemed as good, if not better, by the critics, as they will accuse me of letting my standards drop. You see, Nicola, the confidence has to start from within...'

Pausing, he had jabbed a finger at her chest, adding, 'You have to believe in your talent first! I am sure Matthew will tell you that he is only as good as his last article.'

Nicola had blushed slightly. 'You know about us... being together?'

Paul nodded encouragingly and smiled. 'I had an idea you might be and then I noticed you both at Jack's party and it was confirmed. Don't worry, I don't think everyone has picked up on the fact.'

'Has Lynette?'

'I'm not sure, but if she has my sister will be pleased.'

Paul placed a reassuring hand on her shoulder and Nicola wanted to hug him, but she demurred. From the start of the fresher term, he had consistently been her biggest champion and she adored him for it.

He raised his hand in farewell as a fellow student approached him and Nicola took her leave. She wasn't sure how she felt about her relationship with Matthew being public knowledge, but she was relaxed that it was Paul who knew. As for Lynette, Nicola suspected that *if* she did know, her paramount reaction would be relief.

She sat now in the same cafe at which she had met Matthew several times, after Christmas, prior to him leaving for Paris, when her relationship had been gloriously new and vibrant and exciting. She smiled as she waited for her cousin Martin to arrive. He too had noticed the positive change in her demeanour when they last met, which had been a sharp but welcome contrast to her downbeat mood before Christmas. Martin was a man of the world, albeit his bachelor status was one that he had reconciled himself to. The scars he still bore had become an enduring legacy of the ordeal he had suffered at Festurbet and were as likely a motive as any, he claimed, to deter any woman from contemplating a marriage to him. She had scoffed at this, protesting at him not to be so negative, but he had gently laid a hand on her arm and assured her that it was fine. That his status suited him. According to his doctor the mobility to his left arm had improved to the extent that it would now and Nicola knew as her cousin had told her several times before, that the only battle he had to fight now was the one within himself. The recurring nightmares which still plagued him, during which he felt as if he were back in the trenches, listening to the mortar fire, and the smells of war being engaged around him, his vision blurred by smoke, were images which hadn't yet faded and perhaps they never would.

21

Martin Fearns had been standing at the door to the cafe, watching his cousin Nicola for several minutes, attracting the disapproving looks of several patrons who had to push past him to gain entry, with his smile offering little by way of placation. He carried his stick for additional support but he didn't really need it now. It had become like an emotional crutch if truth be told, which he was as yet unwilling to give up.

He smiled gently as he watched Nicola waiting patiently for his arrival.

He reflected on how much more she resembled her mother, as he had remembered her at all the social soirées they had attended before the war. He had fallen for her, swiftly, but he had lacked the confidence initially to declare himself and then his cousin Clifford Fearns – or Simon as he preferred to be called – had steamed in and claimed her hand or had "stolen" her from him as Martin chose to describe it. He had cursed himself for not having noticed that his cousin's interest was *so* strong as Clifford had always prided himself on the belief that he had his "pick" of numerous eligible girls, so Martin realised that had been his mistake, to have set his cap at someone, but had then procrastinated on following through. He had reached the conclusion that his later resentment of

Clifford which lingered to this day intensified from that moment, although they had never been close, added to which he had enjoyed a cushier war in the Middle East, barely saw any action and in comparison had come out virtually unscathed. There was never, of course, any doubt that Clifford would inherit the estate on the Surrey-Berkshire border that their great-grandfather had bequeathed to his eldest son. That was a fact which Martin's side of the family had been forced to reconcile themselves to half a century ago. He cursed mildly as another patron shoved past him with only a cursory apology and he decided it was time for him to go in. Although his mood felt heavier than when he had set out, he hoped that luncheon with Nicola would make him feel better, as his previous meetings hadn't gone as he had hoped. The medical consultation had been routine but unremarkable with a very matter-of-fact physician telling him he was as back to full fitness as he could hope to be.

He had suffered his share of blunt army medics in the field hospital at Etaples, and then at the wretched convalescent home in Oxfordshire, which had been hell, but he had put on a brave face then, for the sake of the few visitors who had come to see him, who had included Nicola and her mother, but mercifully not his cousin Clifford.

The medical consultation had been followed by a meeting with the publishers Trentham & Westmacott, who he had known of through his friend Daniel Swiffen. The idea of recounting his war-time experiences held little appeal for him, and it had been another idea of Clifford's, *damn him*! It could have been a lucrative enterprise had they been willing to pay a reasonable amount to make it worth his while. He was determined that should he agree, it would have to be for more than what they had offered him today, written on a sheet of paper and slid face down across the desk. It had been pointed out when his sceptical look had been less than encouraging that there were other publishers in London that he could approach, but then he had thrown Daniel Swiffen's name at them and it had got a reaction, but insufficient, he recalled smiling ruefully, to *coax* them into improving their offer.

Hobbling slightly, he approached Nicola's table and she looked up, smiling. He could see her sketch pad on a chair beside where she sat and she removed it so that he could claim the seat, as the cafe was filling up steadily. He liked that she was busy, that her art appeared to matter as much as he believed it should; as much as her mother had wanted it to, and he wondered if there was a young man in her life. She hadn't said anything, but he hoped that if there was, he was worthy of Nicola. Lunch with his cousin was just what he needed to brighten his mood as the walk from the publishers had taken him back in his mind to the trenches, from the noise in the dug-out before they had gone over the top at Festurbet. He had been back there too many times recently and that was a recurring nightmare that he had no wish to revisit.

★ ★ ★

Mercedes Campion was not very happy. She didn't like being placed in what she would describe as a difficult position, forced to potentially compromise one friendship in order to preserve another. Thanks to Laurence Naismith that is where she found herself, sitting in the offices of Trentham & Westmacott, listening to the droning voice of the fastidious but slightly intimidated Austin Westmacott, as he outlined the problem – of which she was already aware – while his mentor Edgar Trentham sat silently beside him observing, his fingers steepled as he tapped them against pursed lips. Mercedes knew Edgar enough to be aware of his reputation within publishing, in which he'd had no difficulty re-establishing himself after his career in politics had been reduced.

She appreciated that he had the company's best interests as his priority but that was not hers. By confirming what Naismith was alluding to, his book would be a betrayal of someone she considered a worthier man than Laurence Naismith. Edgar fidgeted in his seat and Mercedes could tell that he was growing as impatient with Austin's procrastination as she was. She rarely came across anyone less inclined to come to the point.

Edgar laid a firm hand on the younger man's arm. 'Please get to the point, Austin. I am sure Miss Campion has other pressing business to attend to.' Mercedes smiled wanly. She had been surprised to get the call from Edgar, via Cedric Westmacott, as it was known within literary circles that Naismith had dispensed with his agent's services and yet he had a potential deal on the table and with such a reputable house.

Nathaniel Gilbrandsen had been right to think that a legal letter would urge caution upon the publishers and they would be unwise to go ahead without revisions and she doubted Naismith would have cause to refuse as he was unlikely to be in a position to pay back their advance. They were keen to see a return on their investment, but not at the cost of a scandal.

'Can the author substantiate the claim beyond doubt? It is a work of fiction and Naismith has stated that, however we are aware that you know who it is that Naismith is referring to.'

'I wish I knew why Laurence Naismith has been so indiscreet. I know how desperate he is to have a hit, after experiencing so many poor reviews to previous books, but my advice is that unless you insist on revisions, you will be opening yourselves up to unnecessary litigation. Is Naismith worth the risk? Do you consider his book to be that good?'

'I am glad you appreciate the risk to us, Miss Campion. You are in a unique position of knowing all the interested parties and that is why Cedric thought of you. You will of course be compensated for your time, but can you persuade Naismith to retract the offensive portion? He has been reluctant to agree to even the most minor revisions…'

'So don't publish. Let Naismith look elsewhere. I don't think I am betraying a confidence to say he has approached other reputable houses without success. Let him add yours to the list. Do you know why he sacked his agent?'

Edgar shrugged, and Austin made a noise that sounded to Mercedes like a childish whimper. She knew from his father that he saw securing the Naismith name with the house as a feather in his cap. He turned to her and asked, 'So how likely is legal action if we publish as it is?'

Mercedes smiled as she exchanged a rueful look with Edgar. It was clear to them that Austin was in some denial.

'Very,' said Mercedes firmly.

A sound like another whimper escaped Austin's lips.

'I strongly urge you to instruct Naismith to do the required revisions, because if one of the interested parties doesn't pursue an action against the company, the other will. I know them both well enough to be certain.

'What's more, I would make the instructions to rewrite a condition to publish. I probably shouldn't divulge this, but I seriously doubt that Naismith has the means to sue you should you decide not to go ahead with publishing his book.'

Edgar stood to shake her hand and she smiled. 'I thank you, Miss Campion, you have been very helpful with your insight to the interested parties. Naismith won't like what we have to tell him, but my interest lies with the company. If he wants his book to be the success that he believes it is, he has no choice…'

Mercedes shook Edgar Trentham's hand and she couldn't suppress a smile. Although she reserved most of her ire for Naismith, Mercedes had to acknowledge that Nathaniel Gilbrandsen shared some of the blame for his cognac-fuelled indiscretions while he was hosting Naismith, so the real victim in all this was Margot Trevelyan. Mercedes had seen first-hand that Margot didn't regret agreeing to the marriage that her parents had encouraged. She also said Gervaise had proved a much better husband than she had always deserved.

She accepted that if the worst scenario came to pass and Edgar didn't publish the book, Naismith might never speak to her again. She could live with that. Her sister Jayne would likely encourage her to that end. Edgar Trentham shook her hand once more as he saw her out to her taxi.

'Thank you for this, Miss Campion. Cedric told me you wouldn't let us down. That your advice would be sound and that I should heed it.

'Don't worry about Austin. His pride might be wounded if we don't secure Naismith for our list, but the house is bigger than any one author and its survival is my paramount concern.'

Mercedes stepped into the back of the waiting taxi and Edgar waved her off. She lit a cigarette and instructed the driver to take her to her flat.

She sighed heavily. Her prime objective in accepting Cedric Westmacott's commission was to protect her friends and she believed she had achieved that. Suggesting that Laurence Naismith accept the revisions and try to write a better book might be harder than Edgar Trentham had suggested.

From what she had heard, Naismith had found the process a hard slog and he believed it still represented his best work in years. As soon as Nathaniel had confessed his minor indiscretion, she had urged him to contact his solicitors and in doing so, she had chosen sides. She didn't regret it. Because she believed she had done what was *morally* right.

22

Deauville, France – February 1923

Sybil Horton considered herself fortunate in many ways, that despite losing the first man that she had loved to the war, she had through favourable circumstance met Lieutenant Hayden Ballard, who was as different from Miles Savernake as he was as remarkable and yet recently she had begun, without being aware of it, to compare them.

If pushed she would have described Miles as heroic. He had succumbed in the heat of action to an enemy bullet and died almost immediately, as youthful and as beautiful as the poet Rupert Brooke, who many said he resembled. Hayden, she would call brave, because what he had endured in recovery in the aftermath of war demanded a level of endurance many would not have been capable of, and yet his recovery still wasn't complete. He still bore the scars of battle and had a nurse coming each morning to check his wounds, during which she stayed away, walking alongside the racetrack, where the racehorses were worked. The chill of winter hung in the air, but some days there was a weak sun, indicating that spring was in abeyance. Deauville was a racing town and that was part of its appeal for

Hayden, as she knew from what he had told her about his past. She knew he still wanted the miracle as far his recovery went, although his doctors said that was unlikely and that he would have to reach a point of acceptance.

She had been forced to bite her tongue several times, to resist telling him that he was luckier than most. Because she did *love* him, despite the flashes of temper which she found quite scary in their ferocity.

Yet this was the future she had chosen, She had reached a point of no turning back, knowing now that she wanted to become Mrs Ballard.

At one time she had believed during the deepest well of her grief after Miles, that she could never love anyone that intensely again. Then she had been forced to accept what she believed was the loss of her brother, Ralph, followed swiftly by the cruel, unfounded speculation that Ralph might have survived, which was then exposed as an administrative error, but no less painful, when she discovered the truth. Those were the depths from which she had pulled herself back from the brink to meeting Hayden in her role as a VAD, and tending to his medical needs had felt like a balm which brought her to where she was now. Taking their relationship further carried risks about which she had been warned to be careful, as patients could become too dependent.

She didn't recognise a desire to feel needed and she thought Hayden was too strong-spirited to come to the point where he would need her.

Nor was it any foundation on which to build a lasting relationship, that he would rather set her free, if he ever believed that she wanted to be that for him. So it had been his idea to engage the nurse once their relationship had gone beyond a certain point and she had to be convinced that it was the right move, fearful that he might think she was starting to treat him differently. Hayden had told her, soon after she first came to treat him in her role as a VAD, that before the war he had helped to train racehorses alongside his father at their property in rural Ontario. That was the life he wanted to return to, and he had said it with more passion in his voice than she had ever heard him say anything. She stood now at the rail and smiled.

She had little experience of the sport, but listening to him talking made it sound exciting and she would like to go to the races here and at Longchamp near Paris, but Hayden was nervous about socialising too much and he was self-conscious around strangers. She had witnessed him, withdrawing deeper into himself after hearing some barbed comment about how he looked and once she had pressed him on why he was being anti-social and he had snapped. She half turned and saw the nurse take her leave, so she began to walk back to him.

She entered his room, noticing immediately the deep frown pleating his brows and she steeled herself for another of his swift flashes of temper, but he smiled wanly and the letter he was reading almost fell to the floor until she retrieved it and handed it back to him.

'A letter from home?'

Hayden nodded and she smiled. He guarded his privacy and she respected that. If he wanted to share he would in his own time; that was another difference between him and Miles and she had to accept it.

'I noticed you walking alongside the track and I thought you were going to head towards the beach as you are later arriving today.'

Sybil nodded. 'I know. I wanted to make sure I didn't arrive before the nurse left you. As you prefer it that way…' She came to stand behind his chair and wrapped both arms around his neck. She kissed him on the temple and he put a hand on one of hers. She felt his warmth, but how deep that went, she couldn't tell and didn't *dare* to push.

'They want to start me on physiotherapy again, Hydrotherapy to be exact so swimming.'

Sybil nodded. 'How do you feel?'

Hayden took her hand in both of his and squeezed as she came round to face him. 'I will do whatever helps to get me back to where I was physically. I can't stay trapped in this chair forever and I am determined to walk down the aisle and wait for you there, just as I am determined to walk down the gangplank of the liner when I return home with you on my arm...'

Sybil smiled. She wanted that as well, but couldn't escape the fact that her devotion to him had been tested in ways that it never had been with Miles. Her trip back to Cornwall before Christmas had come in the wake of a quarrel – one of their most fierce – and he had been especially harsh and scathing and she had fled, uncertain whether she would return.

She had sought solace with Hugo and Caroline Trevelyan and they had enveloped her in affection making her feel whole again and then on the night of Jack's party she had received Hayden's letter, full of profuse apology, pleading her forgiveness, and then later with Alicia Savernake, she had understood there was no route back into the past. They had to move forward with a future without Miles and so had she, so she had accepted this was where her future was.

'That is still what you want?'

Hayden frowned at her and then as Sybil bit hard on her bottom lip, he smiled.

'What else could I want, but the woman who has helped to see me back to the man I recognise when I look in the mirror?'

Sybil tried to move away, but he held her arm, his grip firm but unthreatening. There was, she knew, a lot to love about Hayden Ballard, but she was aware also that there were parts of him she feared she might never reach. That the mental scars he had might never heal any more than the physical ones that she had seen, but she had to be as honest with herself as she had been that night in the taxi in London with Adam Trevelyan. That by coming back to Deauville, she had committed herself to coming back to Hayden, to putting her faith in love once more and to trust that it would be enough.

23

Matthew Fullerton returned to London, unsure about whether he had squandered the opportunity to enjoy a sustained relationship with Nicola as her letters to the address he had supplied on the Left Bank, ceased suddenly in late February, largely because he had become tardy in his responses. His editor had encouraged him to stay in Paris after the initial interview with Christopher Wood had been submitted and he had been told the response to his article about the artist had largely been positive among their peer group, although he had smiled at the line where she wrote that Paul Crowley had only been mildly effusive in his praise.

He was very conscious on the boat home to Dover that he should have treated Nicola with more kindness and respect and while acknowledging that his trip could not have come at a less opportune time, from the point of view of their relationship, it seemed to have enhanced his journalistic career. Coming after the abruptness of his split with Rosalind, he was keen not to be perceived as someone who wouldn't commit and he didn't want another relationship failure.

Nicola had no reason to believe he had been unfaithful to her while in Paris, although the opportunities had been plentiful. He arrived back in London on a drizzly March morning and was keen to meet with Nicola as swiftly as possible, but realised she would be attending a life class at the Slade. He paused to light his cigarette outside Victoria Station, almost colliding with a man, who turned out to be his brother, Giles.

'Ah! So the Prodigal Son returns!' Giles' tone was heavy with sarcasm, but Matthew refused to give his brother the satisfaction of starting a quarrel.

'Giles.' His tone was matter-of-fact and it lacked warmth.

'How was Paris?' Giles' query was polite.

'Busy! Vibrant! How is life at Fullerton Chase?'

'Well, not vibrant or especially busy as you might have guessed. I do have good news, however, Rosalind and I have got engaged! So you see, she didn't see my overtures as a case of her settling for second best after all, although her mother is still struggling to come to terms with the fact she won't get the wedding she had been hoping for, but it will still be to a Fullerton brother as she had planned…'

If Giles thought his attempt to goad him was working he'd have been disappointed, besides which he was right. Rosalind's mother had never been subtle about her marital ambitions for her daughter – he and Rosalind had often laughed about it – but he had never been prepared to have his future mapped out for him in the manner that Giles appeared to so readily accept, so why his nearest sibling was preening so much, he didn't quite know. He readily accepted the disappointment that his parents felt at him not pursuing tennis as a career and in ending his relationship with Rosalind, but they would still be getting her as their daughter-in-law and professionally they would reconcile themselves to the fact that he had made the right career choice for *him* eventually.

'I never actually said she would see you as the second best option, but that her mother might. I know you will make Rosalind happy, Giles, and I want that!'

Giles sneered, and said, 'Which is big of you considering…'

Matthew drew heavily on his cigarette and a cloud of smoke, concealed his own sneer.

'I am not prepared to quarrel with you in the street, Giles, however much you might relish the prospect. So what brings you to London?'

'The engagement ring. I have had it custom-made at Mappins. Rosalind deserves the best.'

'That is something we can agree on. Have a good day, Giles…'

Matthew moved to edge past his brother, but Giles moved to block his way. He clutched a handful of Matthew's coat, and felt his brother's exasperation.

'What now?'

'It's just that you seem very relaxed about me formalising matters with Rosalind. So have you met someone else? I understand it's a very bohemian world you occupy now. Have one of your artist friends caught your eye, here or in Paris?'

'You shouldn't believe everything you read.'

Giles raised an eyebrow. 'Really? That's a strange thing for a journalist to say. I am merely curious. Having benefited from your failings in romance, I wouldn't want you to lose out a second time, through a failure to commit!'

'You don't care a damn whether I am single or have a string of admirers. Your only interest lies in gloating about what you perceive as my failings. Well, I am doing fine thank you, both personally and, from the article I wrote about Christopher Wood and the artistic community of the Left Bank in general, professionally as well. Now I sincerely hope you and Rosalind have a happy future together. If you chose not to accept that in the spirit it is given that's up to you!'

Matthew looked down with a warning look and nodded. Giles relinquished his hold on his coat and stepped back.

'You mean that?'

'Yes! But you prefer a conflict. Sorry not to oblige…' He

slapped Giles on the shoulder and added, 'I am sure you will thrive in your role as the dutiful son!'

Giles reddened visibly as Matthew pushed his way past and stubbing out his cigarette, he disappeared into the throng of people, without looking back, so that Giles couldn't see his expression of quiet content.

* * *

Nicola had been less than fully engaged in her life class, once again earning herself the disapproval of the tutor. Her mind was fixed on the telegram she had received from Matthew, prior to him leaving Paris. It had said boldly that they needed to talk. So she feared a parting of the ways, proceeded by a quarrel. Neither of which she wanted or would be of her doing. She had stopped writing to him because he simply hadn't found the time to respond. Paul Crowley had urged her not to take the ceasing of a response as any sign that Matthew wanted to finish with her, but she remained unsure.

When they had first got together, she had been content to be the cautious one. To let Matthew do the chasing and respond to his pace, but she had quietly feared their relationship could always be just a brief interlude for him. His absence however had firmed her desire for him sexually, along with a wish to continue seeing him. The rest, of course, was up to him.

He found her at the flat in a pensive, silent mood, pacing and feared he had expected too much from her too soon. That her insecurities which he had endeavoured to eliminate had resurfaced during his time away and that she had gone backwards into thinking herself unworthy of affection. He had accepted that her attraction to Lynette Crowley had been based on heroine worship rather than physical attraction, but he feared that any relapse on her part meant that she was convinced he would leave her at some time, so it would be less painful if she left him first, or because she lacked the confidence to fight for what he believed *they* had. He wanted Nicola to see that they could be as strong as Paul and Jayne were in their relationship along with Jack and Alicia.

'How are you?' he asked, opening his cigarette case, surprised but not angry that his hand was shaking slightly as he lit it. Nicola had to see that this mattered. That they as a couple mattered to him as much as he believed it mattered to *her*.

He offered the cigarette case to her with a nod, but Nicola shook her head.

'I am fine. Although a little distracted in life class, which didn't impress the tutor. How are you?'

'I could be better. I came out of Victoria Station and bumped into my brother Giles. He was in London to collect an engagement ring from Mappin & Webb and he couldn't wait to gloat that he had formalised matters with my ex-girlfriend Rosalind Marriott. I'm not surprised by the news. He has always been interested in her and he wants to make me jealous and then he is angry because I'm not!'

Nicola shrugged. 'Not even a little?'

Matthew shook his head vigorously through a cloud of blue-grey smoke She smiled slightly and Matthew couldn't be sure she believed him.

So he would have to make her see that Rosalind was in his past, whatever the future held for them.

'Your letters stopped so suddenly that I got worried and then I couldn't wait to get back to London to check that we are still OK, that I hadn't upset you as I had feared, but my editor was keen for me to stay… So I'm sorry!'

Nicola shook her head. 'I was – am OK!'

Matthew nodded slowly, absorbing her words. He smiled. 'What about us as a couple continuing as we were prior to Paris?'

Nicola felt her throat going dry. 'Is that what you still want?'

'Yes! Absolutely! I accept the blame if you were starting to doubt me, but I thought of you often in Paris. It took a while to make contact with Christopher Wood and then he hesitated about me interviewing him for an article. It was *so* intense between us just after Christmas that I feared the interest had fizzled out on your part during my absence, that we had failed at the first hurdle, but I still *want* you, Nicola. There were temptations in Paris. I won't lie to you about that. They were thrust in my path, but I resisted them all, because I realised I was comparing them to you, what we had been enjoying physically and they paled in that comparison. I want you to believe that truly!'

Nicola smiled as it surprised her that she did believe him and not just because it was the easiest path to follow. She could see it in his eyes, that he meant it and it gladdened her heart.

Matthew took Nicola in his arms and kissed her firmly, with passion.

She broke the kiss first and stepped back, awed slightly to be with him again after such a time away.

'I feared you had gone back to thinking that you weren't deserving of love, of being happy in a relationship and that was what motivated you to cease writing to me. Now I understand there were misconceptions on both sides…'

Their gaze drifted off to the bedroom and Nicola bit nervously on her lip. She watched Matthew through a haze of cigarette smoke, as he stubbed out his cigarette. There had been a time when they first met, when he had appeared hesitant, unsure of himself within the peer group he wanted to mix in, but now confidence oozed out of him and she felt stronger when she was with him.

The uncertainty which still plagued her at the Slade, when she felt scrutinised unfairly by her tutors, seemed to dissipate when she was with Matthew. She looked again in the direction of the bedroom. Was he thinking the same as she? Did he want to be in bed with her, as much as she wanted to be curled up in his arms? She smiled sheepishly and he gave a sideways look.

'What?'

Nicola shrugged. 'I'm just getting accustomed to you being here again, that I am still occupying your space. We had only been together a few weeks when you left so it would make sense if you had considered our relationship while you were away and decided that what we… had before Paris, was all you had to offer.'

Matthew smiled, but he was careful not to appear as if he were mocking her. He held out his hand and she came to take it. He kissed her, as fervently as before, but this time, he didn't let her break free of his embrace. He held her tighter.

'I hope you feel worthy of my love, Nicola Fearns, because you have it. Completely!'

Then he looked towards his bedroom and he smiled. For a moment Nicola hesitated and then she nodded and within another moment he had scooped her into his arms. His brother, Giles, had tried to make it clear that he was the better option for Rosalind all along, but that was a myth. He had been responsible for severing the link with Rosalind because she represented in his eyes the link with Fullerton Chase and that was part of the past. Despite what Giles chose to believe, Matthew was genuinely pleased that Rosalind had found the happiness with his brother that he hadn't felt able to offer her and now he knew as he carried Nicola to his bed, that it was time to move on.

24

Mercedes Campion handed Nathaniel Gilbrandsen a decanter of cognac and a glass and then she resumed her seat opposite him in her flat.

The man infuriated her so much sometimes through his failure to commit to a decision, or reconcile himself to a point of acceptance and to move on, although she accepted it wasn't an easy situation to navigate.

He couldn't prove his paternity, even if he had wanted to, and Margot had always refused to give credence to the rumours by acknowledging them. Gervaise Trevelyan was a good man, whatever Nathaniel thought of him. He accepted Margot's flaws and as Mercedes knew all of them to varying degrees, it gave her unique insight and she knew that behind his gruff exterior, Nathaniel Gilbrandsen was a troubled man.

'So you have seen the wisdom of not broaching the subject with Margot again? You will return to Spain, without forcing the issue?'

He grunted as he poured himself a handsome measure of cognac, placing the decanter on the coffee table. There was still a chill in the air for mid-March and the fire was banked. Grabbing the poker, he stirred the coal embers to life.

'Nate?'

'Yes! That is my plan. We both know Margot too well to expect her to change tack after all these years, so what good can I do by stirring a hornet's nest? She will never confirm it one way or another and yes, I know I am responsible for the indiscretions to Naismith which gave life to the latest speculation. Whether it's out of loyalty to Gervaise or consideration for the boy, I don't know. It's what it is! I am grateful for the invite to the exhibition. I don't belong in London any more.

'My life is rooted in Spain now and this trip has served only to confirm that. I still want to be buried here, but I am content with my lot – I really am!'

Mercedes smiled. She wasn't convinced, but she would keep her own counsel. She had never doubted that Nathaniel had loved the young Margot Phillips very passionately, because that was his style, but as a husband he hadn't possessed the urge to conform, to blunt his urges and artistic fury to present himself in a better light to Margot's father and that had been his loss.

She stood as he drained his glass. Then reaching for the decanter, he refilled it. Mercedes smiled. 'I hope you won't be so keen to give succour to Naismith the next time he turns up. I doubt he even realises the damage he has done!'

Nathaniel took a long sip of cognac, treating Mercedes to his best smile, recalling how he had painted her more than once during her youth and he would have done her sister, Jayne, as well if Paul Crowley hadn't claimed the honour for himself. He had talent, Nathaniel acknowledged as much and not grudgingly which was unusual for him, so maybe he was going soft. He shook his head. If forced he would back Margot's youngest, Jack, to be the greatest artist of his generation any day, but he would have to want it enough! To be sufficiently ruthless and selfish to go out and claim it, just as he, Nathaniel Gilbrandsen, had and to be content not to count the cost!

Finally he stood, and took the last mouthful of cognac in a gulp.

He took a rueful glance at the near-empty decanter and grinned.

'Don't worry. I bought it for you!'

'I know one thing, Mercy. If Naismith has lost you as an ally he's in trouble! Just as I am certain the publishers are grateful for your input regarding revision. I didn't really want to go down the legal route and your advice has probably saved us all a lot of money and trouble that would have come with litigation!'

'From what I know it is not resolved as yet… but I wasn't going to let an old friend like Cedric Westmacott down by not offering my insight.'

'So has he found another agent?'

Mercedes shook her head. 'I think he approached Gollancz without success, so I think St John has urged him to stick with Trentham.

'Trouble is Naismith is going around London feeling like a wounded animal and we all know what Naismith can be like in that frame of mind.'

Nathaniel nodded. 'Bloody impossible…!'

He made for the door and Mercedes followed him. There was a lot to be said for being remembered as an artist at their peak and although he would still happily joust with Augustus John, the joy that he once had in their rivalry had dissipated with the years.

He knew that he couldn't compete with some of the young blades studying at the Slade now and he didn't believe he would want to.

There is a lot to be said for exile in warmer climes and he was glad he was booked on an early train tomorrow. Smiling, he half turned and took Mercedes' hand between both of his and smiled.

'You know what they say about a guest who has outstayed their welcome, Mercy, besides which I am in danger of feeling overly nostalgic and that usually ends with me embarrassing us both.'

'Take care, Nathaniel. Don't be a stranger…'

He shrugged. 'So come out to Spain for a change. Rent your villa on Cap St Vincent to Naismith at an excessive rate, so he can blow his advance! You know you would be very welcome.'

Mercedes smiled. 'It's a nice idea!'

'So do it! Bring Daphne Milford – Savernake, for company as I will be madly busy!'

He squeezed her hand once more as she opened the door. 'You will hail a cab back to your hotel?'

He nodded and said, 'If you see Naismith, wish him luck with the book.'

Mercedes raised an eyebrow. 'That's very generous of you!'

'He has been very indiscreet at my expense, but I can't begrudge him another potential hit as it may be his last…'

He raised his hand in farewell and turned to leave.

'Goodbye, Nate.' Mercedes closed the door and leant against it, feeling slightly wistful, as she felt in her gut that *unless* she accepted his invitation to go to Spain, she might have just said farewell to the genius that was Nathaniel Gilbrandsen for the last time.

★ ★ ★

St John Crowley sat in the lounge-bar of his club growing impatient as Naismith was late. The reckless error of having sacked his agent just before Christmas was coming back to haunt the author, but St John had little sympathy. He wasn't the type to abandon his friends, but Naismith was being even

179

more tiresome ever since Mercedes Campion's input into the editing process of his novel became public knowledge. He had given Naismith a roof over his head as the delay in receiving his advance meant he had lost his flat, but as a consequence, he hadn't seen either Paul or Lynette for days.

That was their choice to be absent from the Bloomsbury townhouse as he refused to give in to demands and hated being backed into a corner. He summoned the steward and in that moment, Naismith arrived, but his expression was grim and St John groaned as he ordered two gins. He had heard second-hand that Naismith had used up whatever leverage he had in literary circles and rumour had led to him looking desperate. There was, he believed, a contract on the table with Trentham & Westmacott, albeit with a reduced advance, and all it required was for Naismith to swallow his pride and accept it. Naismith took his seat with a curt nod.

'Any luck?'

'Not much...' He paused to glance around the lounge. 'Edgar Trentham isn't here, is he?'

St John shook his head.

'Gollancz are still interested in the outline, but you know how wily Trentham can be.'

'They have offered you a contract, Laurence. Has any other publisher gone as far?'

Naismith shook his head. 'Not yet.'

'So stick to Trentham. They are your best bet!'

'I thought so as well until Edgar got fidgety and brought Mercy Campion into the fray. She doesn't like me and she has pinned her colours to Trentham's mast very firmly.'

St John sighed heavily. 'I believe she mentioned that her father and Cedric Westmacott went back a long way – or was it her late husband? I forget which, but one of them anyway...'

Naismith shrugged. 'Well, I have certainly learnt who my *real* friends are, anyway. Thank you, St John, for your loyalty...

Besides which, Cedric is all but retired now. His name is still on the letterhead, but his input is minimal. Trentham is the power there and he has considerable influence over Austin Westmacott who is as skittish as a newborn foal!'

'Do you think you were a little rash in sacking your agent at the end of last year? With representation this could all be signed and finished now.'

To his surprise, Naismith nodded, taking a long sip of gin, as St John watched him intently. 'I fear you are right, but I wasn't left with a lot of choice. She said that she would only try and sell the book with a major rewrite and that would have rendered it unrecognisable from the original! Also daring to suggest that I was past my best! I am sorry, St John! I thought I would be settled in my own pad by now. Dispensing with my agent was a gamble I had to make, but it doesn't look as if it has paid off… yet!'

St John took a long sip of gin, trying to absorb what he had just heard. A humbled Naismith was a rare thing indeed! He raised his hand in dismissal.

'Your cousins would have returned to you if I wasn't there! I'm not so obtuse!'

'They acted churlishly. It's my house and I will extend invitations as I choose, so please don't fret!'

'Surely it won't be long before Paul can afford a luxurious pad of his own, if the reviews of his Jayne Campion portrait are an indication! Please pass on my congratulations!'

St John smiled. To his credit Paul had tried to be more conciliatory about Naismith returning to the Bloomsbury house, which had surprised him, and although St John knew that his cousin would bask in any praise which came his way, he wasn't sure about how he might react to it coming from Naismith, because Paul was fully aware of his sister's antipathy towards the author and given that Jayne made no secret of the fact that she *loathed* him, she wouldn't have welcomed his comment about her portrait under any circumstances.

25

Deauville, France – Spring

The weather turned distinctly warmer in the early weeks of March, but it had little impact on Hayden Ballard's demeanour as he returned to the melancholic state that he was in when he first met Sybil.

Although she had been forced to drag the information out of him, she knew the return of the nightmares which took him back to the trenches at Vimy Ridge were the root cause for his recent swings of mood. They were less severe than before, but when he was most inclined to self-pity they prompted him to encourage her to give him up as a lost cause and to make her escape, while she still could.

It wasn't what he wanted really and Sybil had no intention of abandoning him now and she dismissed his words lightly when in his presence, but they had the power to cut deep and she felt them in private moments when alone. He was worth the effort though and on that she had no doubt.

She had hoped stimulating his interest in the racehorses which were worked daily on the beach would have a positive effect and it did on good days when he would tell her in more vivid detail about all the premier races his father had won as a trainer in Canada. It gave her a greater insight into what his life had been like, and his voice was lighter in tone and more positive in outlook.

'So what did you want to be, a jockey or to train like your father?'

'I grew too tall and heavy for a jockey so the decision was made for me to that extent. I think I would have wanted to be a trainer…'

Sybil wrapped her arms around his neck and though her cheek was soft against his face, it hurt the scar tissue and he flinched slightly.

Sybil pulled back. 'I'm sorry…'

'It's OK,' Hayden said, pulling her head gently to him and he bent to kiss it. He paused a moment and then added, 'I know I have said this before more than once, but I don't want you to have any doubts about our future. I have become very fond of you, but I don't want our relationship to be based on a sense of gratitude, or for you to stay out of duty. I just couldn't abide that. We Ballards are a rowdy lot and there's a lot of pride there as well; some may say too much pride. We have never seen it as a vice, but I guess it could be to some…'

Sybil took the three steps that brought her in front of him. She took both his hands in hers and squeezed tight. 'What are you saying, Hayden?'

He took a deep breath. 'If it's freedom you want, take it now, before the reality of losing you has the power to break me, perhaps forever.'

Sybil stared at him, and he averted his gaze, but she touched his cheek ever so gently that he turned to face her.

'Is that a touch of self-pity I can hear?' She had folded her arms in a defensive pose and he was ready to respond, when she reached out and placed her finger against his lips. He was smiling, but it was an uneasy smile.

'Because if it is, it won't wash, Lieutenant Ballard, because I have invested too much of myself in trying to mend you, physically and emotionally, just to walk away now. I never thought that I could feel anything for another man after Miles. I certainly wasn't seeking it when I came to find the truth about what happened to my brother and found you. Discovering slowly and surely how you got under my skin. You managed to get me to care deeply for you, probably when my defences were down. So don't tell me now that I have allowed myself to *endure* all this for nothing. For you to send me away out of a misplaced sense of honour, or to make it impossible for me to stay, with your careless conduct or harsh words, because I am not going to walk away and you are going to get better.' She moved in closer and took his hand in hers, squeezing tighter. She bent to kiss him with a fervour that left him in no doubt about the strength of her feelings, that for her there was no turning back and that she didn't want him to offer her that opportunity ever again.

Hayden smiled.

'I guess that's me told! How did I get to be so lucky that Volunteer Nurse Sybil Horton happened to come into my ward that night and decided to confer her compassion on me?'

Sybil shrugged. 'I don't know, just as long as you don't forget how lucky you were that chance fell upon you.'

'So Canada is still an option for you when the time is right?'

She turned to gaze out of the window, trying to stem the flow of tears, as she didn't want to confuse the situation, but she was committed to Hayden, so that meant going where he had to be.

'I never envisaged a future for myself. By the time I realised how much I was in love with Miles, the war had come and then I volunteered, as a nurse. It would seem from what you have told me that your career was mapped out. Horses! I can't say that I am swapping my life's passion for yours, because there was none other than becoming Miles Savernake's wife.

So I hope I have allayed your fears about my commitment to us and yes, Canada is alien territory for me, but I will have you and honestly, there was a time when I had given up on having anyone…'

Hayden offered her his hand and she reached for it with a wan smile and he would take that and for Sybil, the hope that she had laid the ghosts of her beloved Miles and faithful brother, Ralph, to rest was stronger than it had ever been.

26

The Trevelyan marriage went through another malaise in the weeks after Margot had returned from London. She had stayed on after the exhibition, at which a number of her students had shown their work, largely at her behest. After which she contacted Gervaise and encouraged him to join her, once Nathaniel Gilbrandsen had returned to Spain. Yet he declined, despite Hugo urging him to take the break, but once again Gervaise used his old friend Nathaniel as a barrier in their marriage and this combined with Margot's instinctive obstinacy led to an impasse which continued for days which then slid into weeks, with Margot insisting she would return to Cornwall when her students needed her.

Hugo retreated from the situation at Caroline's urging, totally exasperated, talking to his father only on matters relating to the estate.

His younger brother Adam went to see Margot at Mercedes Campion's flat. She gave them use of her lounge, while she retreated to her office.

Adam stood with his back to the fire, looking down at his mother.

'One of you has to concede or is this nonsense going to continue indefinitely?'

Margot stared at him sharply.

'I offered your father an olive branch by suggesting he join me in London once Nate had gone home. He declined, citing the demands of the estate, which your brother is more than ready to meet. Gervaise could have shown a united front by coming to London with me. He wouldn't have had to meet Nate Gilbrandsen. I just don't know what he expects, Adam. I realise that in your eyes – Hugo's and probably Jack's as well – that a chasm has opened between us, but your father sees no urgency to close it, so why am I being portrayed in the poorest light? Art is my life, Adam, always has been and your father knew that when I accepted his proposal. I had to surrender my chance to flourish in the artistic world, largely at my father's urging to marry Gervaise. So he won. What more does he expect? For me to submerge my life into his, in Cornwall, to simply *just* be his wife? He must have known before Hugo came along that it was never likely. I am just not that sort of girl!'

She reached for a silver cigarette box and taking one, lit it.

She sank back in the chair and eager to fill the silence, Adam asked. 'So is it the end for you both? *Finiti!* Divorce?'

Margot looked at Adam sharply, shocked at the enormity of what he was suggesting, as she was that he had asked it. Swiftly her expression changed and she retained her inscrutable mask.

'Don't be so foolish. Your father would never act so rashly. He will sulk awhile longer and then ask me to come back and once I do, on my terms, he will be mollified. All will be well. We shall continue to happily co-exist!'

'Happily?' Adam's tone was incredulous and Margot threw him a withering look with all the menace that he had come to fear, growing up.

'I won't presume to tell you how to conduct your marriage, whenever you find someone willing to take you on, so don't try it with me! We understand each other. I accept that he still resents the fact that Nate has commanded some hold over me, but as a young man Nate Gilbrandsen was hypnotic, mesmerising! A Lord Byron of the art world.

The Rossetti of his day! That animalistic magnetism is quite heady for a young woman. I fell for it and so did Alicia's mother. Yet when I had reconciled myself to accepting Gervaise's hand, I accepted that he had different qualities and I went down the aisle to meet him in St George's, Hanover Square, with an open heart, otherwise I would have refused him and accepted my parents' wrath. We have stayed together; made it work. So what does that tell you? Put the ludicrous notion of divorce out of your head!'

Adam smiled, feeling chastised, but also surprised that his mother had revealed so much when quiet reticence was part of her code.

'So Hugo is worrying for nothing?'

'You know what your brother is like. Besides, he is living with Gervaise's sulking so he sees it first-hand. Now, are you taking me out to dinner so that we can give Mercedes her home back?'

Adam smiled again, and offered Margot his hand, which she took with a gentle squeeze as Mercedes appeared in the doorway.

'Everything OK?' she queried tentatively.

'Everything is fine, Mercy. Gervaise is passing his melancholic state onto Hugo and that is being passed along the line. I am surprised that Jack hasn't come round to offer his advice. You know what my husband is like.'

Mercedes smiled. She had admired Margot for having deflected rumours about her and Nathaniel Gilbrandsen throughout her marriage, but it must have come at a price. She knew Nate believed Margot should have absconded to Spain with him and refused her parents' demands, but she would never have taken such a risk. Nathaniel was always more suited to being a lover than a husband and Gervaise Trevelyan was just the opposite. In her view Margot had made the right choice. As Margot rose and Adam led her to the door, Mercedes said, 'Enjoy your dinner!'

Margot took her friend's hand and squeezed it and Mercedes swore under her breath, sighing with relief as they left. She loved Margot, but her friend knew how to stretch the elasticity of an overdue house-guest and this time she had surpassed herself.

★ ★ ★

Jack Trevelyan had been appraised of the situation in his parents' marriage prior to Adam's visit to their mother and while concerned, he found solace in his work. Alicia was away on modelling assignments and although he was missing her, he enjoyed the time to paint without the distractions she brought him. He had promised to look in on Laura, but had cried off due to work and having heard whispers that she had a lover, he didn't want to intrude. His lover's sister was entitled to her privacy and if she wanted to keep her lover a secret, it was Alexander's business not his. He had no wish to appear a possessive lover, but Alicia's work commitments meant more time apart. So he had begun to envy Paul Crowley having Jayne's company more frequently than he enjoyed with Alicia and Matthew's burgeoning romance with Nicola also left him feeling slightly neglected, but he remained determined to keep any feeling of resentment at arm's length.

So when Adam turned up with Margot at Gresse Street later after dinner, Jack was not in the mood for visitors.

'I wish you had called ahead. I was going out!'

Margot kissed her youngest on the cheek and stood back to admire the decor.

'I have hardly seen you since I have been in London and I wanted to see your flat.'

'To see where your money was spent,' Adam offered with a hint of sarcasm, to which Margot responded with another withering look.

Jack smiled.

'You have been busy with the exhibition, I suspect. Encouraging your students and placating father… I take it Nate Gilbrandsen has gone back to Spain?'

Margot pretended not to hear, but she exchanged a glance with Adam and then looked swiftly away.

'I like what you have done with the design. Very tasteful. Modest! I am impressed!'

'Money well spent then,' said Adam, expecting another withering look from Margot, who didn't disappoint.

Jack ran a hand through his hair, turning to face his mother.

'So why do I feel like I am missing something?'

'Like what?' demanded Margot sharply.

'A decision concerning your future with father? Our family?'

Margot pursed her lips, folding her arms in a defensive fashion.

'Has he been putting nonsense inside your head or is it Hugo's doing?

'Our future isn't an issue you have to be concerned with. We are as solid as we have ever been. Your father is in a sulk and Hugo is bearing the brunt, so I guess he is trying to deflect some of it. I asked your father to come to London for the exhibition when we were all together at Christmas. You heard me and his response. A flat refusal.

'I reissued my invitation after Nate had gone home and he offered another excuse about the demands of the estate. I have remained in London, primarily for my students' sake and Gervaise knows that. He just chose to make it about Nate, because he wanted to!'

Jack looked down, embarrassed, and Margot ran a gentle hand down his arm.

'You both need to understand that after all these years, I refuse to dance attendance around Gervaise's sulking. He has had no just cause to mistrust me and for him to still feel threatened by Nate Gilbrandsen after all this time is just foolish!'

Adam exchanged a warning look with Jack to say nothing more and if Margot noticed it, she gave no indication. The finality of her words however brooked no further discussion on a subject that she considered to be closed.

27

Laurence Naismith finally gave up on the pretence within literary circles that he had numerous deals tabled for what he considered his best novel in years, when in reality he only ever had one.

Despite St John's urging, he continued to hold out on signing the contract, trying Edgar Trentham's patience to its limit. His overtures to Gollancz never amounted to anything more than tacit interest at best and when Trentham took the decision to call the agent that Naismith had parted company with, just before Christmas, and word had got back to Naismith, he knew that the charade was over. He had to accept the revised offer from Trentham & Westmacott or be left with nothing. It wasn't even a fact that other literary agents wouldn't represent him, and the rumours began to circulate swiftly that he, on the basis of his past reputation, had convinced himself that there would be a clamour to represent *him*. He felt humiliated but tried valiantly to conceal it.

Edgar Trentham wasn't easily fooled. The disclaimer absolving the publisher of any blame for ensuing legal action hinted at by Gilbrandsen's solicitor was still a potential deal-breaker on which the house was not willing to budge.

Naismith knew who was behind that and he doubted

he could easily forgive. So when he arrived at a bistro in Bloomsbury and found Mercedes Campion sat between Edgar Trentham and Austin Westmacott, he bristled with indignation. Naismith was already late, when just before he walked in, Edgar consulted his pocket watch and frowning he turned to Mercedes.

'Why am I still bothering with this man? Does he not realise that he is not still the hot property he was before the war? He has no representation and he is only on the brink of getting a deal by trading on old friendships and past reputation!'

'There's also the fact that Pa told you to do the deal!' Austin said, and bowed his head as Edgar frowned at him, his anger rising.

Mercedes stifled a smile.

'I don't know why I have been included. He won't like seeing me here.'

'I don't care. I value your insight and so does Cedric. I understand your discomfort, but please stay. You know Naismith better than any of us and he was never one of my authors before the war. I have solid information that his overtures to Gollancz lasted the duration of one lunch… So there is no other offer. I also spoke to the agent he fired because they weren't sufficiently enthusiastic about praising the novel when he first submitted it. I fear he is in denial about just how good it is!'

As Naismith entered and was led to their table, Edgar gently touched the sleeve of Austin's jacket and said, 'I strongly suggest you leave most of the negotiations to me.'

Feeling chastised Austin blushed profusely, but still nodded silently as Naismith was shown his seat.

'You are half an hour late, Naismith!' Edgar said tersely.

'Yes and I apologise, St John offered me some pre-lunch courage at the club by way of a gin, so I got waylaid…'

Frowning again, Edgar summoned a waiter and then looking directly at Naismith he said, 'So having been buoyed up by Crowley are you ready to sign the contract and the disclaimer?'

Naismith coughed nervously. 'Is the disclaimer still needed, having done the revision you… asked for?'

'Yes,' said Edgar in a flat tone.

The waiter approached to take Naismith's lunch order and once he had left, Edgar handed Naismith a pen and pushed the contract under his nose. He half turned to Austin to check he wasn't inclined to intervene and compromise their position.

Naismith hesitated, recalling St John's advice in the taxi from Northumberland Avenue. 'Sign the contract,' he had urged in an uncompromising tone. He was being short-changed, he knew that, but the lack of a response from agents had left him bristling with indignation but with limited options, and he knew for certain that were it not for Cedric Westmacott, he wouldn't have the deal on the table now.

He snatched the pen from Edgar's hand and signed the contract and then with another cough of indignation he signed the disclaimer.

Tossing the pen on the table, he said, 'It amounts to theft, that's what this is. To think what the Naismith name has earned your house over the years, especially before the war, means that deal is an *insult*! To my reputation and my talent!'

Edgar shook his head sadly. Let Naismith rant all he liked. Other patrons were staring at him as he made a fool of himself. He had got a much better deal than he deserved and sadly his manuscript wasn't the masterpiece that he believed it was. This novel wouldn't amount to a *renaissance* in the literary career of Laurence Naismith and he had to reconcile himself to that reality.

He turned to Mercedes Campion who couldn't conceal her embarrassment. This was not the man that she had known for years and just for a nano-second she almost pitied him.

The waiter brought Naismith his wine and he drank half of it in a gulp.

Edgar Trentham shook his head sadly and rose to leave. He regretted inflicting Naismith on her and he feared she would incur the bulk of his wrath. He would always trust his partner Cedric's instincts, but if it had been solely down to him, he wouldn't have signed Naismith again.

The author had left them through his greed just after the war and then his reputation began to wane and his sales suffered accordingly.

Edgar feared his partner had taken a gamble out of old loyalty and that it was one they could come to regret.

'Not staying for lunch, Edgar?' Naismith eyed him suspiciously.

'Sadly not. I hope you enjoy yours. Ms Campion, are you staying or should I leave Austin to keep him company?'

'I can manage by myself. Thank you! I take it you are paying for this luncheon?'

Edgar smiled benignly. Typically, Naismith was showing his true colours!

'Of course. I shall instruct the maître d' to send us the bill. Good day to you!'

Edgar sashayed his way to the door, and turned to take one more look at the embittered sorry-for-himself-looking figure that was Laurence Naismith and he realised that unlike some of the authors he signed, he didn't really like the man and that he *never* had.

When Mercedes stood to leave, Naismith turned on her.

'Leaving so soon? Having offered your input on my future, I guess your work here is done? Although I understand that with your literary protégés you generally wait until the book is out, so you can bask in their reflected glory!'

He tried to force her back into her seat, but she broke free of his hold.

'What's left of your self-respect, Laurence? Washed it down in middle-ranking claret purchased on your friend's *largesse*. You are a *parasite*! Which I have known for a while, given how often you expect me to offer my villa *gratis*. You even got yourself into this legal imbroglio with Nate Gilbrandsen because you wanted warmer climes in which to write at *his* expense. Yes, he was indiscreet in his cups, but believe me, you are, and forgive the pun, the author of your own mess!'

Austin, feeling uneasy and looking bewildered, got up to leave and Naismith sneered at him. Mercedes threw her napkin down and summoned the waiter.

'I understand Mr Trentham has asked for the bill to be sent to him for settlement? Good, when he has finished his lunch, send him home in a cab. Because I have seen enough...'

Mercedes hesitated a moment and Naismith glared at her. 'You're still here?'

'Yes and I don't know whether St John broached this with you, but I suggested to him you take a trip, maybe start a new novel, just in case this one isn't the hit you have always claimed it would be. Rejuvenate your career, because if you remain in London, you will be a spent force... literary speaking at best. Or maybe just a lush, way past his best...'

Naismith stared at her. 'Where do you suggest? Your villa on Cap St Vincent?'

'No. You will never benefit from my generosity there again, but I will put in a good word with American publishers that don't yet know how you have burnt most of your bridges in London publishing circles...'

'Where exactly?'

'New York! Think about it! Ask St John for his advice, it could be the best move you ever make.'

Naismith bristled with indignation as Mercedes took her leave.

St John had mentioned New York as an option for him in passing, but he had neglected to mention Mercedes Campion's name and now he understood. Truth be told, as much as he resented having to admit it, she had a point. He had over-sold the merits of his novel because he felt he had no choice and while it did contain some of his best work in years, if it failed to capture the public's attention, he didn't know where he might turn next and he was damned if he would let the likes of Edgar Trentham and Mercedes Campion witness his decline.

28

In the weeks that followed the luncheon, during which Laurence Naismith vented his frustration at his publisher, Mercedes Campion managed to rise above the criticism he had levelled at her, to honour the promise she had made to assist him by virtue of using her contacts in the publishing circles of New York for his benefit.

Naismith chose to make it a much more difficult decision than it should have been, but one that he was strongly urged to take when he broached the subject with St John Crowley. This was despite Mercedes' sister, Jayne, encouraging her to cut her losses based on her deep misgivings that Naismith was actually worth all the effort, combined with her assertion that Mercy had done enough for him already for which he was only marginally grateful.

Mercedes had received similar advice from others but she was prepared to follow up with her promise, with the caveat that if Naismith squandered this opportunity, she would never help him again.

'Why bother, Mercy? The man is a *leech!*'

Mercedes nodded. 'Even so, will you ask your friend, Matthew Fullerton, if he will interview Naismith? It might do him some good journalistically.'

'I doubt Matthew needs it, but I will ask.'

Mercedes smiled. She had been contacted shortly after the luncheon meeting which had gone so badly awry by Edgar Trentham who acknowledged that although parts of the novel contained elements that were "vintage", Naismith was still short of his pre-war best, but Edgar was enthusiastic about the New York idea and tried to conceal any satisfaction he gained from the prospect of Naismith being out of the country for a while.

She also confronted St John Crowley in his Bloomsbury home.

He had heard second-hand about how Naismith had embarrassed himself at the luncheon, while Naismith had conceded to him that the quantity of alcohol he had consumed at their club might have been a contributing factor. Mercedes raised an eyebrow.

'Only might? His behaviour was disgraceful! I know he feels he has been offered a poor deal, but it was the *only* deal on the table and if he had tried harder to get representation elsewhere it might have made some difference. Naismith can be an oaf when he chooses. I don't see how you can defend that.'

'I don't seek to do so, Mercedes. You are *right*. He has been his own worst enemy for almost all the time that I have known him. I think the root of his anger is that he thinks his reputation should earn him more leverage within publishing circles… For what it's worth, I think New York is a great idea and I will do my best to encourage him to take it.'

St John didn't reveal that Jayne, allied with Paul, had taken him to task on the very subject as she was delighted at the prospect of Laurence Naismith going to America. 'Just a pity it's not one way…' she had remarked icily.

St John chose to ignore the comment as his cousins had decided to look for accommodation elsewhere for their second year at the Slade.

To Jayne's surprise, Matthew agreed to interview Naismith, citing that as he was still a sufficiently well-known name, it couldn't do him much harm. He doubted the *Daily Express* would take it, but Mercedes was confident that *Strand* magazine would, if she used some influence. St John, like Jayne, was curious as to why Mercedes appeared *so* keen to help Naismith when so many of his other friends had lost their patience.

'Does that include you, St John?'

'Well, given that I don't have your influence in literary circles, yes, but I admit that is a poor excuse. I know he was petrified at the idea of Edgar Trentham pulling out of the deal at the eleventh hour, but I tried to reassure him that as long as he had Cedric Westmacott on side, that was unlikely to happen. He has acknowledged that he was very rash in sacking his agent without first securing other representation, but that has always been Laurence's weakness. Rash decision-making and I just wonder if you are concerned he may ruin his chances in New York and cause you problems over there! I recognise now that suggesting a couple of gins at the club to give him some courage prior to luncheon with Edgar Trentham was a grave error on my part, but I don't want your reputation to suffer.'

'It won't!' said Mercedes firmly.

St John Crowley shrugged. Mercedes smiled benignly and said, 'New York provides Laurence the opportunity to redeem himself, to build a reputation in a country he doesn't already have one and maybe if he doesn't blow it, he can come home with his reputation as a novelist having grown stronger providing his work continues to flourish.

'I fear that by choosing to stay here, he will become more embittered and then anyone who can help him career-wise will lose all patience… Because aside from his writing, what *has* he got?'

St John looked glum, and nodding he said, 'Nothing. I see your point…'

'I am glad. Make sure that he does, as well.'

St John lit his cigar, offering Mercedes another martini, which she declined.

Drawing heavily on his cigar, he stretched out his legs and said, 'You are doing this for Margot Trevelyan's sake as well, aren't you? Or is it Gilbrandsen's reputation that you are seeking to protect?'

Mercedes bristled slightly, but if St John noticed the gesture, he let it pass.

'So you are not convinced that I could *just* be doing it for Naismith's sake?'

'Given the way he has behaved towards you recently, I would have to doubt it.' Mercedes feigned ignorance because she needed to be sure that St John wasn't fishing for information.

'If Nate hadn't been so generous with all that wine he was offering when he hosted Naismith last autumn none of this would have been necessary,' he remarked dryly. Mercedes made a tiny moue with her mouth. St John Crowley was renowned for his cunning, but she was damned if he would get any damaging information from her.

She lacked the faith that he was willing to show in their mutual friend, but he remained convinced that her efforts on Laurence Naismith's behalf were as honest as they were sound and that the person who stood to gain most from the proposed American trip was Naismith, but only if he saw it as an opportunity, or even as an adventure, and not as some kind of exile.

29

Deauville, France – May 1923

The start of the flat racing season had given Hayden Ballard a new interest on which to focus his attention and he embraced it with all the enthusiasm and fervour, albeit just as a spectator, as he had before the war. Sybil had never seen him so engaged in anything aside from his determination to make a full recovery, but she was still a little unnerved by the sudden changes in his mood.

She attributed some of it to the letters he was receiving from home, which he said were becoming more consistent in enquiring about his plans to return to Canada. She didn't know to what extent they were aware of his injuries, but he said they could fund the completion of his recovery over there. He had always been insistent that he would return only when he could walk unaided and he wasn't at that point yet.

There had been more frustration and he had snapped when she said that his family needed to give him more time.

'I am *needed* there!'

She was apprehensive about having him force the issue on her before she was ready to sever links with her life in Europe, however much she was committed to the new one he offered in Canada. For so long now Hayden had been the focus of her energies. His needs filled a void in her life, where before only the corrosive emptiness of her grief had dwelt. He had always wanted to appear worthy of asking for her hand in marriage, but what now for her if the call from home claimed precedence over that? He was no longer the wretched shell of a man that she had helped to nurse back to health and the psychiatrist, who had been assessing him, had said he was in much better shape physically than many of his other patients, but he was concerned there was still a mental block, discouraging him to see himself as he now was and not as he imagined himself to be, or as he remembered.

Hayden could not wait around in Europe for an eternity in the vain hope that he would return to his family in Canada looking exactly as when he had left them. Nor would they expect that.

'Is that what I am doing?' Hayden had demanded of his assessor, icily. 'As you seem to know my mind better than I?' The psychiatrist simply bowed his head, but when Sybil had placed a gentle hand on his arm, he had angrily pulled it away.

'I fear it might be, Lieutenant Ballard. Don't you want to go home? Your family are race-horse trainers, aren't they? I imagine you might want to get involved with the action again rather than just watching it from the sidelines…'

Hayden had looked at him with a faint smile, which could have been a sneer.

'You imagine quite a lot for a psychiatrist, don't you? I always thought cold, hard facts were your priority?'

The psychiatrist smiled back, benignly 'They are, but we would be very dry, unconvincing fellows if we didn't put a little colour into our assessments sometimes. I have come to look upon you as a very strong-willed man, Lieutenant Ballard. If you applied some of that strong will to reconciling yourself to the fact that you are now close to being as physically fit as you are going to be in the short term, then the rest of your recovery… or as much of it as you are going to achieve, will take longer, but it can be attained in the rolling hills of rural Ontario as easily as it can here…' He then squeezed Hayden's shoulder and took his leave. When he had gone, Sybil stood nervously behind him and he half turned to her.

'You have gone quiet. Do you think he is right? That I have developed a mental block about moving forward with recovery, with my life… our future?'

Sybil hesitated and he pushed for an answer. 'Well?' he said tersely.

'I think you want to go back looking as close to what you were when you left and that is what has held you back, why you haven't yet formally asked me to be your wife. The advantage I have is that I saw you at your very worst. As a VAD that was part of the job I signed up for, but your family have been spared that and it's something they and *you* should be thankful for…'

Hayden smiled, his demeanour softening because Sybil was right.

She had nursed him through the worst, and she deserved better from him now. He offered her his hand and she moved closer to take it, as he squeezed it hard, and she let her thoughts drift back to how on so many nights he would wake screaming as he relived his horror in the trenches at Vimy Ridge. Luckily she had often been on hand to soothe him back into the present and eventually he fell back to sleep, then the next day, he would ask if the nightmares would ever end and she didn't have the answer any more than his MO had.

The physical scars had healed with time, but the psychiatrist was evidently still concerned about the mental scars, for which he appeared to have developed a block. He no longer turned his face in revulsion from the mirror in his room, which at one stage, he had demanded be removed in a sudden fit of rage, but he had allowed doubts to linger about the strength of Sybil's commitment, not quite able to believe that he was the man she had fallen in love with, not the man he had been before the war, when he recalled the many girls in Ontario who had cautiously flirted with him, nervous and hopeful that he might ask them out or steal a kiss. He could believe it then, but Sybil Horton had fallen for him as he was now and he still couldn't always believe how lucky he was, especially when the photograph of her former fiancé, Miles Savernake, had fallen out of her purse. He had bent to retrieve it and just for a nano-second he had a slight sense of recognition, which had only been fleeting, yet remembering Miles with his boyish good looks and with his resemblance to the poet Rupert Brooke, had only served to strengthen his doubts that she could genuinely want to build a future with him. Yet she did and he sensed that she was growing tired of having to reassure him. Hayden knew he had to repay her faith and loyalty and he would, mindful of the psychiatrist's words that he was a lucky man.

He had always planned to marry Sybil in Canada, with all his extended family attending, aware that it was an ambition based on his ego, to show off his beautiful bride to the friends he had grown up around, but now he speculated on whether he should do as she had urged and formerly ask for her hand and marry here in Deauville. It would be a bold statement of intent for the future they had discussed at length, and his family would love her as he had come to. Her family had been shattered by tragedy when she had been left with just her brother, Ralph, and it was for him that she had come looking at the American Hospital in Paris when a *crass* administrative error had dangled the false hope that he might be alive, only for it to be snatched away. Hayden knew from the fragments of her history that she had shared with him, that two families had offered her and Ralph a sense of home, but that too had been cruelly snatched away, through Miles' death.

So it was entirely possible that what he was offering her in Canada was the lasting chance of belonging in a family unit that she'd had since childhood. He wouldn't mean that in the arrogant way that it sounded, but it was the truth nonetheless as Sybil had told him, that she couldn't exist on the periphery of the Savernakes world forever, regardless of how much they *loved* her and would want to include her. She needed to move on and he wanted that for her, with him at her side.

Holding her hand tighter, he urged her forward till she was standing at his side. Sybil smiled uneasily and he shook his head slightly.

'How do you manage to soothe my ill-tempered ways even when I least deserve it, as I haven't today?'

Sybil half shook her head and Hayden took a deep breath. 'I do want the future we have planned and yes, I have been hesitant in asking you to become my wife, as I wanted to be sure you hadn't changed your mind. Yet the psychiatrist is right. I have been delaying the time of departure. I want you to come home with me, but not as Sybil Horton, my fiancée, but as Mrs Horton-Ballard.'

Sybil smiled as he kissed her hand and she bent to kiss him ever so gently, as she nodded, smiling. He smiled back, thinking now that he had said it, how much he liked the sound of it, and he knew in that moment, that the time had come for him to *act* on that promise.

30

It came as no surprise to either Mercedes Campion or St John Crowley that Laurence Naismith indulged in one further fit of petulance prior to deciding that he would seize the opportunity that New York afforded him.

On the eve before he was to meet Matthew Fullerton for his interview for which Matthew had secured publication in *Strand* magazine, Naismith dined with St John at their club. He was being his most irksome self and although he had agreed to accompany him down to Southampton prior to passage aboard the *SS Aquitania*, St John found that he wasn't sorry to see his friend go, convinced as he was that the trip could be the remaking of his literary career; a kind of mid-life renaissance as a novelist that he was unlikely to enjoy if he remained at home.

St John leaned back and lit a cigarette.

'So in two days you will be off to New York. Sounds spectacular. I do envy you!'

Naismith grimaced. 'So go instead!' he said in a uncharacteristically flat tone.

'As the contacts Mercy Campion has established for you in New York are entirely literary, as an art critic I am not going to benefit. Besides, I thought you had resolved yourself to going.'

'I am being *punished*, St John! These contacts you speak of are good ones, but she is only trying to salve her conscience for having come down on Edgar Trentham's side. Were it not for Cedric's influence, I probably wouldn't have any deal. What good would her New York contacts be then?'

St John sighed heavily. 'I also think she has done her best to protect you from potential legal action that would have ruined you financially if you had lost. You knew that what Gilbrandsen said to you, when you were both in your cups, can never be proven beyond doubt, so I would be a little more gracious to Mercy Campion if I were you…'

Naismith averted his gaze and took a long sip of cognac, but St John was determined to press his point. 'Did you expect the publisher to put themselves at risk of being sued? I think it's significant that the only publisher who wanted to touch your book is Trentham & Westmacott and you had a connection to the senior partner. Your overture to Gollancz fell flat, didn't it?'

'Will you kindly keep your voice down? You know Edgar is a member here and I don't want word getting back to him about how my approach to another publishing house went… He has been smug enough as it is.'

'It is time you faced up to the fact that you acted rashly and you are fortunate to have a friend who is willing to go to the lengths that Mercy Campion has for you!'

'What if I were to make the kind of splash in New York that Mercedes thinks I could and one of the New York houses decide to publish the original text and be damned for it? I doubt any one of them will be overly concerned about what Margot Trevelyan can claim.'

St John drew heavily on his cigarette. He had to concede that Naismith had a point. There was some doubt that Naismith would secure a deal with an American publisher, despite Mercy's assistance, as he still hadn't secured new representation, but the Trevelyans' reach over there would be limited, but given that Laurence hadn't enjoyed even a moderate literary success in some years, he was going to New York as a virtual unknown so America could be the making of him literary speaking or serve to prove the point that his best days as a novelist were behind him. St John wished his friend well, despite his irksome tendencies, but he feared for him as well. As much as he knew the extent to which Laurence Naismith could be the architect of self-harm, he didn't deserve public humiliation and *he* didn't want to be the friend left to pick over the fragments of Naismith's ruined career.

31

'Damn the bloody man!' Jayne Campion winced as her sister Mercedes tossed her copy of *Strand* magazine across the lounge of her flat. She suppressed a smile as nothing that Laurence Naismith did surprised her, but she was aware that her elder sister had gone to strenuous lengths on his behalf, providing important contacts in America and at the very moment that he was heading to Southampton, the fallout from his interview with Matthew Fullerton, which the *Strand* would doubtless call a publishing coup was filtering into the public's conscience.

Mercedes turned to her sister.

'I thought Fullerton was someone to be trusted?'

Jayne nodded. 'As a friend in a social setting he is, but he is also a journalist and you know that a good story is what matters most to them. Naismith has provided one on a silver platter...'

Mercedes, still fuming with anger, lit a cigarette. She then began pacing anxiously. 'Wearing out the carpet isn't going to help solve this.'

'Don't be flippant, Jayne!' She raised her hands in apology. 'I'm sorry! Should I call Margot in case she hasn't seen the article? To forewarn her.'

Jayne shook her head. 'No, I advise you to stay out of it this time. Let Nathaniel Gilbrandsen clean up his own mess.

It was his fault for hosting Naismith and plying him with endless snifters of cognac and then he was as indiscreet in his cups as Naismith has been on the page. You know what I think of Naismith and I think you have been a saint, by putting up with him all these years. I think you are well rid of him and be thankful of the fact…'

Mercedes nodded, smiling wryly. She knew her sister had never taken to Naismith, even on the most casual basis, but she felt betrayed!

Margot would be horrified and she feared she would feel her friend's wrath because she was close and accessible and Gilbrandsen wasn't.

Despite her subtle hints while he was here, Mercedes had never managed to get Gilbrandsen to say whether he was happy with what he believed in his gut instinct to be true. She had heard his bluster about legal action, but whether he would have been content to stoke the speculation at Gervaise's expense, she could never be sure.

Jayne was right to lay most of the blame on Naismith; she knew that he was a law unto himself! Yet she couldn't rule out the possibility that what Gilbrandsen had described as a cognac-fuelled faux pas when Naismith was staying with him, hadn't been entirely accidental, because Nate had always felt Margot made a mistake by choosing Gervaise, regardless of the fact she would have been ostracised by her family. Reap as you sow and she knew Nate had sown many wild oats before he had taken Margot as his muse and afterwards.

She stood at the window as Jayne laid a reassuring hand on her arm and then took her leave. Mercedes smiled wryly as she took one long draw on her cigarette. It was irrational also to lay the blame on Matthew Fullerton. He had the making of a great journalist and he barely knew some of the people involved. No, this had Naismith's petty thirst for revenge all over it and he likely didn't care what damage his contribution to the article had done. Still seething inside, Mercedes could only hope Naismith made a sufficient success of his sojourn in New York and that he chose to stay longer, as she feared he may have just shot his last chance of a comeback at home!

★ ★ ★

Edgar Trentham was not in the mood to be placated. He knew from his queries to Mercedes, that Laurence Naismith was en route to New York and he arrived at St John Crowley's Bloomsbury townhouse, having first failed to find him at their club two nights in succession.

He had a book to publish which may yet fly off the shelves in the light of the *Strand* magazine article, or may yet become the vital piece of evidence in a case brought against his publishing house that had the potential to lead to financial ruin, despite having taken steps to mitigate that risk. He wanted answers.

'Can I offer you coffee, Edgar?'

St John was being infuriatingly sanguine. Was it possible that he hadn't read the article in the *Strand* magazine or that he hadn't yet heard from Mercedes or simply now that Naismith was en route he had ceased to be St John's problem and that was something to be grateful for?

Removing his hat, Edgar shook his head.

'So Naismith has left a trail of chaos in his wake as he boarded the liner for New York? Never mind the potential for slander against us, his publishers?'

St John held out his hand to offer Trentham a seat. Then he lit a cigarette. He didn't make a habit of receiving guests before eleven in the morning, but Trentham's incessant banging on his front door had left him with little option but to invite him in.

'If there is action against us I cannot proceed with the launch of Naismith's book. He does realise that? The first print run will have to be stored indefinitely and I cannot see any American publishers being that interested in Naismith if he can't guarantee release over here! Or was his desire for petulance overriding his common sense when he agreed to this article…'

'The interview *was* Mercy Campion's idea!'

'So you are blaming her? Even after all that she has done for Naismith.

'The contacts in New York are down to her. *I* brought her into the negotiations for Naismith's book. I told Cedric that we didn't dare touch it without a disclaimer and we took full advantage of Mercedes' friendship with the interested parties. Naismith should be grateful to her for saving his book from the slush pile and if you saw the wider picture, you would have advised him likewise, but I am guessing you are retreating hastily from the scene? Well, I don't entirely blame you, Crowley, but if we go down, we will take Naismith with us. Would he have you to fall back on then? How strong will your friendship be then, I wonder?'

St John sipped the coffee that his valet had discreetly brought him and then stubbed out his cigarette. He had let Edgar burn out his ire and then he smiled.

'Is that a threat, Edgar? It sounds suspiciously like one to me! Is it really in the interests of Margot Trevelyan to sue? I don't claim to know her as well as Mercedes does, but I would guess that a dignified silence might be her best option. We know Naismith is wildly self-indulgent. Does anyone take much notice for very long? This furore will lose its strength as far as I can see as long as the interested parties don't stoke it. With Naismith in New York, I see no potential for that. He did tell me that Cedric Westmacott authorised you to proceed to a deal, so have you got his take on the *Strand* article?'

Edgar blushed slightly before nodding as he had spoken to his senior partner and he had said the same as Crowley almost verbatim.

St John took the blush as an affirmative. Smiling he said, 'I am guessing he is more relaxed?'

Edgar breathed deeply. He invariably found Crowley an odd fish.

He was more of a friend to his brother, Charles, and he had known his younger brother, but Edgar understood that Crowley's principal passion was art, while aside from the business it was always politics that had motivated him.

'I don't know why people always assume that I will take responsibility for Naismith's lapses of judgement. Yes, he is a friend, but have you ever been expected to take some of Charles' errors upon your shoulders? And he is your flesh and blood. What about Mercedes? No, I didn't think so!'

Edgar rose tentatively. As far as Crowley was concerned the meeting was over and despite heeding Charles' advice on how to deal with him, Edgar had come away with little satisfaction. He had to concede that Crowley had a point. He wasn't involved in publishing like Mercedes was, so he had little motive to overreach himself on their behalf, or even on Naismith's. He would have to wait and hope that any threat of legal action was just bluster, unless he was inclined to take a trip to New York himself and to confront Naismith there! The idea was *unpalatable*!

He stood, retrieved his hat and half bowing at his host took his leave, and just missed St John's sneer of triumph.

32

Margot Trevelyan agreed tacitly with her husband that they would maintain a dignified silence if approached on the subject of Naismith's article in the *Strand*. It was however the only issue on which they could find common ground. While she blamed Naismith for what she perceived as spite on his behalf, Gervaise laid the blame at Gilbrandsen's door, for failing to accept what he couldn't possibly prove beyond doubt to be otherwise, especially as he claimed to have reconciled himself to that fact more than two decades before. Until he invited a struggling novelist into his home and saw an opportunity to use him as a conduit for his own ends. That, in Gervaise's eyes, was *unforgivable*. They both reacted with joy to the news that Sybil Horton had become engaged to the Canadian that she had told them about the previous December, with Gervaise saying it was long overdue that this Lieutenant Ballard finally realised how fortunate he was.

Margot reminded him gently to consider the Savernakes, who might not view the news so favourably as it represented a severing of the link with Sybil that was bound to reprise memories of their son, Miles.

A sentiment that Hugo agreed with. Gervaise was surprised as Margot had never struck him as the overly sentimental type.

'How do you mean exactly?' he had queried.

'Well, as long as Sybil remained unattached, she represented a link to Miles, but now that she has become engaged to this Hayden Ballard, it is a sign that she has moved on, as she must, but Alexander and Daphne will be reminded of what they have lost and the part that Sybil and Ralph played in their lives as they did in ours. Jack has told me how much Alicia still grieves for the brother she adored and that she sees Sybil as an integral part of the past she still likes to cling to.

'Don't forget how much we liked Miles when he came here to stay with us!'

Gervaise gave her a rueful look, then nodding he said, 'You can draft the telegram of congratulations to Sybil. You are better at that sort of thing than I am…'

Margot smiled. From the few occasions she had been with Daphne Savernake, she knew how the woman struggled to manage her grief whenever the anniversary of Miles' passing came around.

She dealt with it very differently from her husband and daughters, she knew that. It was a strained relationship as she admitted to having been jealous of Daphne Milford when she was sitting for Nathaniel as she saw her as a rival, until Alexander Savernake asked for her hand. Of course Nathaniel had ticked her off, telling her that she had nothing to be concerned about, until of course her parents had forged the understanding with Gervaise and she feared she had lost Nate forever, but meeting him again in London recently had confirmed it wouldn't have worked long-term with Nate as he wasn't the marrying kind. She liked to believe that he would have tried his best for her sake, but they could have come to resent each other or worse and she wouldn't have wanted that. In his own oblique way, Gervaise was trying to say that Sybil's engagement was a good outcome for the Savernakes as well. That letting go of the past was a crucial part of the healing process, that she too needed to jettison the rose-tinted memories she'd had as a youth, of which Nate was a part, and to accept that she had made the right choice in Gervaise Trevelyan.

She thought about the words she had reiterated to Adam, that she and Gervaise would be fine, they had an innate understanding, but suddenly she felt the need for reassurance.

'We will be OK, won't we?'

Gervaise smiled, put a hand on her shoulder and squeezed it.

'After all these years, I should bloody hope so!'

★ ★ ★

Chelcombe Place, Chelcombe Lacey – May 1923

Alexander Savernake took the news of Sybil Horton's engagement better than he had expected to, appreciating that Margot Trevelyan's telegram arrived ahead of the letter from France. Daphne stood behind him as he read it aloud and when his voice began to falter, she offered him her hand.

Sybil Horton's words only confirmed the affection they would always have for her, when she explained that committing herself to another man after Miles was never going to be easy, but that she wanted them to have no doubt that she had found with Hayden Ballard, a joy that she had never expected to feel again. Alexander looked at the framed photograph of the boyish-looking Miles in his uniform and he ran a shaking hand across the top of the frame and then biting hard on his bottom lip, he let the letter fall onto the desk and turned away, as Daphne picked it up and began reading aloud.

'To yourself… please.'

She nodded silently. 'The Trevelyans knew at the same time, so Alicia will know as well.'

Alexander nodded. 'She will have Jack to support her…'

Daphne folded the letter and placed it on the desk. She could see the stray tears in his eyes, although he tried to conceal them, just as she could feel them welling in hers, so she sighed heavily. Sybil owed them nothing. Miles had died knowing that she loved him and always would, but she couldn't be expected to live her life with affection only in abeyance, lived through the prism of memory of a youthful passion she had nourished and then lost. It was in many ways the final severing and her new life in Canada awaited her. Daphne would write on their behalf, telling her that she could go with their blessing, with the proviso that she was entirely happy with her choice.

She half turned to speak to Alexander and realised that she was alone, that he had gone stealthily, so that she couldn't hear him, but she knew where he was heading before she even saw him striding across the lawn. Sighing heavily she picked up the framed photograph of Miles, as ever youthful and smiling. Was it ever any surprise that Sybil Horton fell for him? She only hoped that Lieutenant Hayden Ballard measured up to what Sybil deserved, that he realised how lucky he was. As for Alexander, she had hoped that when this day came, as they knew it would, he could reconcile himself to the reality of it, but instead she feared that far from setting him free, saying farewell to their beloved would-be third daughter, Sybil, had served only to *expose* the deep well of his grief again.

33

London – June 1923

As the last scorching days of May slid effortlessly into June and the final weeks of term at the Slade School of Fine Art, tentative plans were made between Paul, Lynette and Jack about what they should do with the long summer break. Paul had stated boldly one evening that he would like to work in a flurry of activity, which he would like to do in warmer climes.

If this was intended as a hint to Jayne to encourage her elder sister to rent them her villa at Cap St Vincent, she remained tight-lipped on the subject, but Paul remained hopeful. Jayne had been worried about where their relationship was going recently and had voiced her fears to Lynette, as Jayne hoped she wasn't only ever going to be an artist's muse to Paul, as her sister had briefly been to Nathaniel Gilbrandsen in her youth. Lynette had responded with only mild reassurance, as she made it a policy never to interfere in her brother's romantic relationships, on the understanding that he wouldn't have cause to invest in hers.

Paul was surprised by a letter which arrived for him at the Slade as it was a commission to paint a portrait. He was given a time at an address that looked vaguely familiar and on arrival one scorching Wednesday afternoon, he was advised to set up in the main living area by his client who was in the bathroom. She emerged moments later, revealing herself as Laura Savernake, dressed in a silk kimono, much like the one that Jayne had worn to her sittings with him, which had left little to the imagination.

So Paul knew that like Jayne had been, Laura, Alicia's younger sister, was naked underneath. Swallowing hard, he said, 'This has to be a mistake!'

Laura smiled mischievously as she stepped out of black silk pumps and made her way to the chaise-longue.

'No mistake, you have proved that by accepting the invitation. I take it the fee I have offered is acceptable?'

'Yes, very generous, even so I cannot accept this commission!'

'Why?'

'Because you are Alicia's younger sister and I value her as a friend. Because I am not comfortable seeing you like that… under-dressed and I have no wish to incur the *wrath* of your father. I take it Alicia is entirely unaware that you have invited me here to paint you?'

Laura bit her bottom lip and smiled, ready to disrobe, but Paul averted his gaze.

'No, but only because she doesn't need to. You were not the only artist I wrote to at the Slade, but you are the one I want, because I know that I can trust you. I could hardly ask Jack…'

Paul gulped. He had made no preparation because he had no intention of staying, but he was intrigued by her motivation.

'So why do you want your portrait painted, especially like this? You hardly expect your father to hang it at Chelcombe Place?'

'You are asking a lot of questions, Paul. Did you have the same reservations when you painted Jayne? That portrait has done wonders for your reputation as an artist of great talent, so painting me like that could promote you further!'

'Or it will get me ostracised by my friends, along with your family and I don't find the prospect appealing.' He folded his arms and looked at her straight in the eye, adding, 'Besides which, you have swerved my previous question: who is it for?'

Laura moved on the chaise-longue and the kimono slipped, revealing her décolletage, and when Paul looked away, she laughed slightly. She could trust him she knew, his discretion wasn't in doubt and discretion was something that Antonio was ferocious about, given what he always referred to as his 'position' at the embassy. She was however growing tired of the subterfuge. She didn't want to be his secret lover. It was kind of tawdry, like she was someone to be ashamed of, but she also feared that she was already in too deeply, cared too much now for Antonio Viaz to be strong enough to demand more, to insist that he be seen with her in public and to stand strong, if he refused to comply or he just walked away.

She wanted this portrait as a gift for Antonio. As a token of her love and devotion to what they had, even if on the surface it amounted to precious little. One thing she could be certain of, however, was that Paul Crowley could be trusted to act like a gentleman with her. That is why he was here. Now she only had to convince him to accept the commission.

'OK, if that is the condition you have laid down, because I want this and to have you paint it, I will tell you. It is for my lover... Antonio Viaz!'

That Paul's expression didn't change impressed her, although he did raise an eyebrow.

'Who?'

'He was a guest at Jack's flat-warming last December. We have been seeing each other ever since. With total discretion, of course...'

Paul shook his head vigorously. He shoved his hands into his pockets and gazed at the floor. He was lost in thought for what seemed like an eternity.

'Is the portrait his idea? Are you being *coerced*?'

Laura shook her head. 'No, it's my idea. A surprise gift for him.'

She quirked an eyebrow and asked, 'So, will you take my commission or should I look... elsewhere?'

There was a hint of menace in her voice and he pointed at her.

'Don't try that. Just don't! I won't be blackmailed into accepting. This will be for private viewing only? It won't be exhibited anywhere? That is vital, Laura, if I am to put my name to the canvas.'

She smiled, raising her hands in mock surrender. 'OK! If that is your only condition, I can wear it... I guess Jayne wouldn't want to be outshone by your latest subject.' The mischief in her voice was obvious and Paul knew he had to lay some ground rules.

'You are not in competition with Jayne... For a start she is over twenty-one and you are not and I must be insane to even contemplate this, but I don't want you looking elsewhere and getting a stranger and being exploited in all kinds of ways. So I will give it some serious thought and make a decision.

'Not this afternoon though. I need more time to absorb this before I commit.'

Laura let her bottom lip drop, so that it looked as if she were sulking, although in truth her mood was pensive.

'OK, Paul, as you wish, but answer me this, please, if I were not Alicia's younger sister, or a total stranger to you, would there be any reticence on your part?'

Paul shook his head smiling and he turned to the window, shielding his eyes against the afternoon glare. 'I have to admit, Laura, that you are very subtle in coming to the point and in challenging my misconceptions about people's character. I clearly had you marked wrong. You know your father will go mad if he finds out about this and that *I* was involved...'

'That I have taken a lover, or that I am paying a friend of ours to paint me in the neo-classical style as a gift to the aforementioned lover, whose desire for discretion borders on the obsessive?'

Paul smiled again. 'All of the above I suspect. Is Alicia aware that you are seeing anyone?'

Laura shook her head. 'She spends most of her time at Gresse Street when she isn't flitting off to Paris. Which wasn't one of the conditions of me coming to London to live with her, so as far as our father is concerned, Alicia has every reason to want to keep my secret. I don't think she would begrudge me having a lover. The only person we all know who saw me chatting to Antonio at Jack's party was Matthew Fullerton and he seemed too interested in Nicola that night to come to any firm conclusions.

'There was another chap there who came with Antonio. Stretton, I think his last name was, very arrogant in that posh kind of manner… He was quite taken with me as well.'

Paul smiled wanly, nodding. 'You *were* popular that evening.'

'I need this to work, Paul. I *can't* lose Antonio. I won't!'

'So it's that serious between you?'

Laura nodded. 'It is for me…' Paul looked at her and the crestfallen look was all too evident and he knew the signs. Laura Savernake was smitten.

'Give me a couple of days. I will have a decision.'

Laura nodded without speaking and half turning she watched Paul leave her flat. He walked most of the way home, thinking how much he regretted even going to the address supplied. His curiosity had got the better of him and now he had a decision to make, but if he hadn't gone, it was obvious Laura would have looked elsewhere.

Her whole plan was flawed in his view, but she was *so* determined to press on and have her portrait done, that to protect her as Alicia's younger sister his decision was almost ready-made for him and he didn't appreciate being painted into such a corner. There was also much more that he would like to know about Antonio Viaz.

He knew enough second-hand gossip about "Kit" Stretton to know that it wasn't a reassuring connection to have to come to terms with, but the youngest son of the Earl of Broxbourne wasn't the issue here.

He would have to talk discreetly to Matthew Fullerton and on the basis of what their friend told him, he would make his decision. Whether Laura liked it or not, he wouldn't be compromised to satisfy her whim.

34

In the days that followed, Paul Crowley agonised over what his decision should be regarding Laura's commission, aware that if he approached the subject from an entirely objective point of view, he should accept and have no qualms about doing so, but it wasn't as simple as that. What scant fragments of information he had gleaned about the nature of her relationship with Antonio Viaz, from what she had been willing to share, concerned him deeply.

He feared Laura was subjecting herself to censure at best, in her bid to present her lover with a gift in the hope that she might hold on to him for longer and it filled him with unease. He couldn't take Jayne into his confidence, so his only option appeared to be Matthew Fullerton who, having seen Laura and Antonio Viaz together at Jack's party, might have greater insight, so he arranged to meet Fullerton one afternoon at a cafe on Coventry Street, close to the Trocadero.

They sat opposite each other in a secluded booth, and Paul slipped a sheet of paper with the name of Laura's lover on it, face down across to Matthew, who smiled at the intrigue being played out before him. He read the name and raised an eyebrow.

'I am taking an educated guess that the "X" in this equation is Laura Savernake?'

Paul tried to keep his expression neutral, but wasn't certain that he had succeeded and when Matthew smiled, he had his answer.

'Relax, Paul, you haven't betrayed any confidences. I did notice them chatting at length at Jack's party, but I wasn't aware how fixed they had become. I suppose I expected whatever spark there was would have fizzled out, but the fact that you are aware suggests otherwise. So how long have you known?'

'This week.'

'Really. In what respect?'

'She has offered me a commission to paint her portrait in the neo-classical style as a gift to him. So whatever spark you saw hasn't fizzled out. Not on Laura's part anyway.'

Matthew whistled through his teeth. 'For how much?'

'More than I expected her to have the means to offer and that I should feel comfortable about declining… What do you know of him? Viaz, I mean. I understand he came to the party with the youngest Stretton?'

'Not the most respected of company, but harmless enough.'

As a waitress brought their coffee, Matthew opened a cigarette case and offered it to Paul, who shook his head.

'So what do you have of any note on Viaz?'

Matthew shook his head. 'Without doing some digging, not much. That could be tricky, unless it's done with absolute discretion. I wasn't surprised to see the youngest Stretton at Jack's party – he seems to get invited on the flimsiest of associations, but Viaz is different. From what I saw, he was very guarded all evening and *crucially*, he left before your press arrived! I shall try to unearth what I can. Will your decision to accept the commission depend on what I discover?'

'Possibly. Although as she seems so determined to gift him this portrait, she might go to someone who doesn't know her and so won't feel obligated to be as trustworthy, and then Laura will have no reason not to tell Alicia that she came to me first if something did go awry.'

'So you are tempted on those grounds?'

Paul nodded.

'I see your dilemma…Of course, the most reliable source would be Adam Trevelyan as he exchanged nods with Viaz as he left, but I can see why that's not an option!'

'Indeed,' said Paul tersely.

Paul finished his coffee in a couple of gulps and half rose to shake Matthew's hand. 'I appreciate your discretion on this. Anything you can find out about Viaz will help in coming to an informed decision.'

Matthew pulled a face and Paul raised an eyebrow. 'What?'

'If what I find out is sufficiently bad, will you tell her?'

'If she needs to know to save herself from any harm. Absolutely!'

'She may not thank you for demeaning her lover in her eyes. If she is *so* invested in him as this commission suggests, you could turn out to be the bad guy!'

'That is a chance I will have to take! It is Alicia's sister we are talking about here. What other decision is there?'

Matthew nodded and rose as Paul took his leave, no closer to a firm decision than he had been when he had left the Savernake flat, two days before.

Deauville, France

Lieutenant Hayden Ballard was in much better spirits from the moment he resolved to ask Sybil Horton to become his wife and to return with him to Canada. Although there was no hint that she would decline his proposal, he was racked with nerves until the moment that she said yes. He had grown fearful that moving to Canada might have been a deal-breaker for her, as that was the crucial part of the plan for him and one that he wouldn't shy away from.

The psychiatrist, Dr Emile Rykhard, was pleasantly surprised to see him in such good spirits the next time he visited and Hayden explained that tentative plans had been made to book passage home, at which point, Hayden had reached for Sybil's hand, which he took with a squeeze and explained that he wouldn't be making the journey home alone, but as a newly married man. Sybil had smiled positively as Hayden spoke of picking up the reins of his life before the war at the family's racehorse training operation in rural Ontario. If Dr Rykhard was looking for any sign of hesitation, he didn't telegraph the fact and Sybil showed none or that she had any reservation, that this was the future *she* had chosen. This was no pretence, there was no hint of charade.

So Dr Rykhard shook Hayden's hand warmly and congratulated him and then he turned to Sybil. His gaze held hers and there wasn't a flicker of doubt. He left his patient that day believing he could call Lieutenant Ballard a successful case and he hadn't always been confident of such an outcome.

When a telegram arrived for Sybil, saying that Alicia Savernake having been told of her engagement was travelling home from her latest modelling assignment in Paris, via Deauville, Hayden became suddenly quiet, not sure whether he was ready yet to meet someone so significant in Sybil's past. A member of the family she had told him so much about, into which she would have married if fate had dealt her former fiancé a different hand. She tried to reassure him that there was nothing to be concerned about. He was the future she had committed herself to, but the Savernakes remained important to her, reminding him that they had welcomed her and Ralph into their home, when as orphaned adolescents they had nobody else to turn to.

'Absolutely nobody?'

'There was a sister of my father's, in Singapore I think, but nobody closer and if that aunt had been inclined to take us on she showed no sign to our parents' legal representatives. There were two options for us, an orphanage or the Savernakes. They took us on.

'Ralph was boarding at the same school as Miles and there was sufficient money to pay for another two terms at most. We were destitute! So while you have nothing to fear from the Savernakes, I have everything to be grateful to them for, and as such I *remain...*'

Sybil said the words as gently but as firmly as she could, but the intention to leave her fiancé in no doubt of the importance of the Savernakes to her was non-negotiable.

'It will be OK!' Sybil said and Hayden smiled, because he felt he had no alternative but to trust her. Ever since he had asked for her hand in marriage, he had felt grateful that she had said yes, but he was conscious that he had to move on from that if they were to enjoy a marriage of equals. He looked at her with a raised eyebrow and she smiled.

'Everything that I have told you about Miles' family should convince you there is nothing to be concerned about. They have been aware this day would come, ever since we lost him. That I would move on, find someone else to love. So when Alicia sees for herself how happy we are, how can it not?'

Hayden had demonstrated an amazing capacity for adapting to new situations so why he felt so threatened by the prospect of meeting Alicia, she didn't know. In quieter moments, she sometimes succumbed to the urge to draw comparisons between Miles and Hayden, but she couldn't totally succeed, because the contrast was too great. There was boyish, flamboyant Miles, forever fixed in her mind as eternally youthful, and the quiet, determined Hayden, who had been gifted the opportunity to recover against the most enormous odds and had needed all that determination to overcome as he had.

There was a short rap on the door and with an encouraging nod from Hayden, Sybil went to open it. She had warned Alicia not to be alarmed by Hayden's facial scars as he tended to be piqued by those who reacted adversely on first sight and as the scars were fading now, she didn't want Alicia to be shocked. As Sybil welcomed her in, Hayden stood to greet her with the aid of his stick. His leg wobbled slightly, but his hand remained steady as they shook. Alicia took a deep breath, marshalling herself not to react on first sight of him.

She took the seat he offered and smiled wanly. Sybil stood behind them nervously. It was as important to her that Miles' family liked Hayden as it was that he understood the vital role they had played in her life. Meeting the Ballards would also be a test for her and so she understood the hesitance on Hayden's part, but for Alicia it represented a significant breaking of a link with the past, seeing her moving on, however happy they were.

Hayden laughed mirthlessly and said, 'I must be quite a sight if you are lost for words.'

Alicia bowed her head blushing, fearful that she had done the one thing that Sybil had urged her against and reacted adversely to Hayden's injuries which were not as bad as she had feared.

Alicia shook her head. 'I didn't mean to make you feel uncomfortable, Lieutenant Ballard... I *am* sorry! I shouldn't have come.'

Alicia stood to leave and then she felt Hayden's hand on her arm. He smiled and it was a smile that started in his eyes. Gentle and reassuring.

'Well, I will feel uncomfortable if you persist in addressing me as Lieutenant Ballard. It's Hayden, please.' He indicated the seat she had just vacated and with an encouraging nod from Sybil, Alicia sat down again.

'I have been informed that your family took Sybil and her brother, Ralph, into their home and treated them as family. That this happened before she and your brother fell in love and were then so cruelly parted by the ravages of that bloody war;

that perhaps I wouldn't have the confident, beautiful fiancée that I have been so fortunate to come to know, were it not for the kindness your family showered upon them when they had needed it most?'

Sybil turned her head, fighting back tears that she never expected to shed and Alicia similarly overcome, bit her bottom lip and nodded.

Hayden took her hand in both of his and held it there. 'Then I thank you on their behalf, because meeting Sybil Horton and convincing her to share my life has been my greatest privilege.'

Hayden gave Alicia's hand one last squeeze and then smiled encouragingly as she let go, gently sipping the cognac that Sybil had poured for her. Alicia had come prepared to say a last farewell to Sybil, not sure of what to expect from meeting the man that she had decided to share her life with, but Hayden hadn't just surprised her, he had laid any fears to rest that Sybil would be looked after, and *loved* as Miles would have loved her and that on the behalf of her family, it was time to say goodbye.

Alicia finished her cognac in several small gulps, smiling at Sybil and then at Hayden. When it was time for her to leave, Sybil followed her to the door.

'I am sorry if I made him feel uncomfortable to begin with… I am glad that I came, to have had the opportunity to meet Hayden. To say farewell and to wish you all the happiness, *because* we do.'

'I knew that I was falling for Miles, long before he showed his interest in me. I guess you knew it too. I dreamt of what it would be like, walking up the aisle at Chelcombe Lacey Church to meet him, with you and Laura behind me as my bridesmaids…' She paused, took a deep breath and continued, '… but it wasn't meant to be, but Hayden is right to say that it is thanks to your family and the Trevelyans that I am the person I am today, ready to take on the challenge ahead of me, in a new country, by giving us the succour and the love, in your homes, and for that I will always be grateful.'

Alicia bit hard on her quivering bottom lip and hugged Sybil to quell the flow of tears and when they parted she went to leave quickly, but Sybil held her hand and then kissed her on both cheeks.

'We will always be sisters, Alicia. Where it counts...' she paused and placed her hand on her heart, '...in here.'

Alicia did leave then and Sybil watched her go, climb into the back of the taxi and it drove away, without its passenger looking back once.

Sybil came back into the room where Hayden was sat and he offered her his hand.

'Thank you,' she said.

He pleated his eyebrows and said, 'For what?'

Sybil smiled. 'Just thank you...'

35

Paul Crowley came to a decision very swiftly that, despite his initial reluctance, he *was* going to accept Laura Savernake's commission to paint her portrait. Firstly out of respect for his friend Alicia, and because he could paint her in a tasteful manner, not entirely in the style that she had asked for, but which would allow her to emerge with her self-respect intact. Matthew was taking his time in getting some background into her Spanish diplomat lover, while he was being very coy with Jayne, saying only that he had received a paid commission and leaving it thus, so she remained curious.

'As long as she doesn't outshine me,' Jayne said as a throwaway comment, which had been a curious response as Paul had used considerable deftness of touch in persuading Jayne to sit for him, given her initial reluctance, however as her portrait had become a much acclaimed piece of art, she had been happy to bask in its reflective glory. The kind of portrait that Laura wanted, however, was entirely different. She wanted to provoke a reaction in Antonio Viaz, but Paul was concerned it might not go as she planned.

He was concerned for her that the gift she had planned could precipitate the very outcome she feared most, the abrupt end of her relationship with Viaz.

At the next meeting at which he told her he was accepting her commission, he had asked what prompted the idea, what she thought it would do for their relationship and Laura said she wanted it to be more transparent, but Antonio was insisting that discretion remained paramount. It led Paul to think that Viaz might be engaged to another woman or worse, already married. He kept these thoughts to himself as Laura said she had told him who her lover was because she felt she could trust him with the news, so he hoped now that Matthew's queries didn't arouse suspicion.

When Matthew sent a telegram to meet at the same venue on Coventry Street, Paul was nervous, as his worst fears were confirmed and his expression turned grim.

'Can't you warn her gently?'

'I doubt she would listen. She is already too deeply invested.'

Matthew nodded, exhaling heavily on a cigarette, his expression equally sad.

'He wouldn't marry her. His choice has been made for him, mapped out since his adolescence and I have been led to believe that her family is better connected than his. Career-wise, he has always been very focused thus his obsession with absolute discretion and worse, his time at the London Embassy is limited. He will return to Madrid in due course, marry and await his next assignment, which will likely include a promotion.'

Paul bowed his head. 'So Laura is *just* an amusement to him. A passing dalliance?'

'We feared as much. My source has confirmed it.'

'Your source is reliable; this won't get back to Viaz?'

Matthew shook his head. 'What about the portrait? Will you do it?'

'Yes, out of loyalty to Alicia, because I don't want Laura going to some sleazy stranger who will do what she thinks she wants because she is in love and then she will spend ages regretting it. I will only take a portion of what she is offering as well.'

'It would have been better had they not met at Jack's party, or that I had chance to warn her… about Stretton at least.'

Paul shook his head slowly. 'She told me she had the measure of Stretton, so I doubt that would have held any sway. You recognised Viaz, so can you blame a girl like Laura falling for him?'

Matthew stubbed out his cigarette and shook his head.

'Any plans for tonight?'

Paul nodded. 'St John has invited me and Lynette for dinner. She has convinced herself he is going to make some big announcement, but from where she gets such an idea, I can't imagine. He is in something of a malaise, so maybe a holiday is on the cards. Right now my thoughts are on Laura. She doesn't know that I have told you, but I didn't want the burden of being the only one to know. I do appreciate this.'

Matthew shook the hand Paul offered and took his leave.

★ ★ ★

The Crowley Townhouse, Bloomsbury – Same Evening

St John Crowley had been trying to decide how he might broach the subject of his forthcoming trip for days. He had sounded out Mercedes Campion about it, urging absolute discretion, given her sister's relationship with Paul. He realised Lynette had convinced herself there was something behind the dinner invitation, but he had left her to speculate all she liked. He had asked Mercedes directly whether she thought a working trip to America might benefit him as much as it appeared to have with Laurence Naismith and she was thrown. St John sipped the lunchtime martini she had mixed for him, smiling at her shocked face over the rim of his glass.

'I don't know. What has brought this idea to you?'

St John shrugged. 'I am stagnating here, that's for sure. I am rarely on the guest list for the important artistic soirées as I used to be. When did you last turn up at an event and see me there?

'You can't recall and there's the problem. I don't host as many so I think those who still have influence with new artistic talent have possibly leapt to the conclusion I have become bored with it all.

'Which I haven't but I need to prove myself and I wondered if you thought New York or any city out west might do for me in artistic circles what New York, largely thanks to you, has done for Naismith.'

Mercedes reached for the lapis lazuli box on her coffee table and retrieved a cigarette, which she lit swiftly. She had been caught on the hop and she knew St John liked to shock as much as she hated being his victim.

'Aside from the fact that I advised him to go for his own sake, to get him out of a fix, I can't see that you need the boost. Won't a holiday do the trick? Reinvigorate you?'

St John shook his head. 'It's fresh motivation I need. I am strongly inclined to go, but I appreciate your perspective.'

Mercedes shrugged. 'So do it!'

St John was still reflecting on his meeting with Mercedes later, as Lynette and Paul sat opposite each other at dinner, as their cousin drained his glass.

'St John, what is it, this mystery that you are peddling which is the motivation for tonight's invitation?' St John smiled benignly and Lynette frowned. 'You're not seriously ill, are you?'

St John laid a calming hand on her arm, as Paul draining his wine glass, lit a cigarette.

'I wanted to catch up with both of you as there is a plan

fermenting in my mind to take a trip to America, much as Naismith has done, in the hope it will revive my career. Someone who claims to be an important influencer of artistic talent has to be able to claim some influence and I have lost mine, so I need to regain it. It is my view that in the eyes of London's artistic press, I have become jaded, perhaps bored by the array of talent before me to promote, critique, whatever it is I am meant to do. That doesn't include you, Paul, because they would expect me to be biased in your favour and would factor that in, but you have proved you don't require my expertise and have flourished accordingly. Mercedes suggested I try Europe, but that doesn't sound like much of an adventure. I need a fresh impetus and America provides it!'

'Are you going because of Naismith?' asked Lynette, her scorn evident.

'No, Lynette. I am going for me! Call it selfish indulgence if you like, because that is what it amounts to. You can have the run of the house until term finishes and then you have arrangements made for your second year at the Slade, so I feel no obligation to anyone!'

Paul patted his cousin on the shoulder, and smiling, he said, 'Good for you, St John!'

'Why?' said Lynette struggling not to make her question sound like an interrogation.

'Because contrary to what Dr Johnson once claimed about London, I am tired of the old haunts. Artistic soirées in Fitzrovia that I don't get invited to any more. Long lunches at the club; they are just not as enticing as they used to be! I need to create a splash, discover a new artistic talent, just waiting for the right kind of patronage so the critics can claim the old St John Crowley is back to his scintillating best!'

St John raised his wine glass in a toast and Lynette and Paul joined him. Her brow was still pleated in a frown, but she was sufficiently placated that it wasn't about Naismith. Yet unlike her brother, she felt a little abandoned, as if another link to the past was loosening its thread, albeit temporarily.

'You will be coming back?'

'Of course, in time. Six months, maybe. A year at most. It will fly by… You will hardly notice me gone.'

'As if that is likely. When do you go?'

St John hesitated and then took a deep breath. 'I sail in six days. For New York!'

'So soon! So you have been planning this for a while?' asked Lynette.

St John shook his head.

'I only decided for myself today, after a lunchtime martini with Mercedes.

She is the only person aside from you two that I have told. As for the speed in which I have acted, I didn't want to be talked out of it, once I had decided, by either of you, or more significantly myself, because that would be the easy option. The lazy one and career-wise, I don't think I can afford to be self-indulgent. As you know, finance isn't an issue for me and this house is paid for. I have to go to see if firstly I can still pick out an artist of talent and then be sufficiently *motivated* to make them a star…'

Paul smiled, shaking his head at the breathtaking swiftness of it all.

He had never expected his cousin to have the capacity or the will to surprise him *so* startlingly.

Lynette was less enthusiastic and was convinced there was more to it. St John exhaled heavily on his cigar, hugely satisfied with his evening's work. After he had left Mercedes' flat and called at the Cunard shipping office and booked his passage, telling the two cousins who were the only relatives who really mattered to him, was always going to be the hardest task. Convincing Lynette that he wasn't seriously ill was an obstacle he hadn't been expecting, but he believed that he had put that concern to rest and now he was convinced it was the best decision he had made in years. There was no turning back and those he knew in the artistic world, who thought that St John Crowley had lost his touch, could think again. Like a phoenix from the ashes he *would* rise again.

36

Late June 1923

When news of St John Crowley's decision to leave London on an indefinite trip filtered through to his friends, acquaintances and professional associates it caused a considerable stir, not least because it was so sudden. There were those who had known him for years, who chose to see it as an act of desperation, whilst others claimed to have noticed the professional lethargy that he now freely admitted to.

Despite his cousins' surprise at the urgency of his departure, he knew that if prolonged, he would likely delay, or worse change his mind.

It was imperative he did this now, or he probably never would. Paul was largely supportive of his cousin's decision even though he was acting rashly and that he would likely return within weeks, but Lynette felt differently. She was convinced the malaise under which St John was existing was deep-rooted and she feared they may not see him again for months, maybe even years. St John had arranged for the Bloomsbury townhouse to be let once the term at the Slade finished and his cousins left for the French Rivera as Mercedes had finally agreed to let them rent her villa on Cap St Vincent for July and August.

Jack and Alicia had confirmed they would be coming and they were trying to persuade Matthew Fullerton to come as well, and that invitation at Paul's insistence had to include Nicola.

For Paul, the final weeks threw him into a flux, with St John's departure coming at the time he began seriously working on Laura's portrait, a commission which was financially welcome, yet still filled him with unease. He hardened in his determination that he wasn't going to paint her exactly as she wanted, because he firmly believed she would regret it afterwards and everything that he had been led to believe about her lover, Viaz, told him the lifetime of their affair was finite, but the legacy of the portrait that *she* had wanted wouldn't be. There was also the chance that if the Spanish diplomat was as conservatively minded as Matthew had suggested, the choice of subject would come as a shock.

Nicola meanwhile was still hesitant about joining them for the summer and Matthew's efforts to convince her were failing to have effect. Lynette was dismissive, saying she should be left to her own devices, but Paul managed to convince Nicola on a Friday afternoon, as she was preparing to leave for her family home near Bagshot.

Her cousin Martin was joining them which meant it would be a tense weekend. He had recently secured a tedious desk job at the War Office that was in his words only just bearable, but as Nicola's father had told him, with little family money spare, and the Civil Service role for which the pay could be described as adequate at best, he might want to revise the idea of writing his war-time memoirs. Nicola told him it was an idea worth thinking about and that she would solicit Matthew to assist him should he decide to go ahead, and that he should consider selling the portrait she had done of him, but he firmly shook his head.

'No, I shall treasure that.'

'At least until I am famous and that will hike up the price…'
She said it with a twinkle in her eyes, but Martin was glad to
see her more confident in her demeanour and believing in the
artistic gift that she possessed.

The Savernake Flat – June

Arranging a time for Laura to sit for him was proving the
trickiest aspect of fulfilling her commission and it caused Paul
considerable frustration in the last weeks at the Slade. He
didn't want to arouse suspicion by skipping classes and as Laura
demanded total discretion, she had to check and then confirm
Alicia's schedule of modelling assignments before any sitting
was arranged. During one such session she felt the need to
convince him that Antonio's affection was as genuine as hers
and she grew quite defensive on the subject, which led Paul to
believe she was having to convince *herself* as much as him.

When she asked for a preview of the work in progress, he
refused flatly, saying it was his policy never to show a subject
the work until it was complete. That it was non-negotiable as
far as he was concerned and when pushed he did say Jayne had
seen hers before the unveiling at Jack's party, but only once and
after it was complete.

'So you expect me to see mine the same time as Antonio
does?'

'If a prior showing can't be arranged, yes, but I usually
schedule it otherwise. You are confident that he will appreciate
this gift, in the style you are being portrayed?'

Laura, shrugging out of her kimono, nodded, biting on her
bottom lip as she took her place on the chaise-longue. Paul was
nervous as well, as he wasn't depicting her exactly in the neo-
classical style, but he remained certain that although initially

annoyed she would come to see it was the right choice on his part. Matthew Fullerton's insight about Viaz worried him as he doubted the Spanish diplomat would happily accept the gift in any guise. As Matthew alluded, Viaz was biding his time with Laura, having fun from his dalliance with her while he was in London, but Paul feared that once he was back home in Spain, Laura would be swiftly forgotten by Viaz and her self-confidence as a desirable young woman would be crushed.

The very least he could do, in defiance of her wishes now, was to leave her self-respect intact and hope she would thank him, given time.

'I hate his obsession with secrecy. Surely a diplomat is entitled to a private life. I have lost count of the occasions we have arranged a rendezvous, only for him to phone to say he couldn't come or to just not turn up. How many receptions can one embassy have?'

Paul smiled, shrugging his shoulders. 'Seems strange that you a single woman and him with no commitments can't be open about their relationship. Has he ever taken you out to dinner?'

Laura shook her head. 'That would never happen. He laid out the rules the first time we met again after Jack's party. I almost told him to go there and then, but I guess I must have liked the idea of being a "mystery woman" as I lack the courage, but I have to admit it is beginning to wear thin.'

'So the portrait as a gift is supposed to what?'

'Show him what he has and that many men in his position would value it and treat me with respect rather than just as a guilty pleasure…'

'If it doesn't?' He kept his tone neutral.

Laura shrugged. 'Then my gamble will have failed…' She sighed heavily and then added, 'To be frank, I am not even considering that as an option. This has to work, Paul, so please make me your masterpiece; your career-defining work!'

Paul smiled benignly, his focus on the canvas, so she couldn't misread anything into his expression.

'No pressure then…' he commented lightly.

★ ★ ★

Two days prior to his departure, St John Crowley had luncheon with Charles and Edgar Trentham at their club. It was a rare trip to London for Charles, and he felt out of place, while for St John, gazing around he realised the club looked as jaded as he felt. Where once before the war it had buzzed, now an uneasy quiet fell, like the fog of cigar smoke over the whole place and he realised suddenly just how much he was looking forward to going away.

'You can tell Naismith that his book's publication is on schedule.'

St John forced a smile. 'If I see him I shall but can't you wire him the information? The first conclusion that my young cousins leapt to was that I am going to New York because I was missing Naismith…'

'As if that could be the case,' said Edgar dryly.

'Exactly.'

'So why are you going?' asked Charles bluntly.

'To discover what America has to offer, from an artistic point of view. To see if I can spot real talent and promote it with my contacts over here, whilst also establishing myself as a patron/critic over there.'

'Tricky challenge,' said Charles, swirling his brandy snifter gently.

'I don't know but I am relishing the challenge.'

'Good for you!' said Edgar.

'What are your long-term plans?' asked St John.

Ignoring Charles' sneer of derision, he said, 'Unless the Liberals make it back into Government, I shall continue as a publisher and be happy to do so. With Cedric no more than a name on the brass-plate, I think his son, Austin, still needs a guiding hand.'

'Naismith told me he is as skittish as a young colt!' exclaimed St John.

'That is because Naismith can be a bully when it suits him. He tried to bully Austin, but it didn't work with me!'

St John realising he was on shaky ground paused to draw heavily on his cigar.

'So what will constitute success for you in America, Crowley? Hope to unearth a new star of the canvas like your cousin, or will you bide your time and then try to come back unnoticed and pick up as you left?'

Edgar stared at his brother with a withering look. 'Ever the ruthlessly direct?'

'I see no point in prevarication. Crowley is confident that he can make a splash in the American art world and I am curious as to how long he is going to give it before coming home and hoping that he hasn't been missed too much. You did at least keep your hand in when you were part of the Asquith Government, and you weren't divided by an ocean…!'

Edgar turned on his brother, but fearing an embarrassing scene, St John sought to placate him. 'It's OK, Edgar, Charles' query is quite valid and I would say a renewed sense of purpose is my primary aim.

'I feel listless in London now. I lack the motivation to go out and seek the talent like I once did. If I was overlooked for an artistic soirée, just a couple of years ago I would put the word out to demand *why*… Now when I am not invited I accept it with a shrug.

'Take the retrospective exhibition that Mercy Campion curated for Gilbrandsen! I was included for just one event, and no, I am not Gilbrandsen's biggest fan, but I would have demanded to go and once there I would have made my point…'

He shrugged, continuing, 'Now I think, so what? I need to get out there. Demand to be heard and *read*.'

Edgar nodded, as he understood what was driving St John's decision.

An aversion to being overlooked. The great enemy that was boredom.

Charles shrugged, indolently. 'Well, I wish you luck, Crowley.'

What he left unsaid was more telling though, because St John knew him too well. Charles Trentham believed that he was going to need it. For him though remaining here and wondering "what if" could be his greatest omission!

37

As the last days of June faded into July, summer became more sultry with a heat wave that provided a foretaste of what they could expect on the Riviera. The academic year at the Slade School of Fine Art wound down to its conclusion and plans were made for the following year. Nicola Fearns decided after much urging from her cousin Martin, backed up by Matthew and Paul, that she would be coming back for her second year. A decision that Lynette suggested was always likely and with some derision she dismissed the accompanying drama with a sneer. Paul couldn't understand why his sister was still *so* dismissive of Nicola and didn't attempt to get to know her as he had. She also had a few young blades paying her some attention, one of whom was "Kit" Stretton, whose name raised a few eyebrows, but was met with cold indifference by Paul.

Jack Trevelyan, like Paul, was planning to use the time in Cap St Vincent to do "a serious amount of painting", as he described it, and to spending more time with Alicia, who had returned from her last assignment in Paris, deeply affected by the meeting with Sybil as it was, as she described it, a significant shift from the past.

'Sybil is moving on with her life, as she should, so we must move on with ours…'

The lump that had lodged in her throat as she spoke, however, was significant to Jack as saying it wasn't as easy to come to terms with as Alicia appeared to be suggesting. They had been lying in bed, having just made love and Alicia had said that Hayden Ballard was a kind man, decent and that she had no doubts that he loved Sybil, but he wasn't Miles and that was the point. Until recently Chelcombe Place was still a home from home for Sybil. Somewhere she could go back to and gain comfort from just *being* should she need it, or derive strength if she was struggling as she had been the previous Christmas.

Jack had run his fingers down Alicia's arm, as she cushioned her head against his chest. Although he would never say it aloud, he felt that Sybil's future in Canada could be a good thing for Alicia, forcing her to look ever more forward, while still conscious of her brother's memory and what he had represented to her.

His sister-in-law, Caroline, had been equally saddened by the news of Sybil's decision to live in a new country, until Hugo had made her see that it was the right decision to help Sybil cope with all that *she* had lost and to begin anew.

Alicia had gone slightly stiff within his embrace and as she turned round to face him, Jack had seen the tears welling. Stroking her hair gently, he wiped her tears away with his thumb pad and then he kissed her ever so gently on the forehead.

For Paul, the final days of June had been hot, hectic and *demanding*.

He had finished painting Laura's portrait and had delivered it to the flat the following afternoon. He was in a pensive mood, as he still didn't know how she would react to the fact he hadn't painted her entirely in the neo-classical style as she had wanted. He had decided he would not take the remainder of the fee, but that he had no regrets in choosing to spare her dignity, even if she wasn't happy now.

'I think you will come to value my discretion on your behalf. Maybe not now, but at some point in the future.'

'How, Paul? When the portrait is a gift for my lover and only he will ever see it…'

'Are you sure? Can you seriously trust this man *so* explicitly? That your generous gift won't become the subject of embassy gossip? Laura, he has nothing to lose, it's you that has everything!'

He pleaded with her with open arms, but she had remained rigid.

He folded his arms. 'If you don't like it, I can take it away, pay you back what you gave me…'

'It's not about the money, Paul…' Her tone was curt.

Paul nodded. 'No, but I would have paid it back anyway, because it's about your self-respect, Laura, and what it would do for Alicia and your parents. You may have invested a lot of trust in Antonio Viaz and that's fine, but would you trust "Kit" Stretton so avidly? What if he were a guest of Antonio's and he saw the portrait, hanging in your lover's bedroom. Would he be so honourable and discreet?'

For a moment Paul thought his words had struck a chord in Laura, but the moment was gone and it had appeared transient at best.

With her arms folded in a defensive pose, she half turned and murmured, 'You have done enough damage from my point of view, so I think you should leave. You know the saddest part is, I came to you because I thought I could trust you! I could have given this commission to a total stranger…'

'Yes, you could and they may have painted you in the neo-classical style and charged you double what I was willing to take and it still wouldn't have guaranteed you the reaction you want from your lover. So I hope for your sake, Laura, that when you show this to Viaz you are not too disappointed by his reaction.'

Paul half bowed and took his leave.

Laura Savernake half turned to look at the portrait and a half-sob broke free. Sadly Paul was right, because there was so much she didn't know about Antonio Viaz, because all she had was what he had chosen to reveal. Everything about their relationship was conducted on his terms and in the beginning, in the cold, dark days of winter, the intrigue and the secrecy had been part of the excitement along with the amazing sex, because he was an accomplished lover. She had never asked how he was so good at giving pleasure in bed, but she had assumed it came from visiting brothels, but what if she were just one of many current paramours from a long list of exes? She had considered approaching "Kit" Stretton to ask him for details about Antonio, but she knew that word would get back to Antonio as "Kit" couldn't be trusted and she wasn't even sure that he would tell her what she wanted to know about his friend. So, however much it galled her, Paul was right. She could bide her time about gifting him the portrait, but at some time she would want a reaction from him and she needed to know it would be the one that she craved and not as Paul had so cruelly predicted.

She lifted the portrait and replacing the cover, stored it in her wardrobe. Alicia was so rarely here now that she had no fears it would be discovered before she had a chance to show it to Antonio.

Her fiery-tempered but equally charming lover. In the six months they had been together, she had offered herself to him completely and freely, but had fallen short in what he offered of himself to her.

She didn't think she could ever get as close to Antonio as she would have wished as he had shown no inclination to let her in.

So she feared that ultimately their relationship was built on mutual sexual attraction only and thus was sadly doomed.

38

Antonio Viaz gazed at the portrait of Laura again, with a critical eye, shaking his head slowly. He remained tight-lipped, but Laura didn't need to hear him say that he didn't like her gift, because she could tell from his demeanour. All the fears that Paul had shared with her during the hours she had sat for him, were being realised. This was the man she believed herself in love with, yet now he seemed like a stranger, only considerably less charming than he had been on the night they met. If this provided him with the motivation to end their relationship, would her gesture have been worth it? Finally he half turned to her and Laura could see the anger glistening in his deep brown eyes.

'Who painted this?'

'Paul Crowley. The artist who unveiled his portrait at the party, hosted by Jack Trevelyan, on the night we met.'

Laura wanted to fill the silence with more conversation, but felt it was wise to remain silent. Finally she said, 'You said you were impressed by that portrait.'

'That was an entirely different situation. You tell me that you are presenting it to me as a gift, so where am I supposed to

251

hang it? My bedroom wall, or in the main salon of my parents' home in Seville? Where exactly is the most appropriate place for such an ugly, invidious work of art?'

He turned on her angrily, dropping the framed canvas onto her chaise-longue with sneering contempt for it, curling his lip and with little regard for any damage his temper might do.

Laura folded her arms in defiance as he came closer, she averted her gaze from him, but Antonio cupped her chin with his hand and brought her gaze level with his.

'So I am ugly now, am I? Not so ugly when I am gracing your bed.'

He laughed mirthlessly. 'Not you. The portrait; the fact that you chose to be depicted in that way and to have paid for the privilege. It astounds me that you should be so lacking in judgement.'

Laura lit a cigarette and turning away went to pour herself a gin. She offered him the bottle of cognac, but he shook his head.

'I cannot accept this gift, of course. So sadly your poor judgement has cost you whatever you paid, but worse than that it leaves me wondering about our future as a couple, whether it would be wise of me to continue seeing you for whatever time remains for me in London.

'I have been informed that my posting at the embassy here is coming to an end, so now might be the best time to sever our relationship and to part, hopefully, on good terms.'

Laura turned on him, her eyes blazing with anger. She could have easily succumbed to tears, but she knew they would have had no impact on Antonio and she didn't believe him worthy of them. She was angered by what she saw as an over-reaction to the style of portrait she had chosen, but it was the sheer hypocrisy which had underpinned his condemnation of her decision to gift it to him that angered her the most along with the hurt.

'So I have exhausted my use to you, is that it? I am being cast aside over one small error of judgement, or perhaps that was in your mind when you called to say you would be coming here tonight. After all, I hadn't mentioned a gift until you arrived. Have I been widely discussed among your circle of friends, have our illicit trysts been the topic of conversation or was I always too sordid a detail in your life for you to admit to? More of a dirty secret than a guilty pleasure?'

Antonio shoved his hands into the trouser pockets of his well-tailored suit and rocked backwards and forwards on his heels, his breath laboured.

'You are being hysterical! Irrational!'

She sneered derisorily and turned her back.

He admired her spirit, because there were few employees at the embassy who would dare to speak to him thus and he knew none of his parents' staff would ever display such courage, but surely Laura should have known that their time together was finite. That another diplomatic posting would come along eventually and he would have to go. Would she have followed him to Spain? Become a mistress he provided for, at a tiny apartment in Seville? He doubted it. Perhaps using his disapproval of her choice of gift was a convenient means of exit and she was too smart not to reach that conclusion, but this day had to come and she should have realised that and to have been content with the time they'd *had*. Laura turned to face him.

'So this is your tactical withdrawal? The polite way of leaving the scene with your dignity intact while attempting to restore some of mine. Well, how typically diplomatic of you!'

'I am trying to make this as easy as I can... I did say at the start that our time together would have to be limited. I believed you understood that. My work at the embassy, the demands of my role...'

'...Were an excuse, Antonio, not the rationale that you have sought to make them. Our relationship was based on sex, pure and simply. When you wanted to have it with me, then I saw you, otherwise the last-minute cancellations were your exit clause. Who knows, perhaps I was just one of many women… I see now that it would be a lie to say that we made love. The fact that I confessed to loving you probably flattered your ego, but I doubt it ever went deeper than that!'

Antonio lit one of his hand-crafted cigarettes and smiled uneasily.

He felt awkward. Laura's words which contained a lot of truth were making him feel uncomfortable, but instinct told him to remain the urbane diplomat.

'I really hoped that we would part amicably, avoid the emotional reaction and I really believed you would be above all that. Sadly I have misjudged you on that count as well.'

Laura shrugged nonchalantly, watching via the mirror as he made for the door. He half turned. 'What will you do with the portrait?'

'Honestly, I don't know. I only planned it as a gift for you, but as you won't accept it, I will probably discard it. Nobody ever knew of our affair from me anyway, so I guess your reputation will remain intact along with your family's exalted status, for you to bask in once you have returned home.'

Antonio bowed his head.

'*Adios*, Laura. I wish you only the very best. I truly hope that you find the happiness you deserve.'

He leaned in to kiss her, but Laura shook her head and then averted her gaze.

Antonio Viaz left. He walked out of her life and Laura took one last fleeting glance at the portrait he had rejected, just as he had *so* cruelly rejected her. It was only when she heard the front door click, that she choked on a half-sob. Then she looked at herself in the mirror, then once more at the portrait and she felt her bottom lip quivering as finally she succumbed to an avalanche of tears.

39

The Campion Villa, Cap St Vincent – July 1923

Paul Crowley looked down from the wide terrace, shielding his eyes from the glare of mid-afternoon sun, to where Laura Savernake sat on the edge of the jetty in a one-piece black swimming costume, her knees pulled up and her chin resting on them. The haunted look in her eyes was all too evident and Alicia had almost given up trying to find out what was bothering her younger sibling.

That Paul had his suspicions, but didn't think it was his place to divulge, racked him with some guilt. He was surprised that Laura had even made the trip, as there had been some doubt that her father would sanction it, while he doubted she would want to, if as he suspected the relationship with Viaz had ended and not so well for Laura.

He felt a shadow across his peripheral vision and saw Matthew Fullerton come to stand aside of him.

'Doesn't look too happy, does she?'

'I am surprised that she came along. I take it Viaz has returned to Spain?'

Matthew shrugged. 'It's not been confirmed by my source,

but I am guessing that, unless he terminated the relationship with Laura, either way, which judging by her mood is a safe bet.' He paused and Paul knew there was more. Dabbing his brush into his palette, he nodded.

'Worse may yet come for Laura, because my source hinted that when his posting in London ended he was going home to Spain and a formal engagement was imminent...'

'Damn.'

Matthew smiled wanly. It was to Paul's credit that he had invested so much concern for Laura's well-being during the process of fulfilling her commission. He had never treated it as just a financially beneficial commission and if he hadn't feared that she would have sought out another artist, he would have happily declined.

Jayne approached them, lighting a cigarette which she put between Paul's lips, and she smiled. 'So what are you two conspiring about in hushed tones?'

Paul returned his full attention to his work, pretending not to have heard what his girlfriend had said, so Matthew covered.

'We were just remarking on how sad Laura looks and that maybe persuading her to come along wasn't the best idea for her.'

Jayne nodded. 'Alicia has told me she can't get to the root of what is bothering her, but knows there is something. She feels guilty that she has been so busy lately that she has been a neglectful sister and she doesn't want their father to discover why.'

Matthew shrugged and Jayne took a large gulp of her drink.

'Give Laura a day or so and she will be OK. Who wouldn't be in surroundings such as these?'

Paul looked at Matthew and nodded. 'Jayne is taking the credit for convincing her sister to rent the villa to us.'

She looked at him with her eyebrows raised. 'Of course.

Absolutely! What other reason could have swung her around to the idea?'

Paul winked at Matthew.

'Well, your sister is a great supporter of artists. I am guessing that having her property associated with another Crowley masterpiece could also be a factor!'

She smacked him playfully in the arm, as he bent to kiss her, but she walked away. Paul shook his head, laughing, while Matthew, puffing his cheeks with air, shook his head, but their relief at swerving the conversation away from Laura's romantic tribulations had been achieved.

Laura Savernake never revealed to her sister the cause of her sadness despite the constant urging. Laura had been feeling melancholic for the entire two weeks after Antonio Viaz had abruptly ended their relationship to the time they had travelled to the Riviera.

As they both suspected, their father, Alexander, had been uncertain whether Laura should be accompanying her sister and friends, but he knew she wouldn't want to spend the summer at Chelcombe Place and that would curtail his own plans. So still sceptical he had acquiesced. Laura hadn't been convinced that a month-long holiday would help her heartache, which she was determined to keep to herself as she knew she could trust Paul's discretion. However, it was an opportunity that might never come her way again, so she had decided to accept.

She felt she could rely on Alicia to respect her privacy and believed she would be too preoccupied with Jack anyway, but thus far, both Paul and Jack had been painting in a fever of activity by day, leaving the women to their own devices. For her part, she realised now that she had placed far too much faith that Antonio's feelings for her would ever be as strong as those that she had for him. Having told him as they parted that she loved him, which had been responded to with a shrug, almost as if it were just a routine thing to say, had been all the confirmation she had needed to know that he had never truly cared for her at all. She had been a dalliance. A distraction from the routine of his role at the embassy, nothing more. Since arriving in France, she had vowed never to make that mistake again, but the *hurt* remained.

She had been warned, of course, to be aware of his patrician attitude.

His friend "Kit" Stretton had advised her to enjoy Antonio's attention while she could, on one of the very few occasions that he had been willing to escort her socially and only then to a very intimate gathering with people that he knew really well. By then, of course, she had been too heavily involved to take heed of Stretton's words, but sitting now with her legs dangling from the wooden jetty she wished that she had. For the time being she wanted to be left to lick her wounds. She couldn't see any way forward that filled her with any optimism for where she could go next. Her modelling career had stalled, although she took some blame for that, in not having pushed herself as hard and as effectively as Alicia had.

Thankfully her family were as yet unaware of the extent to which she had fallen behind in her ambition to follow Alicia, as a much sought-after model. Her sister just had an instinctive gift for modelling, which she doubted she could ever match.

When Jack was encouraged by Alicia to go down to the jetty and cajole Laura into opening up about the cause of her bleak mood, she was reticent to divulge anything and she didn't understand why Alicia was so determined to force the issue. Jack tried his best and she felt slightly sorry for him, but she was determined not to be dragged into what would be an awkward conversation for each of them, so she told Jack as politely as she needed, to leave, which with some reluctance he did, climbing back up the stone steps with an indolent shrug. When Alicia looked at him with arched eyebrows, Paul shot him a sympathetic look, to which he responded with another shrug, while Laura shot her sister a dark warning look which explicitly said, "Leave me alone!"

40

The Campion Villa, Cap St Vincent – Two Days Later

Laura was left entirely to herself after Jack's failed intervention and although Alicia continued to fret, Jayne and Lynette urged her to let Laura work out whatever it was that troubled her. While they sat in the warm sun, or swam, Paul and Jack remained engrossed in their work for most of the day, each claiming their own particular territory within the grounds of Mercedes' property, while Matthew was content to remain within the group, to work on his column and the short fiction pieces in which he had recently discovered an interest in writing. Nicola had been very impressed, encouraging him to write more based on what he had let her read, saying with her tongue in her cheek, that he might be able to give Laurence Naismith something to think about, but Matthew had shaken his head, smiling that he doubted fiction was something that he was planning on pursuing to any serious extent.

'I gave up tennis to pursue a career in journalism, so writing fiction will be a sideline at best. Besides which, don't distract me by trying to shift the focus onto me. I hope you have decided to go back to the Slade for a second year.'

'You should. You have the talent!' Jayne added, while Matthew waited for some barbed comment from Lynette, but none came. Nicola nodded.

'I probably will. My family have been very encouraging on the basis of what I have produced in my first year, although I suspect that some of the tutors at the Slade won't be sorry not to see me back.'

'I have heard you say that previously, but you could be wrong,' Matthew commented gently, but Nicola shook her head.

'I do believe their attitude to those who gain entry by the bursary system differs from other students. I don't suppose Paul's place there has ever been questioned.'

Lynette smiled from her lounger. A barbed comment was in her mind, but a look from Matthew compelled her to refrain. He had tried to decipher her expression, but her dark glasses hid it and Matthew decided to let it go, although it was obvious to him that Lynette had never properly forgiven Nicola for her initial reaction to her, which Lynette had convinced herself was a "crush" while Nicola admitted it was an embarrassing error on her part. No malice had been intended and Matthew felt Lynette should be over it by now.

Matthew had kept in contact with one of the sources who had supplied most of the reliable information about Antonio Viaz, so after luncheon he went to the local post office, to see if there was any communication for him. His editor knew that he was taking a month-long holiday, but had been promised some travel-related pieces, but there was something which confirmed what his source had implied that a formal engagement between Antonio Viaz and the daughter of another prominent Spanish family had been announced in a Spanish newspaper. He suspected this would be the last thing Laura needed to see in her current mood, aside from that fact that if she reacted to it, she would have little choice but to finally confide in her sister about what happened with her diplomat lover.

Matthew read the letter with disdain, as his source was telling him that the engagement had been based on an understanding between the two families for many years. Basically a union of "arrangement" so confirming what he and Paul had always suspected, that Laura represented a brief dalliance for Viaz, before committing himself to marriage. That no matter how willing she had been in the relationship, she had effectively been *used*. Matthew shuddered slightly shaking his head in dismay at what he had read but also afflicted by a surge of guilt. He had pointed Laura out as she had stood in the corner of Jack's living room at Gresse Street, when "Kit" Stretton had asked who she was. If it had been the youngest son of the Earl of Broxbourne who had started courting Laura, from that night onwards he would still have urged caution upon her, but louche as Stretton was, he would have been an improvement on the arrogant, patrician Spaniard who had captured her heart, as at least then she would have been spared this heartache.

He took his time walking back to the villa, thinking then of how he should broach the subject and whether he should mention it at all.

Aside from Paul, he couldn't guess at what the rest of the group would have to say, although Alicia was the one who having her sister's welfare at heart, was the next person to be considered.

The Campion Villa – Late Afternoon

Matthew sought out Paul on his return from the post office, showing him as discreetly as he could the information his source had provided.

Paul's expression was grim, but he was not surprised. He continued cleaning his brushes after another satisfactory day's work. He looked down at the lower terrace to where his sister and the other women were soaking up late-afternoon sun.

'Should we tell her?' Matthew asked, his tone grave.

'You mean should I tell her?'

'You did say that the fewer people she thought knew about her and Viaz being lovers, the better it was for her.'

Paul smiled.

'True, but you have seen how she has been since we arrived; how concerned Alicia is. If she is told of his engagement and reacts badly how can it be kept from the others…? I am only guessing that she still wants to be discreet, she might not care any more, but I doubt she wants to dwell on it.'

'I feel especially guilty as I pointed Laura out to Stretton at Jack's party last December. I did so thinking he wanted some female company as he had come alone… I didn't ever imagine that it would come to this…'

'Laura's error was that portrait. I feared he would be shocked by it… Sounds like he was *appalled*. It wouldn't have altered the outcome from what your source has told you, but it would have spared her some of the pain…' He paused, pointing down to where Laura lay on the wooden jetty, seemingly oblivious to all around her. Paul nodded, adding 'Do you really think she is ready to hear this regardless of which of us tells her?'

Matthew nodded, but his pleated brow told another story. 'Would you prefer she reads it in the papers? Imagine if it was Lynette or Jayne?'

Paul nodded. His instinct was to urge caution, but he got that Matthew felt he needed to tell Laura, whether for her or to assuage some of his guilt, he wasn't sure, but Matthew's motives for candour were compelling.

Matthew took a long, deep breath, patting Paul on the shoulder.

'I will tell her. I shall try to be as discreet as I can about how much you confided in me at the time you accepted the commission, but she needs to know and I think she deserves to hear it from a friend…'

Laura groaned to herself when she saw Matthew coming down to see her. She wondered who her sister would enlist next in a bid to cajole her into joining them, when all she wanted was to be left to herself and her *misery*, but there was something in Matthew's expression that told her he wasn't coming on Alicia's behalf and she was suddenly alarmed.

The sun was still hot. Although it was beginning to dip towards the horizon, it threw glints of light on the water in which she was dangling her legs. Her hands palm flat on the wood of the jetty, she leaned back as Matthew approached, but she managed a smile as he offered her a cigarette and lit one himself.

'May I?'

'Please do. I was hoping that everyone had got the message, that I craved solitude.'

'I think you should know that Paul confided in me that you had offered him a commission to paint a portrait of yourself as a gift for a man…'

He paused, his head bent and Laura had to suppress a smile on the fact that he was embarrassed on her behalf '… you were in a relationship with.'

'My Spanish *lover*, you mean. I believe it was you who pointed me out to him at Jack's flat party.'

Matthew nodded. 'I thought it was Stretton who had asked me, but I could have been mistaken…'

Laura shook her head, 'You weren't, it was Kit Stretton, but it was Antonio's eyes I was looking into that night and he was gazing back at me and we… well, clicked. Sadly for me I was more invested in the relationship than he ever was.'

'I am sorry!'

'For what? That I fell heavily for a man who wasn't worthy of me? That is hardly your fault. I have had time to think, and

I know I wanted it… him, too much to think rationally, so whatever guilt you may be feeling, let it go. You have nothing to reproach yourself for.'

She pushed her shoulder against his and smiled, but he didn't smile back, so she looked blankly at him and Matthew produced the sheet his source had sent him.

'I think you should read this. I hesitated about telling you, and I discussed it with Paul before coming down here. The last thing we wanted was for you to see it in the papers and wonder why neither of us had told you.'

As he handed her the sheet, he stood and turned back towards the villa. Laura tucked her legs beneath her and read about the Viaz engagement and a myriad of emotions tumbled around her once more. She still blamed herself, partly, but she could see the person who had behaved in a totally dishonourable way was the sneering patrician diplomat that *she* had taken as her first real lover and that was a gigantic error that she had to *own*.

They took Laura's decision that she wanted to be excused at dinner with good grace. Alicia was inclined to pursue the matter, to get the answers she wanted, but she demurred at Jack's urging.

Jayne was in an exuberant mood, downing several gin martinis and then sitting on Paul's lap during coffee, while Nicola was absorbed within herself, focused on a sketch that she had done of Matthew, and the outline for a large canvas that she had planned on the subject of trench warfare, that she wanted to paint as a tribute to her cousin Martin, for all the moral support that he had given her.

Laura stayed in her room, thinking. She had a lot to think about.

The news of Sybil's engagement and forthcoming marriage had been a shock, but she had not felt it as strongly as Alicia, who had always been closer to the woman that their brother was destined to marry, while she had been too engrossed in her relationship with Antonio, but if the news that Matthew had brought her this afternoon told her anything it was that she had never *mattered* to Antonio Viaz, so he was not worthy of any more of her time. She did however want to make a splash, a statement of intent, about where she wanted life to take her next. A late-evening swim might be a good idea, so retrieving her costume, she headed out via the kitchen so as to avoid questions from the rest of the group and went down to the jetty, on which she had spent most of her time since arriving in Cap St Vincent. There had been moments – thankfully all too brief – when she had thought of diving in and sinking to the bottom of the sea bed and perhaps perishing there, as an alternative to feeling the pain of heartache, but now she had no such thoughts, because she wasn't willing to waste any more energy on her former lover.

She was going to *thrive*. It was as simple as that and once the holiday here was over, she intended to seriously promote herself as a model, eager for whatever assignments she could get and to approach her career with the same single-minded determination that her sister had applied to *hers*.

Standing with arms outstretched she dived from the jetty into the sea and after a few strokes she lay floating. The bathing raft wasn't too far away and she could swim to that, and swimming in the cooler evening was a joy, thus she felt a greater sense of freedom than she had felt in days. After a while the others came out to the garden, Paul lit a cigarette and Matthew joined him and then they noticed Laura, lying on her back, floating towards the bathing raft. Suddenly he panicked and with Paul behind him they ran down the stone steps to the jetty, both determined to jump in and rescue her.

Alicia came out amidst the commotion and she wanted to join them, but Jack held her back, and despite initially struggling within his arms, she settled. Paul took hold of a long punting pole and held it out, but Laura shook her head.

'I am *fine*. Leave me to swim!'

'The hell you are. Alicia is frantic, so come on, grab the pole, or one of us will be forced to jump in and rescue you.'

'I don't need rescuing. I am fine!'

With that Matthew threw off his shoes and leapt in, swimming towards Laura, who for a moment considered swimming away, but she didn't and within minutes she was in Matthew's arms as he led her back onto the jetty. Alicia looked at Jack, as if he had any answers, but she was confused as to why her sister had taken a late-evening swim and why Matthew and Paul felt obliged to rescue her. There was too much going on about which she would *demand* answers and Alicia was not alone, because in front of her, Nicola was wondering the same and what Matthew's involvement meant for *their* relationship.

★ ★ ★

When Paul and Matthew returned to the terrace, with Laura trailing them, Jack tossed a towel in Matthew's direction and he muttered thanks, meanwhile Alicia pushed past them to grip her sister by the arm.

'What were you doing out there?'

'Swimming!' She turned to Matthew and Paul, adding, 'I hope you are both satisfied now? All your discretion has gone to waste because now I will have no choice, but to tell her. Well done!'

She pushed past her sister and Jack, and stormed into the villa.

Alicia, with her eyebrows raised, turned to Matthew.

'Well?'

'It is Laura's story to tell, but you have been worried about her and she hasn't been for a swim this late since we arrived.'

'Not good enough, Matthew, but you are right that it's up to Laura to tell me. Paul, can you offer any pearls of wisdom?'

He shook his head, looking furtive and determined to avoid their gaze. Matthew reached for Nicola's hand, but she pulled away. He looked at her confused.

'Nicola?'

'It's you, isn't it? You are the reason Laura has been *so* sad this whole trip. Are you her lover as well as mine?'

'What?!' shrieked Alicia in disbelief.

'No. You are wrong, Nicola.'

'Am I?'

'Yes. Look, I will explain to you separately from what Laura has to tell her sister, however much she might not want to...' He paused to look at Alicia.

'I don't think Alicia is going to give her a choice, but you need to understand, Nicola, that I would never see someone else romantically while committed to you.'

'Do I? On your word alone?'

Matthew nodded. 'Yes, because the alternative is that without mutual trust we don't have a chance. Right now I need to get changed. Wait here and you will get the explanation you deserve.'

Nicola turned away. She was conscious of Lynette's snort of derision and Alicia's fermenting anger. It took Matthew ten minutes to change and return to the terrace, but it felt like an eternity to Nicola, who sat on a lounger with her arms folded, biting her bottom lip. Alicia, still angry, with her arms folded paced up and down the terrace, resisting Jack's attempts to placate her.

Matthew took the seat opposite Nicola and grabbed her hands, although she was reluctant.

'You are way off the mark, accusing me of being with Laura. I think we have all been aware of how unhappy she has been, but it wasn't my place to betray a confidence. All I can promise you is that her unhappiness is not because of me!'

'No, it's because of an arrogant Spanish diplomat called

Antonio Viaz, along with my infatuation with him and the naïve belief that by gifting him a portrait of myself I could hold onto him. I learnt just this afternoon courtesy of Matthew that the patrician Viaz has announced his engagement to a woman that he has been destined to marry since they were adolescents. So you see, Nicola, I have been an utter fool in the cause of love, so I would urge you not to do the same.'

As Laura began to speak, all eyes on the terrace had turned to her.

Alicia had uttered a cry of anguish on her sister's behalf and pushed past Jack to approach her, but Laura held her off.

'I didn't want to tell you as yet, Sis, because you seemed so upset about saying farewell to Sybil. I didn't really want to come here as I feared my mood would drag you all down and that is exactly what has occurred. However, Alicia being the big sister she is wouldn't let it go, so here I am! I just hope that after tonight, we can enjoy the rest of our month here in our own ways… minus the drama.'

Laura came towards them, but she bypassed her sister and took both of Nicola's hands in hers. 'Whether you choose to trust Matthew after he has told you his version of events is entirely up to you, but I would hate that his efforts to be a good friend means the end for you both.'

Paul took a long gulp of brandy, and turned to Alicia.

'It was me that Laura approached about the portrait and because of our friendship, I was very reluctant to take the commission, but she made it clear that she wanted it as a gift for Viaz. I insisted on knowing who it was for and that was a deliberate piece of subterfuge on my part as I passed his name to Matthew and asked him if he could make some subtle queries to a contact of his and he came up with the information we needed, but Laura was still *determined* and I didn't want her to be painted in the neo-classical style by a stranger, so I agreed!'

Nicola looked at Paul.

'So what has it got to do with him?' Nicola pointed at Matthew, who had tried to allay her fears without success.

'As I said, Matthew provided me with the background and Laura never explained what had taken place between her and Viaz when they last met, because it's not our business, but we could tell she wasn't happy and that Viaz had let her down. I know from conversations that I have had with Matthew that he cares very deeply for you, Nicola, so I would urge you to think before you throw it away.'

Nicola shook her head slowly. 'I was convinced you had started something with her. Look at her! How beautiful she is! I came to the conclusion that you had grown tired of me, as I always feared you would.'

Matthew smiled. He took both her hands and helped her to her feet, caressing her cheek. He didn't care that they had an audience, Nicola had to learn to believe in herself. About her looks, her artistic talent, her worth as a human being and he wanted to help her in that, if only she would let him.

'I can't keep making allowances for your insecurities, Nicola. I am in love with you. When we hooked up at Jack's party last December, a night that has come to be so significant for most of us, in varying ways, I knew what I was taking on and how lucky I was to realise it before it was too late, before one of those fellow students at the Slade claimed you as theirs.'

Nicola bowed her head, blushing profusely. She wished that Matthew had said all that when it was just them, minus their audience, but she conceded that she had forced his hand.

She looked across at Paul, and he nodded silently, smiling. Matthew cupped her chin, to bring her eyes level with his. 'Only you can decide on your own worth. To realise that if I ever gave you good reason to walk away from what we have, then *I* would be the loser. If you would find someone else once you had healed… but believe when I say I am *not* prepared to put us at risk. For anything or anyone…'

Nicola averted her gaze, but Matthew shook his head. 'Not any more. Look confident, be proud of who you are.'

He offered his hand and she took it, letting Matthew lead her into the villa. Alicia turned to Laura and said. 'We need to have a long talk, Sis. I need to know why you felt you couldn't come to me about this stuff with Viaz. With all due respect to Paul and Matthew...' She paused, bowed her head and looked across at Paul as she continued '... I am grateful to you both, but, Laura, we are flesh and blood, I want you to know in your gut that I am always here for you...'

Jack came to stand behind Alicia and kissed her cheek. Gripping her shoulders, he whispered in her ear and she nodded, walking hand in hand inside. Jayne followed and Lynette approached Paul.

'Well, you are a dark horse, Brother!'

Paul shook his head.

'Not tonight, Lyn.'

'I was going to compliment you on having Laura's best interests at heart. You could have done irreparable damage to your friendship with Alicia and Jack by saying yes, but you did it out of concern for Laura and not wanting her to go to a stranger. You stepped up. Very commendable!' Paul smiled uneasily. He pointed to Laura who had remained on the terrace. She looked at Lynette, smiling awkwardly.

'I am *so* sorry, Laura, I thought you had gone inside...'

Laura shook her head. 'You are OK! Paul *is* a hero. You are right to commend him. I was so blinded by my love for Antonio and what I foolishly believed he felt for me, that I never saw the wider picture. Or the true implications of what I was asking of your brother. He accepted my commission with honour. Took less money for it than I had offered and then I was ungrateful and wretched to him. I cannot imagine what Antonio would have thought of what I originally asked for, given how much I could see how he hated the portrait that I gave him.'

Lynette moved to give Laura a hug. Paul took her hand. 'You are OK? No late-night swim planned?'

Laura smiled as she shook her head. 'No, you can leave me on my own and rest easily.'

Paul and Lynette took their leave and Laura watched them until they were inside the villa, then she walked to the end of the terrace and leant against the balustrade.

She smiled as the cool evening breeze hit her cheeks. She could hear the chirping of crickets, the buzz of mosquitoes, and she took a long, deep breath and then she looked down at the worn photograph of Antonio Viaz that she had been gifted with considerable reluctance on his part in the early days of their relationship. She understood that it was only ever about the sex for him. He never wanted anything else and he gave nothing but his time, but only then when it suited. In fact, it was clear that he never cared for her at all. She placed the worn photograph on the stone balustrade and when a sudden gust of wind took it away, she smiled. She was free of the foolish infatuation for a man who had never proved himself worthy. She might be on her own for now, but she was in the company of friends, and she too would have what Alicia and Jack enjoyed, Paul and Jayne, and Matthew with Nicola. So too would Lynette Crowley whenever she was ready. The important part for her, Laura Savernake, was that she had decided to set herself free.

EPILOGUE

London – Spring 1928

Lynette Crowley alighted the taxi on Charles Street, and gazed up at the impressive facade of the house in which her brother rented his flat. In a good part of Mayfair, within proximity of Berkley Square.

It was an indication of just how well he had done professionally in the last five years. She rang the bell and waited, having been told that his very efficient personal assistant, Miss Budd, would be down to greet her. Paul pursued his artistic career from home, but he had retained the studio, where he had worked throughout his years at the Slade, thus retaining his link with Fitzrovia. He had graduated with distinction from the Class of 1925 and since then he had barely looked back. Their parents had of course been flushed with pride, but not entirely surprised by his success as Paul had always been their "Golden Boy".

Their cousin St John had written consistently via his column in the *Daily Sketch* on Paul's progress since, striving always to adhere to objectivity. He had returned fully refreshed from his sojourn in the United States so much so that she and Paul had speculated on whether he might have remained there, but he had returned with a jaunty spring in his step, the professional malaise from which he had been suffering all but forgotten. Miss Budd appeared suddenly and opened the door, her appearance pulling Lynette out of her daydream, and smiling she ushered her inside, they took the lift to Paul's flat and she found her brother on the floor counting canvases resting against the wall. He had another well-publicised and much anticipated exhibition scheduled for tomorrow evening and Lynette was as excited on his behalf about that as she was about her forthcoming nuptials.

She stood at the window which offered a view of the Square Gardens.

It was an unusually hot day for April and the bright, warm sunshine matched her mood.

Paul had come home with a healthy, swarthy look from his most recent trip, and they hadn't seen each other in a while. He turned to her. 'Hello, Lyn. You look well! Being betrothed evidently suits you.'

Lynette smiled gently, touching his arm. Only Paul ever got away with shortening her name. She didn't especially like it, but was inclined to let it go. 'Oh do stop it! I am *no* different. St John sends his regards by the way. He is looking forward to the exhibition as much as I expect you are… Jayne also sends her regards.'

She waited for Paul to respond in any manner he wished, but when his silence stretched, she said, 'I said Jayne sends…'

'Just leave it, Sis, please.' He had wanted his tone to be neutral, but he knew it had been anything but neutral, so Lynette raised her hands in mock surrender. He knew that Lynette had wanted it to work for him and Jayne Campion, and she had been most upset when they had parted.

Neither would go into much detail as to why it had gone wrong, despite her efforts as she would have liked to have had Jayne as her sister-in-law above any other girl that she had seen Paul with.

It saddened her that he hadn't realised just how good a fit Jayne was for him, until it appeared to be too late.

'She looks well on her recent European trip. Of course, now that the villa at Cap St Vincent has been sold, that link to the past has been lost, but she enjoyed the Italian Lakes.'

Paul smiled. He was determined not to take the bait, but Lynette was unperturbed. Mercedes' indefinite sojourn in Spain had been a shock to all who knew her, but most especially to Jayne and he did empathise, but that was no grounds on which to continue pursuing a relationship which appeared to have run its course.

'It's not just Jayne that is missing Mercedes. I understand from Alicia that Margot isn't coping well. Her and Gervaise may have fought some titanic battles during their marriage, but his death has left a gigantic void.'

Paul nodded, his brows pleated in a frown. A lot of momentous events had occurred in the lives of people they knew well in the last five years, but Lynette had always been practical in her approach to life, so he was perplexed as to why she was talking as she was now. What she didn't know and he wasn't going to reveal, was that he had seen her from the window overlooking the square for the entire time that Nicola Fearns had been here and that she only alighted her taxi once she had seen Nicola leave. He recalled a conversation that he had had with Jack, shortly after Gervaise suffered the first of two strokes, the second one of which had sadly proved fatal, when Jack had been summoned to Cornwall and against Margot's expressed wish, Gervaise had told him that he may *not* be his biological father. Gervaise's argument had been that he had wanted to be set free by the possibility of the truth, even though he had always looked upon Jack as *his* son, as much as he had with Hugo and Adam. Jack hadn't revealed to his mother exactly what Gervaise had said until after his death, but it had caused a rift.

Lynette was strolling around the room, gazing at his canvases. 'Are all these going to be exhibited?'

Paul shook his head, smiling.

'Is Jack coming tomorrow evening?'

'I have reason to believe he will try. Depends on whether he has booked passage from Spain in good time. Adam said he will look in, so there will be one Trevelyan present. I know the Savernakes are definitely coming, that's Alicia and her parents and I suspect Laura will if she can…'

Lynette raised an eyebrow, but Paul chose to ignore the subtext.

'I always thought that you and Adam Trevelyan might have become a couple.'

He raised an eyebrow, wondering if Lynette would react negatively, but she smiled serenely. 'You need to accept that I am entirely happy with my choice.'

Paul nodded. 'Well, Jonathan Teijans is quite a catch, given his family's connections. You have chosen very wisely, from the social status point of view. Our parents must be flushed with pride.'

'What they are is extremely happy, because they can see that I am happy, so your attempts to goad me are a waste of time.'

Paul took both her hands in his and squeezed them tight.

'You are aware that we have ribbed each other all our life, but I am very happy for you, Lyn. You have been forced to remain in the shadows, due to our parents' inflated view of my artistic talent, topping anything you achieved despite my efforts to the contrary, but this wedding will be your chance to shine. So I shall see to it that I remain firmly in the shadows.'

Lynette poked him in the arm. 'You will be centre stage where you belong. No arguments!'

Miss Budd coughed gently to attract their attention and Paul half turned.

She handed him some papers requiring his signature, for which he swiftly obliged. Lynette left them briefly to gaze at a particular portrait as she recognised the subject as Laura Savernake, who had transformed her life and career in the last five years, to the extent that nobody within *haute couture* circles dismissed her as just being Alicia's younger sister any more.

Alicia's marriage to Jack and a break from modelling had been beneficial to Laura, but her success was largely her own and due to determination and hard graft.

'Are you showing that one? It's amazing!'

Paul smiled. 'Is that the artist or the subject you're referring to?'

Lynette quirked an eyebrow. 'Both. I understand there are rumours about the state of her second marriage?'

Paul shook his head as he consulted a list that Miss Budd had handed him.

'I wouldn't know, Sis, because I pay no attention to such gossip. Laura's problem is that she never valued herself highly enough, and that's why she was prepared to commission me to paint her thus. Now it's very different, she rates herself very highly as a model, and professionally that approach has born abundant fruit, but does she still see herself as being worthy enough to be happy?' He shrugged, adding, 'I think she needs to take Alicia as her example, or her parents.'

Paul handed the list he had checked to Miss Budd and went to pour two coffees, one of which he handed to Lynette.

'What is it, Lyn? You are not entirely happy, I can tell. There is plenty of exuberance on the surface, but go deeper and I detect some melancholy. Could it be pre-wedding nerves?'

Lynette shook her head. 'No. I am certain that marrying Jonathan Teijans is the best decision I have made. Let's face it, I have dated some dullards. No, I am just being foolishly nostalgic for the past.

'When we were at the Slade, everything seemed so much

simpler. There was the overhang from the war, I know, and we were being encouraged to see ourselves as the lucky generation to have escaped the carnage in the trenches, but even taking what happened on that month-long "hols" at Mercy's villa, there was a sense of being care-free and we have lost it now…'

Paul sipped his coffee and listened intently and then he said, 'Unless we have just grown mature and progressed with life.'

Lynette nodded, but with a rueful look. 'Maybe. Probably. Just ignore me, as I said, I am being overly nostalgic. It's what Jayne was saying at lunch the other day, but I know what her problem is, she's missing Mercedes. She doesn't get the dynamic between her sister and Nate Gilbrandsen and she thinks Mercedes should have come home once Jack had arrived.'

'She rents her own place in Spain, though, doesn't she?'

'Yes. As I said, ignore me. I am being foolish!'

'Foolish is one thing you are not. I am concerned that it's not part of a larger symptom. Perhaps not taking the woes of our friends upon your shoulders would be a good start. Jayne will find what she is looking for and if she needs to make contact with me, she knows where to look. There is one person from those days that you haven't mentioned.'

'Who?'

'Matthew Fullerton.'

'Oh yes. Is he coming tomorrow night?'

Paul shook his head. 'I doubt it, if he thinks Nicola will be. He took that break-up badly. I did *urge* Nicola not to act rashly, but I think in the end they outgrew what they had meant to each other, and of course, her recent success has changed her.'

'For the better?' asked Lynette and Paul was prepared for malice in his sister's tone and was surprised there was none.

'As an artist yes, and it is long overdue. *Carnage at Festurbet* has got to be one of the best artistic depictions of the trenches, but as the person we knew back then, I am not sure and it is sad that Matthew had to suffer along the way.'

Lynette nodded as she finished her coffee and completed her viewing of the exhibits.

'I have asked Alicia to be my maid of honour and she accepted, so you and Jack will get to be reunited at my nuptials, even if he doesn't make it to the exhibition.'

'By doing so prove the press wrong who said that we couldn't remain friends if we both vied to be the best artists of our generation...which I have become, of course.' Paul bowed theatrically and Lynette laughed.

'I suspect Jack will dispute that claim now that he has Nathaniel Gilbrandsen as a tutor!'

'Do you believe that he could be Gilbrandsen's son?'

Lynette shook her head. 'I hope not, for Margot's sake. Alicia says she has suffered enough, but it cannot be proved either way beyond doubt, so it is a matter of what Jack believes and I think he should continue to believe that he *is* Gervaise's offspring.'

Paul smiled. 'All very neat.'

Lynette smiled and held out her hands, which Paul took in his.

'Are you heading back to Wiltshire or staying in town?'

'At the Centurion in Piccadilly. St John did offer me my old room at his townhouse, but I figured it was easier to stay at the Centurion should Jonathan want to dine with me there.'

She kissed her brother on both cheeks. ' Good luck for tomorrow night. I am sure the exhibition will be a huge success and forget my foolish craving for nostalgia! I will be fine!'

Paul watched her leave and then from the window as she hailed a taxi on Berkeley Square. Lynette had always seen herself as a "fixer" of other people's problems and he hoped now that she had learnt to be a little more selfish.

He half turned to find Miss Budd had reappeared and he smiled.

'Has Miss Fearns responded to my invitation?'

Miss Budd checked the list, shaking her head. 'Not as yet.'

'OK! I will call her myself. Any other confirmations?'

'The Savernakes are definitely coming, along with Alicia Trevelyan and Adam Trevelyan. Jack Trevelyan is still only a possible... as is Jayne Campion'

Paul smiled wanly. He hadn't wanted to reveal to Lynette how much he hoped that Jayne might be inclined to accept and it appeared she hadn't confided in his sister either.

Miss Budd smiled and Paul nodded. 'Thank you. You have done a superb job arranging the invitations for this exhibition.'

Miss Budd took her leave, flushed with pride at receiving praise, as she knew that some employers who had hired her via the agency, had reported back that while solidly efficient, she came across as a cold fish, so to receive fulsome praise from an artist as accomplished as Paul Crowley was a boost to her confidence.

Paul watched her leave him and then he stood at the window, hands shoved into his trouser pockets. He had come a long way in just five years and Lynette was wrong to say that an indulgence in nostalgia was foolish, because he felt an inclination to look back to that idyllic summer of 1923. To the villa at Cap St Vincent which, once Laura had reconciled herself to the reality of her doomed relationship with Antonio Viaz, had been a glorious time.

He wished it were possible for them all to meet at his exhibition, but he accepted that it wasn't, but he could salute those days by exhibiting the seascapes he had done that summer, so that he could keep an eye on Laura Savernake as she sat down on the jetty without anyone else knowing that was what he was doing.

He had done some of his best work on that holiday as had Jack and it was little wonder, because they had been their *golden* days.

In the sunset of their youth, when their careers were blossoming and confidence was sky high. When it might have appeared to those looking in, as if they had possessed a Midas touch.

SELECT BIBLIOGRAPHY

Sebastian Faulks, *The Fatal Englishman: Three Short Lives*, Hutchinson (1996)

Michael Holroyd, *Augustus John: The New Biography*, Vintage Publishing (2011)

Richard Ingleby, *Christopher Wood: An English Painter*, Allison & Busby (1995)

Evelyn Waugh, *Vile Bodies*, originally published by Chapman & Hall (1930), Penguin Classics Edition (2000)

ACKNOWLEDGEMENTS

I would like to thank the staff at Crawley Library, for their continued interest in my writing and for their assistance in finding most of the titles listed in the Select Bibliography for this novel. I appreciate as always the support of family and friends in my various writing projects and to one friend in particular, I hope that she appreciates me "borrowing" her name for one of the characters in this novel.